C000132976

Star
SURVIVOR

LISA BRACE

The Book Guild Ltd

First published in Great Britain in 2024 by
The Book Guild Ltd
Unit E2 Airfield Business Park,
Harrison Road, Market Harborough,
Leicestershire. LE16 7UL
Tel: 0116 2792299
www.bookguild.co.uk
Email: info@bookguild.co.uk
Twitter: @bookguild

Typeset in 11pt Minion Pro

Printed on FSC accredited paper
Printed and bound in Great Britain by 4edge Limited

ISBN 978 1916668 386

British Library Cataloguing in Publication Data.
A catalogue record for this book is available from the British Library.

For my husband, Owen and my children, Dylan and Bethan. Thanks for giving me the time to write, the space to create, and the regular WhatsApps to check I'm alive.

Chapter One

Zoe held her breath as the helicopter hung in the air like a toy. Minutes ago they'd dropped what felt like twenty feet when she and her three fellow passengers had clung together in terror. Zoe had hoped for reassurances from the pilot who had chivvied them all onto the helicopter, but all she'd heard was crackling static and occasional doom-laden phrases like 'air pocket' and 'might land safely' through her headphones.

It didn't help, of course, that her heart was thudding so loudly Zoe could hear that above anything else. She tried to distract herself by concentrating on the other three celebrities sat in the cockpit with her, all reflecting the same terrified face as hers. Well, almost all. The only male of the group, who Zoe was sure was Toby Masters, the ridiculously successful children's author who had just made the front pages of all the tabloids after being caught with yet another married woman, looked like he was taking a laid-back Sunday drive in the country. Zoe moved a little to look sideways at him under his sunglasses – he was asleep. No wonder he was so chilled. Mind you, if she'd drunk as much as he smelt like he had, she'd probably have slept through impending doom too.

Zoe was diverted from the sizing-up of Toby, in his pale cream chinos and scruffy leather jacket, all of which worked to lend the forty-something an air of musty sexiness, by the sounds of retching opposite her.

'Sorry,' said the woman with a smile, who Zoe had mistakenly assumed was a PA to one of the stars when she'd first arrived in the cockpit, but who introduced herself as Emily Chase, an Instagram influencer. If Zoe hadn't recognised her, she didn't give it away, instead plastering on the smile which had saved a thousand incessant press junkets and interviews, and saying 'of course' knowingly. Not that a mumfluencer was a bad thing, just not of interest to a twenty-year-old with her career ahead of her and zero plans for a family any time soon.

Rain hit the window next to Zoe so hard it seemed fake, like someone had thrown a bucket of water over them and they were safe in a studio. It felt a bit like when she'd filmed a fight scene for her last movie and she was meant to be underground in a sewer. She'd got so cold that day the team had hidden heat packs within her clothes, only for them to leave rectangular burn marks across her torso.

But this wasn't pretend. This was hanging-by-the-fingernails, try-not-to-look-down, hope-and-pray time that the four of them would land safely and then be whisked away to the plush lodges, for when they weren't on camera pretending to be "surviving" on an island for *Star Survivor UK*.

'Why did we say yes to this?' screeched the last member of the cockpit. June something; Zoe was sure they'd met before but couldn't place where.

'Sorry ladies… and Toby, this is the best I can do.' The sound of the pilot speaking through the headphones brought Zoe from her thoughts, and woke Toby up. 'You're going to have to jump out – I can hold it like this for just a few minutes though, so do it fast. It's not far… I promise… but I can't land. If I land, I may not be able to make it off.'

Zoe looked uncertainly at her fellow passengers as the rain hammered on the windows, but then, all of a sudden, the air whipped around her face as the door was thrown back by Toby, whose six-feet-plus bulk filled the small cabin as island debris hit her in the face. Wobbling on his feet a little, Toby sat on the edge of the helicopter then looked out and back at the three women.

'See you on the ground, ladies.' He smiled, waved and then disappeared from view.

*

'Shit. He did it,' Emily gasped, looking up from the brown paper bag she'd been clutching, full of vomit and the non-digested sludge of the Jaffa Cakes she'd inhaled on the flight – concerned it would be the last bit of normal food she'd be allowed before the bootcamp-style diet began that she'd agreed to do whilst on the island.

Throwing up in the helicopter was a kick-start to reducing calories which she so desperately wanted to do, she conceded. Though she wasn't sure where to leave the bag now it looked like they'd have to actually jump out of the bloody thing.

If her girls could see her now. She'd love to see what five-year-old Cherry and three-year-old Ivy would say if they knew their mum was about to jump out of a helicopter.

'You all need to do it. Now. Otherwise I'll need to leave with you on board. The weather is getting worse.' The pilot's voice was still calm, but there was an underlying tone of panic in it. He's contracted, of course, Emily considered, to get them to *Star Survivor*; if he didn't, she suspected he wouldn't get such a well-paid job again.

'Fine. We're going,' Emily heard a female voice reply through her headphones and looked up to see the world's most famous face beaming at her, giving her the thumbs up. It was very, very difficult to stop staring at Zoe, even whilst the helicopter shuddered and struggled against the wind. Her thick dark hair wound around her head, large brown eyes framed by long eyelashes, her rosebud lips a dark pink that no lipstick could get close to and tawny brown skin with not a blemish on her. The hours and hours of training Zoe had done in her latest role as the first female Bond – a sensational bit of casting if ever Emily heard of it – meant she looked seriously toned. Emily sucked in her belly a little bit more and shrunk under Zoe's gaze, aimed at her and June, still firmly positioned in their seats.

'We have to go, c'mon.' Emily watched as Zoe wrenched the headset off her head and flung it on the seat.

It was all right for her, of course, as an actor who'd been in numerous films – plenty of which were action ones – she was probably used to jumping out of vehicles. Or at least onto a crash mat. The closest Emily had got to a crash mat was when she'd tripped over a yoga mat at the one and only class she'd attended, a trip that left her with a visit to A&E and a dislocated shoulder.

Standing, holding the edge of the door, Zoe almost seemed to laugh at what she saw and shouted loudly, her voice carrying on the wind to the two remaining women. 'It's cool, not far at all.' Then vanished over the edge.

'And now she's gone,' June spoke up, 'If we don't jump, it'll be her and Toby that get all the good coverage; we'll be seen as the lazy or cowardly ones everyone'll make fun of. Memes and such.' She spoke clearly to Emily as though the younger woman had never come across social media.

'Yep, aware of memes. And GIFS. TikToks. Stories. Reels, you name it. I know it,' Emily replied, the adrenaline of the situation beginning to fuel her.

June smirked a little and Emily realised how sour she looked when she wasn't all smiles for the TV. There were wrinkles around her lips which Emily hadn't noticed on TV before either.

'Come on, ladies. Honestly. It's go now or come back with me. I don't care, but I can't hold it like this for much longer,' the pilot yelled.

Emily looked at the leaves whipping past the open door and took two strides over to the side.

'Got your stuff?' she asked of the older woman whose kaftan was so large Emily was concerned it would get caught in the blades if she wasn't lucky.

5

'Yep.' June dangled the tiniest handbag in Emily's direction, a teal bejewelled creation that no doubt cost hundreds, but was, Emily decided, the sort of thing she'd bring to a restaurant, not as carry-on. Not like her, she thought smugly, hefting her rucksack, which had almost been removed from her and put in the hold until she'd demonstrated, with her own tape measure, how it was within the right dimensions. Emily had been relieved to have as many bits with her as possible in the forty-hour flight she'd endured in Economy Plus. Though it had just dawned on her that maybe she'd been the only one not in Business…

'Go.'

June shoved her out of the door, and quickly jumped out after her. Emily landed with a thud and then laughed. It had been less than a couple of metres, not far at all.

Zoe came running over and hugged her.

'Well done, you did it. Can't believe he didn't say how close to the ground we were. Honestly, I was so nervous,' she said with a giggle and Emily joined in, the adrenaline leaving her system in waves.

'I'd never have known – you're clearly a brilliant actress, which, *of course,* you are. What with all the films and awards and, er, do you have any awards? I know you were nominated but…' She tailed off, embarrassed at how much and how little she actually knew of the woman standing in front of her, a polite smile on her face.

'Sorry. It's just a bit weird, I was watching you just now.' Emily flushed with embarrassment. 'Sorry, I don't mean watching YOU, I meant watching you. On the plane,' a red flush was going across her neck, 'on a film. I watched you in a film. Sorry.' She giggled.

'It's fine, I knew what you meant. Are you okay?'

Emily nodded, whilst pulling her shorts out of where they'd become embedded in her thighs, cursing not buying a better wardrobe. Fortunately the pause was filled by a little moan coming from June who was dusting her kaftan off, a pair of high heels dangling from her hand.

'Well, this outfit's only fit for the bin.' She paused, taking an X-ray look at Emily's oversized T-shirt and too tight shorts. 'But at least it'll have company.'

Yikes, Emily thought, June Sharp was sharp by name and even sharper by nature. The other half of TV's most famous daytime duo seemed like she was going to be hard work. She looked sharp as well. Rail thin, with that ridiculously expensive, floaty red kaftan swamping her tiny frame and only serving to make it look even smaller. The shoes – Emily clasped her hand to her mouth to stifle her laugh – silver Choos by the look of it. She only had stilettos? Even though they weren't expected to actually have to *survive* on the island, Emily knew the producers wanted them to make it look as though they were prepared to. Otherwise why would people vote or watch the show? But, Emily considered, gazing at June, she didn't look like she'd cope in River Island, much less a deserted one.

'The runner who took me to the helicopter and took my phone told me the production team are meeting us five minutes down the path with golf buggies, to get us down the track and into our lodges,' Emily mentioned, hoping that would cheer the older woman up.

Whilst Emily could tell her own linen shorts were more creased than an old man's balls, Zoe still looked fresh. She was dressed in a pair of denim cut-offs with an oversized white shirt tucked in, accompanied by some pure white trainers, accentuating her lean, long legs. Emily thought she was playing the part of fake deserted celebrity pretty well.

'Hi, I'm June,' the fifty-something blonde dimpled at Zoe and gushed, 'I know who you are, of course.' She paused to stare at Emily. 'Not sure who *you* are though, couldn't hear properly in the helicopter.'

'I'm Emily Chase, nice to meet you – and no, I doubt either of you have heard of me before. I'm a mummy blogger and Instagrammer,' she explained, almost apologetically, then remembered her agent, Angie, telling her why she'd been put forward for the hotly anticipated UK version of *Star Survivor* following its enormous ratings win in the US.

'I've smashed 1.5 million followers this week and have a book coming out in a few months' time. Toby has the same agent as me, although I don't think he knows who I am,' she admitted.

'That reminds me,' Zoe pulled a face, 'where is Toby? He jumped out first – I'd have thought he'd have waited for us.'

*

'Fucking fucky fuck-fuck. How the fuck am I meant to be on a fucking show with a fucking broken fucking ankle?'

Toby tried to bear weight but it was no good and the pain made him cry out.

'Fuck. Why the fuck didn't I let one of the women jump out first? Maybe the one in the heels. Or the red-faced, giggly one? Couldn't have let Zoe fucking Stenson

8

out first could I? Not a national fucking treasure who looks like Bambi.'

Toby had known as soon as he'd leapt out of the helicopter he'd misjudged the jump. It wasn't the height – that was relatively close to the ground – it was his wave at Zoe that did it. He'd missed a step, fell heavily on his right ankle and the pain had shot instantly through.

He leant against a tree and sobbed a little forlornly as he realised it would all have been caught on camera and he'd be a laughing stock. Again. Toby thought of the GIFs. The memes. He groaned. He'd be on the *Big Fat Quiz of the Year* as the question *'Which "celeb" broke his ankle stepping ten centimetres out of a fucking helicopter?'*

'Shit,' his voice echoed around the eerie quiet. 'Where the fuck am I? Where are the girls? Women? Whatever. Where the fuck are you?'

He listened for any kind of response but heard nothing in reply. Shaking his head he criticised himself for not paying attention to where he'd limped to when he'd tried to get away from the helicopter. At the time he could barely see a metre in front of himself because of the dirt and shit being kicked up by the blades. He had dragged and limped his way across the open space the helicopter had hovered by to a fallen log and sat there, waiting for the women to jump out too. Toby had thought if he had Zoe with him, all the cameras would be trained on her, so there would be less interest in his embarrassing injury.

But the island debris blown by the wind had been so thick he couldn't spot them. Even now, with the helicopter gone, the rain was so heavy he could barely see a thing.

'So much for a fucking idyllic island. I'm going to

be having some serious words with the production team when I get to the l—,' Toby began, ready to have a full-on diva tantrum, when he realised. 'Fuck. Hang on. I don't need to try and find my way to the lodges.' He looked to the trees, hopeful a camera would pick up on him. 'I'm waiting here until someone comes and picks me up in one of those golf buggies. In fact, come and get me before the girls. I'm sure they've not got an injury like this.'

Toby breathed out slowly and felt the tension in his shoulders loosen. What a dickhead. He'd been panicking for no reason.

'Shit.'

He paused and looked at the trees again.

'If I said anything out loud just then, anything about anyone or, erm…' He struggled to remember what he may have said or done in the last few minutes. What if that entire diatribe has been caught on the microphones hooked up everywhere?

'And I wasn't crying. Not really. Just, y'know, there's a lot of pollen around and it got… into… my… eyes. Okay?' Toby nodded at where he thought a camera was and grimaced.

'But my ankle does really fucking hurt and I don't know how long it's been since the helicopter left. Ten minutes, maybe fifteen? But someone should come to find me now. I know the weather is bad, but you can see I need help here, okay?'

The panic was starting to prickle at the back of Toby's head. Just a little. He really needed some painkillers. And a whisky. Ideally together. His head felt a little fuzzy, and he shook it a bit then realised he was really thirsty. The last time he'd had a drink was on his final leg of a forty-hour journey that had started at Heathrow, and that hadn't been water.

'Look, chaps, it's been twenty minutes now I think.'

Shifting on the tree-trunk he had settled on, Toby looked around for the cameras. He assumed they must have been cleverly embedded in the middle of the palm trees, or in the flowers. Angie had said they were minuscule, but he'd assumed he'd see them.

'HELLO?' he tried shouting at one of the brightly coloured flowers. He'd hoped the sound that came out would be strong and manly, not at all in pain and not in the least bit panicked or frightened. But it came out sounding like a cat that had been punched in the balls.

'Hellloooo. Can anyone hear me? I've managed to… ah… do something to my… foot. To my ankle, actually,' he tried again, this time at a palm tree. Maybe he'd been speaking to the wrong foliage. He was beginning to wonder if he needed to just be honest. Maybe he should howl and scream and insist on being seen, then at least they'd come and sort him out.

'Guys, come on. I think it's been at least half an hour now, this hurts. A lot.'

To distract himself from the pain, Toby decided to give a running commentary, maybe then the production team would give him lots of airtime because he sounded so poetic. And maybe they'd come and pick him up. He cleared his throat and considered what to say.

'It's really quiet,' he began. 'Like. Really. Fucking. Quiet.' He thought maybe he needed to try a bit harder and looked around for inspiration.

'It's loud at the same time, I mean, so… there's all these noises I've never heard before and they're all competing against each other. The trees are creaking. In the distance I can hear the crash of waves, and I know, given how small this island is, that the beautiful white sandy beaches can't be far from here.'

He paused to take in the sounds around him, congratulating himself on the narration and thinking how he'd enjoy his own travel show one day.

'I can hear ticks and clicks and howls and cackles and I'm pretty certain there's a million ants around me. But there's nothing else. No overhead sounds of planes. No music. No snippets of conversation.' Toby cocked his head to one side. No buzz of a generator. Nothing. Bit weird.

Had to be at least forty-five minutes now, he thought, then an unpleasant realisation crawled into his mind, along with the ants across his hands, that there may not be any cameras this far away from the main set. And that meant there was a chance no one knew where he was. They might have assumed he'd walked to the lodges and it would be a while until they'd realise he wasn't there.

Looking at his watch he realised he'd been waiting for an hour.

'Fuck, ow, what the actual…?' He looked about and saw mosquitoes everywhere. Both of his legs felt like they were burning, like he had heat rash and someone had rubbed vinegar onto it. He realised he'd been bitten everywhere.

'Shit.'

If no one knew where he was – then that meant no one was coming for him. Whatever had happened at the lodges, no one had realised he wasn't there. Toby knew he needed to get there himself. He needed to crawl if that's all he could do. Then he could get patched up. Then he could shout and scream and demand care and attention.

'Then I'll call fucking Angie, tell her we're suing and they can get me off this fucking island tonight. I will not be made a fool of,' he muttered to himself grumpily.

Scrabbling in his rucksack, he realised the light was starting to fade and other eerie noises were starting to fill the forest. It was a shock when he remembered handing over his phone to a producer before he began the last leg of his journey from Auckland to the Cook Islands, ahead of the fated helicopter ride. It wasn't just the lack of communication, it was everything else that came with it.

Like a torch.

Then, Toby remembered with relief he had packed whilst his mum oversaw. She'd been so excited about his trip and, because she loved the American show so much and believed he would actually be surviving – as he hadn't told her anything else – she had insisted he pack a load of things he wouldn't have thought to. It was with relief his fingers touched the torch she'd told him to put in.

With the light in his mouth, Toby rummaged in his bag for anything else which could help. He found a long-sleeved top, which he pulled on to help protect his arms from being bitten any further and the worn T-shirt he'd changed out of whilst in the car from the airport, which gave him an idea. Toby remembered the half hour he'd spent talking to Bear Grylls once at a boring publishing evening. One of those nights when he and other celebrity authors were wheeled out and had to 'press the flesh', whilst drinking cheap champagne and making small talk with other, more lowly, authors who were desperate to be known. Toby tried to remember Bear's life lessons he'd given him at one of those evenings, and made a makeshift bandage with his T-shirt, tying a stick crudely around his ankle to try and ease the discomfort. It worked. Sort of.

Before Toby tried to take his first step, he went to do up his bag and his hand brushed over the miniature whisky he'd nabbed on the plane when his handler wasn't watching. The sheer wonderfulness of finding it was enough to make him want to cry, again.

He downed it in one and, with the heat burning through him and the tiniest hit of adrenaline that he might come out of this situation looking fucking awesome, he began to gingerly take steps through the forest in the direction of the sea, with the hope that he'd find the lodges, or a member of the team along the way.

They'd taken over the entire island; someone would pick him up soon.

Wouldn't they?

*

'Ouch, shit, sorry,' Emily said for what, to her, felt like the millionth time in half an hour. Zoe – as in mega-bloody star – looked back from where she was leading and smiled.

'You okay, Em?'

For a plan that was beginning to feel less and less like a good idea, the fact that the most recognised woman in the world was now calling her Em, was pretty bloody cool.

'Sure, fine. Just, y'know. It's a bit dark, isn't it?' she replied, trying to sound peppy. The three of them, deciding Toby had made his way to the lodges already, had decided on a route they thought was going to take them to their paradise.

'It's not as easy as I thought it was going to be,' grumbled June, slipping in her sky-high shoes, something which Emily had already begun to block out. They'd been walking for over an hour, and all of them were beginning to panic that they'd chosen the wrong route out of the glade. But it hadn't been clear. They were sure the production team had said there would be markings on the trees to subtly help them find their way. There hadn't been any though.

Zoe had suggested that maybe the production team had wanted to make things look more realistic.

There was a snap and an 'Oof' from June, who was behind Emily. The older woman had stumbled, again.

'Zoe – Zoe, I think we need to stop; I'm not sure June can go much further tonight. Maybe the team will come and find us if we stay still?' Emily yelled and tried to attract the superstar's attention, but she'd disappeared over the brow of a sandy bank. Looking behind her, Emily could see June was still making her way – slowly, but she was there. Suddenly, Zoe reappeared on top of the hill, her slender shape emphasised by the silhouette being thrown on her by a moon as bright as a Tiffany's diamond.

'Come on, look what I've found.' She disappeared again.

'The lodges,' Emily exclaimed, suddenly finding energy to get moving and June picked up her pace as well.

As they made their way to the top of the hill, the sandy bank gave way to a clump of palm trees where groups of coconuts lay on the floor.

'It looks so authentic,' June breathed out, heavily, her heels sinking into the sand. As they burst through the trees, the claustrophobia of the forest disappeared and in its place was a bay bathed in silvery moonlight, the navy sea rippling into pure white sand. Gentle waves lapped at the water's edge. The storm from earlier had gone and in its wake was a stillness which reached into everywhere.

But there were no lodges.

Zoe had discarded her rucksack and taken off her trainers and was preparing to paddle in the water.

'Come down, it's beautiful,' she exclaimed. Seeing the water, Emily's feet felt suddenly hot and swollen in their socks and trainers and she longed for a paddle too. She was aware of the straps of her tightly packed rucksack digging into her shoulders and the need to drop everything, so she bolted to where Zoe was and threw her stuff down next to the A-lister. Soon, the two of them were splashing and crashing in the sea, kicking water at each other and screaming with laughter.

Emily felt exhilarated. What would Matt and the girls think of her doing this? Dancing with Jay Bond?

'Are you joining us, June?' Emily asked of the older woman, who had taken off her heels and was sitting nearby.

She shook her head. 'No thanks darling, I'm waiting for them to bring us to our beds. I need it.' Her gaze kept shifting from left to right, waiting for support to arrive.

Taking in the view and thinking how spectacular it was, Emily spoke quietly, 'Do you think anyone is coming?' She said it calmly, but her heart was hammering because despite its beauty she knew as soon as they'd made it to this bay they were still in the wrong place. Zoe had stopped wading and was also staring out at the horizon, her arms glistening with water droplets.

'I've been thinking about that too. Do you know what I think they've done?' she asked, a slight smile on her rounded lips.

Emily shook her head; she still couldn't believe she was having a conversation with this woman. She and Matt had date night every Friday, and it usually included watching a Zoe Stenson film – she'd been watching Zoe grow up on screen for years.

'No, what?'

Zoe's posture was statuesque; she held it like she had for the navy film she'd been in five years ago. All she was missing was a greenscreen and lots of people pretending they were on a ship. She looked keenly at Emily, her eyes locking on.

'I think it's a bit of a trial.'

Emily's mouth opened in a small 'oh' but Zoe continued.

'I think, rather than us just making our way in a super-easy fashion, they wanted to add realism to it – make it more British – and have us "survive" the first night on our own. I think, all we need to do is get through tonight and in the morning the support teams and production people will be here to take us to the lodges, and when we are found, we can be like "Fuck you, we did it".'

Emily was stunned at the suggestion and her heart pounded with the fear of what might happen, but it was June who piped up first.

'But where will we sleep? What will we eat? What about all the animals who live here and want to kill us? What about water? A fire? I've seen those real survivor programmes – we're not equipped for any of it.' Her speech seemed to take the last of the fire out of her, and she lay on the sand, sobbing.

Emily made her way out of the water and sat next to June, feeling the sand cling to her legs, and she smiled as Zoe sat on the other side of her.

Rummaging in her bag, Emily found what she was looking for.

'Here, take this,' she said, offering a tissue which June accepted gratefully. The TV presenter sat up and blew her nose in a rather noisy way.

Zoe watched Emily and smiled.

'It's just one night we need to be equipped for. We're three women with three bags – there's bound to be a bunch of things we can use to cope overnight. It'll be fun – like Girl Guides. I never did get to go,' she enthused. The other women didn't look too convinced.

'I got expelled from the Girl Guides,' admitted Emily,'I couldn't tie the knots right and kept giggling when the instructor kept telling us to put the bunny in the hole.' There was a pause, then all three women laughed loudly.

Hiccupping with tears, June was grateful to the both of them.'Thank you. Sorry for losing it, it's just I–' she broke off as a bird screeched overhead. It startled Emily too.

'Come on, I think we should get to somewhere dry

and flat – I don't think we need to be in the trees, but somewhere just away from the water's edge. Then we can pool our stuff together.'

The three women traipsed further up the beach and found a decent-sized dip in the sand, which could give them a little shelter. Before they sat down, Emily realised she had one thing which would immediately be of benefit to them.

'I have a raincoat in my bag – we can use it to sit on, less sand in all our bits and pieces,' she suggested, shyly. She was a little daunted by the strong personalities she realised she was going to spend the night with but was determined to make sure she didn't fade into the background. If this was a test, then she didn't want to give the producers any reason not to show her favourably. One thing Matt had kept reminding her before she'd gone away was that the producers saw her as a celeb, and she needed to think that way too.

Once sat in their sand bunker, they took it in turns to delve into their bags and see what they had which could be useful. Emily went first, undoing her tightly packed, black nylon Superdry rucksack, and listed what she had.

'I've got a bottle of Evian, some paracetamol, tissues, anti-bac wipes, erm...' she realised how dull her stuff sounded, 'hands up who's a mum, eh?' She shrugged her shoulders. But Zoe shook her head.

'No, this is perfect. You've got lots of useful bits. Any chance you've got some food?'

Emily wondered if Zoe was suggesting she was... what? Hungry? Or fat? Looking at the younger woman, she decided she was only trying to be sensible.

'Erm, I've got a bar of chocolate, a cereal bar and… a packet of Jaffa Cakes – the small ones,' she added hastily. She wasn't being edited into a walking tuckshop.

'I'm glad I got lost with you,' June enthused. 'Ky bag has a lighter and some ciggies.' She saw both the women raise their eyebrows, 'I know, I should vape but I hate the whole idea of a cloud of candyfloss air surrounding me.'

Emily smiled.

'On the plus side, a vape wouldn't do much at lighting a fire for us – would it?'

June also had a bottle of hand cream and a handful of plasters squashed into her bag.

'That's it I'm afraid, I didn't even decide what went in there. Tom packed it for me.' She shrugged.

'Is Tom your husband?' Emily asked, intrigued. Matt would never risk packing her bag for her.

June looked horror-stricken.

'No, he's my PA. I'm not married. Not anymore.' She paused. 'My ex-husband, Jack, is referred to as The Bastard for numerous good reasons.'

Mortified, Emily remembered something in the media last year about the most famous of TV marriages hitting the rocks. She realised how far apart her world and that of the most well-known face of daytime telly was, recalling seeing June's harried face splashed across numerous magazines in the little shop at the end of Emily's road where she'd do her hangover shopping.

Zoe's bag contained a script she was learning, bottled water, travel sickness tablets, a small pack of rice cakes, some painkillers, two pairs of sunglasses, a toothbrush and a mini toiletry set.

'Not much food, is there?' grumbled June, looking at their survival pack.

'No, but we may as well eat what we have, and then tomorrow, when they find us, we can enjoy whatever we want,' suggested Zoe.

Emily nodded and tried to smooth things over with June, hoping she'd forgive her the divorce faux pas.

'In the meantime, I think we should get a fire started – it'll help us stay warm and the production team will get some good shots of us looking like survivors. We should do it properly though.' The other two looked blank, so Emily rushed on. 'You know, grab some kindling, build it up big, then light it so it looks really impressive. They can get some good shots of us against it. It'll look pretty atmospheric.'

The others nodded and June became animated.

'Oh, I know, we could tie scarves on our heads, apply some make-up as war paint.'

Zoe laughed and joined in.

'Yes, and lots of whooping around the fire and hollering.'

'Okay, I'll grab some kindling, I can light a fire well too – I was taught how to build a campfire before I was kicked out of Guides,' Emily exclaimed. This was just like when she, Matt and the girls went camping. She just hoped it wouldn't include an ant infestation and a 4am wake-up call when a horse took a piss against their tent.

'I'll help,' Zoe offered.

'And I'll dig out some make-up for us, get us into commando mode,' said June with a laugh.

A little later and the three women were screaming and hollering and dancing around the fire.

'I feel so strong, so empowered,' Emily called over the roaring flames, in between yelling and laughing. Who knew being a celebrity would mean this much fun?

'Yes! I feel like a warrior,' Zoe agreed, whooping, acting a little more like her twenty-five-year-old self for the first time since Emily had met her.

June's reply was to rip off all her clothes and go running into the velvet-black water.

'Get a load of this,' she yelled, her voice lost to the black sky, her pearly-white behind shining as bright as the full moon hanging dramatically over the ocean.

*

Stretching herself out, June groaned at the aches and pains making themselves known from a night of very little sleeping on the beach. The mosquitoes had bitten her legs badly and, whilst Emily's coat had softened the space they were lying in, the sand hadn't yielded much to her body and she felt bruised all over.

A huge racket of birdsong from the trees made sure she wouldn't be sleeping any longer and, on spotting Zoe sitting a little further away, she moved to the megastar.

'Morning,' June said lightly to Zoe, who, despite the late night, still looked unruffled. Her white shirt was tied around her waist, exposing a taut navel, and her hair was piled on top of her head in a loose bun, leaving small tendrils to escape around her ears and the nape of her neck.

'Morning,' the A-lister replied softly. The two sat on the powder-white sand, looking across the bay where cool blues and icy-white foam mingled together like a retro cocktail, leading their way across the lagoon to another sandy beach and an island covered in palms and emerald-green fronds a mile or so away.

'This is stunning, isn't it? Paradise really.' June felt the need to break the silence between the two of them, and instantly regretted it, realising she was blowing her promise to herself to act incredibly cool and totally fine with the fact the world's most famous face was sharing an island with her.

Zoe looked at June and smiled serenely, her skin dewy with youth.

'I was awake for the sunrise; and it was mind-blowing, I've never seen anything like it anywhere in the world. I felt very connected to nature.' She laughed at herself. 'Sorry, I promise I'm not some kind of spiritual type,' she thought for a second, 'not that it's an issue if you're spiritual of course.' Zoe looked out to the water again, then added, 'And even if you do just like to dabble, that's fine too.'

She breathed out unevenly, and June recognised what the problem was. They had no idea where the cameras were, or how their conversations were being picked up ,and Zoe was worried about offending anyone. Of course, June could well understand it; after the two weeks Zoe had just had, she was clearly on a charm offensive to try and win over her adoring fans once again.

Now wasn't the time to bring *that* up though. 'She's sleeping well,' June said, changing the subject and looking in the direction of Emily.

'Yup, she said since having kids she can sleep anywhere.' Zoe grinned. 'Must admit, I'm quite jealous.'

'Same, never got around to having children and now it's too late,' June admitted, a little sadly.

Zoe looked in horror at her. 'Oh, no, I meant I wish I could sleep anywhere – I'm not ready for children yet.'

She patted June's arm to try and ease the awkwardness the conversation had brought to them.

'I need my eye mask, ear plugs and white-noise machine before I can even begin to think about sleeping.' Zoe leant in and confessed to June as quietly as she could. 'You'd think with all the planes and all the hotels I've been in these past few years, I'd have adapted to a disrupted sleep pattern but it's just got worse.'

June enjoyed the frankness of Zoe; it was refreshing for a star as huge as her to be so real. Maybe she was doing it for the benefit of the cameras, but something about the way she was speaking to her made June feel like the younger woman needed to get the words out for once. Whether or not she was heard by millions.

'What's it like? Your job?' June heard herself ask, and saw Zoe flinch. The older woman remembered the non-disclosure agreement they'd all signed, with hundreds of things they'd all agreed not to discuss with each other whilst on the show – she thought of it a bit like a prenup but more to do with information not being shared, instead of money – and realised she'd overstepped.

'Sorry. I didn't mean... I don't want to know what it's like to be you,' though she would have liked to ask, she admitted to herself. 'I mean...' She faltered, aware of sounding like a sycophantic fan (which she was) or nosy (which she was) or prompted by the production team to "press Zoe's buttons" (which she wasn't, even though

24

they'd asked). Zoe hadn't said anything, which should have been the indicator to June to stop, but she wanted to clarify her question. It was the thirty years of presenting which did it. No question left unturned.

'I meant, what is your job – as in, being an actor – like? Not what's it like to wear loads of fabulous clothes or meet other famous people or be given expensive things. None of that. What's it like being someone else?' she re-asked, clenching her fists in her lap so tightly she thought her acrylics would puncture holes in her palms. The words felt like they were being carried away on the light, warm breeze to be swallowed up by the sea and the silence between the two women felt interminable.

Then, Zoe cleared her throat, stretched out her legs from the tucked position she'd been in, and eyed June, with a slightly raised eyebrow.

'I love acting. I love being allowed to be other people and for audiences to like it too. Acting someone else's life is much easier than managing your own – don't you think?' She smiled softly at June. The tension which had crept into the older woman's shoulders, filling them, and her, with worry at getting off on the wrong foot with this goddess, dissipated into the air along with the shrieks from the brightly coloured birds overhead.

'I think I'd love a chance to be someone else. Just for a bit,' June admitted, and then worried she'd come across as too introverted. Too against type for the usual smiley June on *Wake Up*. This was meant to be a chance at a new her, not continue with the sad old one. She made sure she gave her trademark deep laugh, flicked her hair a little and looked back to Emily who was waking up.

'Reckon we should have a chat with sleepyhead over there and make a plan. I could do with swapping this,' she indicated her floaty chiffon dress that had begun to look grubby around the edges, 'with something a little less stained and a little more Sienna Miller, and this,' she showed Zoe her empty water bottle, 'with a cup of something ground and from Brazil.'

Nodding thoughtfully, Zoe stood up with June to walk over to Emily.

'I've been thinking about that. It's odd that no one has come for us yet.' June caught up with the younger woman's longer strides and pressed a hand on her elbow to slow her down, picking up the conversation as they fell in step.

'They must have their footage of us all "surviving" now. It must be time for them to get us along to the lodges.' She paused again and held her hand to her flat stomach which showed through the gap between her shirt and shorts. 'I'm beginning to get pretty hungry – aren't you?'

June nodded, though she hadn't eaten a full meal since 1993.

'You don't think—' June broke off; she didn't want to sound stupid, but at the same time she'd had this thought and it had been niggling at her, a whisper at first, but now it was getting louder. 'You don't think that maybe they've split us into a men versus women sort of thing?' Zoe looked sharply at June, and she continued. 'What if Toby was told to make his way, and they wanted to see who could survive better.' She had a further thought and grabbed Zoe on her wrist to make her slow down and listen.

'What if he's already got to the lodges – as well as the other celebs – and the joke's on us... not being able to follow signs…' She tailed off in the horror that she was being made a national joke. Again. She'd had plenty of that the last couple of years since her intensely high-profile divorce from The Bastard.

Zoe stopped. Her posture was straight and tall, her arms crossed in front of her body. June thought wistfully of the days when she had toned upper arms. Now she had to find clothes to hide her bingo wings on TV.

'You think we've been split into gendered groups and the idea was to see which group would get to the lodges first?' June nodded her agreement and Zoe continued, 'And you think we may be the last to get there?' June nodded mutely.

'Fuck,' the younger woman exclaimed. 'Shit. Sorry guys. Sorry. That'll be bleeped. June… you might be right. But if so—'

'We need to get our arses in gear and find the lodges too?' June finished for her.

'Exactly.'

SLUMMIN' IT ON THE ISLAND

THE husband of Instagrammer and famous mum, Emily Chase, has taken over her social media accounts, announcing that she has joined this year's cast of *Star Survivor UK*.

Matt Chase posted a series of stories to Emily's *Slummin' It Mummin' It* Instagram page yesterday where he announced he had said goodbye to his wife a few days ago and the children were already missing her.

During the short videos, which showed their famous kitchen where Emily shares many of her live videos from, Matt looked full of smiles and pride.

He said:

"So we can finally announce that our Emily, or SIMI as you guys all know her, has said yes to a huge adventure and is going to be on *Star Survivor*.

"She's packed for every eventuality but we're pretty certain she'd be fine whatever she's up against – as long as it doesn't involve spiders!"

He added:

"The girls and I are super excited about how she gets on, and I'm only a bit jealous that I'm doing the dad-at-home bit whilst she gets to be on a sunny island somewhere.

"We'll be rooting for her and as soon as phone lines are open, make sure to call to keep her safe. We want to crown her Queen of the Island!"

Matt has said he'll be looking after SIMI's social media accounts until she returns and has already apologised for the feed.

He said:

"It won't be as pretty as you guys are used to, and I'm a bit rubbish at uploading things, but this'll be my adventure and I'm sure you will all be super kind to me."

Other celebrities confirmed include prolific children's author Toby Masters and popstar Cyan.

Chapter Two

Zoe wiped her forehead with a tissue she'd found in her Louis Vuitton backpack. The nineties-style mini-sack had been gifted to her on a shoot a little while ago, and she'd been thrilled to receive the must-have item – even posting a cutesy photo of it. However, compared to Emily's enormous rucksack, it looked a bit ridiculous in their current situation. She realised it looked like she wasn't used to needing a bag big enough to fit anything of use in.

The heat was increasing rapidly and, despite moving back to the shade of the palm trees a little way from the shoreline, the sun was scorching the earth around the three women and beads of sweat were streaming down Zoe's back.

'We need to find the lodges soon. We need water. We need food. We need shelter.' She was building momentum when Emily joined in.

'We need cold showers and even colder champagne.' She smiled – trying, Zoe thought, to cover her anxiety. 'So, what are you thinking?'

The thought did occur to Zoe: why, when she was the youngest of the three, was the decision-making falling to her? But as plans did need to be made, she decided to do what she could.

'So, erm, I think…' The other women were looking at her, their gaze making her nervous. 'I think we should split up, right? And, like, I'll go that way,' Zoe indicated the left of the bay they were in, 'around the rocks, I think. And, erm, Emily, I thought… that you could go, erm, go to the right – through those trees, and see if you could find anyone that way?'

June and Emily were nodding in agreement with her, maybe she *was* being decisive. 'And I thought that you; June, you should stay here because…' She hesitated over saying it was because June was older and more likely to be susceptible to the extreme heat. Plus she had ridiculous shoes for trekking anywhere. She tried a softer reason. 'Ah, because we need someone here in case the producers come looking for us and don't know where we've all gone.'

June nodded, mollified. 'I could look for anything useful here too – in case we do end up here for another night,' she said.

Zoe smiled and nodded, anything to make June feel a little more useful. 'Good idea.'

'We should go now, it's only going to get hotter,' Emily suggested, and Zoe bobbed her head slightly, a knot of anxiety in her stomach.

'Good plan.'

31

June divided what was left of Zoe's water between the other two's bottles, shaking her head when they both suggested she kept some back. Emily dove into her bag and found a scarf to tie around her head to keep the sun off. Wishing she had something too, Zoe looked in her own bag for inspiration.

Emily was watching her closely as Zoe felt about in the recess of the tiny leather bag.

'I'm sure I've got something, like a spare T-shirt to wear,' she explained, and then her hands alighted on something small and cotton. 'Ah, brilliant, here we—' her words broke off as suspended from her index finger was a tiny, pure-white thong.

Guffawing with laughter, Emily wheezed at the sight of the knickers. 'Yep, useful, very, very useful.'

'Maybe you could use them as an eye patch?' June suggested. 'You could be a pirate on this island.' She laughed too.

Zoe shook her head. 'Y'know when you wish you'd packed your own bag?' She laughed. 'Maybe they'll come in handy,' she added hopefully.

'Yep, maybe we can use them as a catapult for when we go feral,' Emily suggested. Zoe laughed again, her insides squeezing so hard she couldn't breathe. She hadn't laughed so much in months.

'Here, use this instead,' Emily suggested, producing a blue T-shirt out of her bag. She shrugged at Zoe's raised eyebrow.

'I like to be prepared. I'm just annoyed I didn't pack the toilet roll I'd usually bring – and it's a pity I wasn't able to bring full-size sun lotion on the plane.'

'You are the most prepared person I've ever met.' Zoe accepted the T-shirt in admiration. 'Thank you.' She wound the T-shirt around her head as a bandana, accepted the half bottle of water June had given her, and stood up.

'Okay, so… I'm going to go,' she said, with more confidence than she felt. Turning to Emily, who was preparing herself too, she said, 'Only walk for an hour. If you can't see anything, turn around and come straight back. We don't want to lose you.'

Nodding, Emily smiled. 'Aye-aye cap'n,' she giggled. 'Sorry, couldn't resist.'

June did a mock salute in their direction.

'Be off with you or she'll make you walk the plank.'

Striding away, Zoe smiled to herself. The programme would be more bearable than she'd thought with these two along for the ride and would hopefully mean she came out of it doing much better in the press than last week.

Rounding the bay, she quickly found her route was blocked by rocks of every shape and size, many jagged and unwelcoming. Thoughts of media coverage and naked photos disappeared as she was confronted with waves crashing against the rocks, white foam licking its way across the stones nearest the ocean. Quelling her nerves with a deep intake of sea air, she began climbing her way across the rocks but had only climbed over one large rock when her foot slipped and she fell hard.

'Fuck.' She gingerly felt down and saw blood across her hand from a cut on her right leg. The bleeding wasn't heavy and when Zoe stood to see if she could bear weight, although it stung, it didn't hurt too much.

She unwound the T-shirt from her head and tied it

around her leg to stem the blood and instantly felt the searing heat through her hair. It was intense and she could feel her skin burning.

'Come on, Zoe, keep going. Think of the long shower you'll have,' she said out loud, surprised at how quiet her voice was in comparison to the shock of waves throwing themselves over the rocks.

Moving as best she could, the makeshift bandage on her leg hampering her movements, she worked slowly but methodically to climb up and over the obstacles in her path. Waves crashed regularly over her and she wondered, fleetingly, if this was it. And if it was, would she be remembered for anything other than her last headline?

Just as she'd missed her footing on yet another rock, Zoe looked up and caught a glimpse of a bay even more postcard-ready than the one she'd left, which gave her the will to speed up and climb over.

As she scrabbled down the rocks, palm trees waved at her and the ocean looked coolly inviting after the heat of the climb. She considered running into the water, but remembered she'd promised she'd find the lodges, and the treeline at the back of the beach looked promising.

Making her way to the forest, which trimmed the sandy beach like a perfect finish to a stunning cake, she burst through to find the lodges – convinced they'd be there.

But there was no sign of anyone. Not a runner. Or a hairstylist. Or a producer.

It was as desolate as the bay she'd left June in.

Zoe pushed through a dark-green canopy of leaves and couldn't help the huge grin spreading across her face when she saw the most ridiculously idyllic pool. A waterfall cascaded into the deep depths of the water, which reached some fifteen metres or so across. The pool was fringed by delicate ferns curling their way to the water's edge, splashed with hints of pinks, oranges and yellows, courtesy of a collection of beautiful tropical plants.

It looked like the setting for a hair commercial Zoe once starred in. But this time the pool would be a welcome refreshment, rather than the tepid bath she'd cavorted in for the hair shoot for so many hours that her legs had begun to pucker.

'Hello...'

Zoe's voice bounced around the forest, hitting the water which was continuing to look even more inviting, with glints of sunlight dancing across its surface.

'Hello, anyone there?' Zoe tried again. There was still no response.

She stepped closer to the tranquil pool. Zoe needed a drink and she was hopeful the water would be safe. Kneeling closer to the edge, she scooped up a little of the water and licked it, tentatively. It was incredibly crisp. And not salty. Which meant she could drink it.

Lying on her stomach, Zoe lowered her head to the water and sipped at it. With one last glance around her and knowing for certain no one was around, Zoe stepped out of her shorts and T-shirt, jumping quickly into the water.

'Shit.'

Her shout echoed around the private glade, followed by a gleeful laugh as Zoe dove fully into the pool, enjoying the shock of cold as it enveloped her. She twisted and turned in the water, luxuriating in the cool embrace that washed away the sweat, the blood, the sticky sand. It was bliss.

'Thank you,' she yelled as she floated on her back, feeling the water cleanse her scalp and hearing her voice echo back to her ten times over.

Knowing she needed to find the others, Zoe regretfully pulled herself out of the pool and dried off as best she could, remembering to refill her bottle to help her on the return walk. She wasn't looking forward to the rocky return though and now she was out of the water, the pain in her leg was returning.

As she was taking a swig of water, a shaft of light caught her eye.

Hesitating for a second, but deciding she may have a better chance of finding the lodges if she followed it, Zoe strode towards the glimmer. On pushing through the trees, she realised daylight was making its way through them and highlighting a path, trodden down by something – humans, maybe?

Zoe paused. She could either return via the rocks, which were hard work, painful and in many ways incredibly dangerous. But at least she knew she'd find the others if she returned that way.

Or she could test this path and see where it took her?

Looking back at the bay and seeing a large wave crash over the rocks, she made up her mind to follow the path.

Happily, the going was easy, with just a few low branches to push out of her way and, after twenty or so minutes, Zoe burst out onto golden sand.

Blinking to try and manage the amount of light burning her retinas, reflecting off the sand, Zoe tried to get her bearings when she heard a shout.

'Zoe. Oh gosh, you're back. I'm so happy, you've been over three hours – I was worried about you.' June was running down to Zoe, arms outstretched and she returned the hug she was enveloped in.

'Did you get lost? Are you okay? Any lodges?' June held Zoe's arm to get her attention and looked concerned.

'I'm… I'm fine… no, I didn't find the lodges.' June looked crestfallen. 'But I did find a much nicer beach – and fresh water. Here, try.' Zoe gave her bottle to June who fell upon it greedily.

'It's amazing. So crisp. I'm sorry, I've not left much.'

Zoe realised June was embarrassed at her gluttony and quickly sought to reassure her. 'It's okay. I think we should go there, it's not far – as I've just discovered,' Zoe laughed, sitting on the sand, pleased at how near the other bay was, but regretting going around the rocks in her haste before. 'Get Em, and we can make a move. I think you girls are going to love it.'

June looked down, worry across her face.

'She's not come back yet. I was beginning to panic about both of you.'

'But I said walk for an hour and then come back.' Zoe was concerned. She'd had a tough walk – what if Emily's had been worse? What if she was hurt?

'Should we…?' June's suggestion faded away, as she grabbed Zoe's arm again.

'Look… it's…'

'Emily,' they both shouted, running towards a

stumbling figure coming out of the forest on the other side of the bay.

'But she's got… hang on… is that…?'

Emily fell over and next to her, Toby slumped heavily onto the sand.

*

'Fuck.'

Emily heard the exclamation from the other side of the beach and saw Zoe and June race closer to where she was sat on the sand, taking in huge lungfuls of air with Toby lying down next to her.

'So… thirsty…' Emily gasped, and Zoe immediately handed over the rest of the water June had left. The other two women watched as she drained the bottle and wiped her forehead with the back of her hand, trying to stem the river of sweat making its way down her face.

'Come on, we should get in the shade to cool down,' June suggested and Emily nodded as Zoe pulled her to standing.

'You're going to need to help him though,' she indicated Toby who was still lying motionless, 'he's hurt his ankle and is in an incredible amount of pain,' she explained.

Toby was conscious, but looked exhausted. The well-groomed face they'd seen twenty-four hours ago on the helicopter,was etched with a greying stubble, and dirt was splattered across his cheeks and nose. He had a dried cut on the left side of his face, where blood had hardened in a sticky mess, and his trademark quiff hair was decidedly ruffled.

'Hi.' He crinkled a smile at Zoe and June as they pulled him to his feet, his face wincing with pain. Zoe pulled Toby's left arm around her neck, and June did the same with the right. With Emily staggering gingerly, they slowly walked to the shade of the palm trees that were swaying in a gentle breeze.

On any other day this would be a selfie moment, the place was so eye-wateringly beautiful, but none of the four could see its beauty. Settling in the relative cool of the shade, Zoe asked the questions on her and June's lips.

'So, what happened – and where did he come from?'

Emily stretched out and took her T-shirt off to get some cool air on her body and discarded it on the sand. She sighed and cast a glance at Toby who looked forlorn.

'I started walking through that bit,' she indicated to the right of them, 'and it was seriously hard-going. I mean, there's *no* chance there are any lodges or anything that way. I had to hack my way through all these vines and branches with my hands,' she showed them the cuts on her palms, 'and it was clear there was no path through. So, I turned around to make my way back. But I must have taken a wrong turn somewhere, because I found myself in a clearing and he,' she indicated Toby with a brief nod in his direction, 'was propped up against a fallen tree. He was so still I thought he was dead.' Toby looked at her in surprise. 'Why else do you think I shrieked when I saw you? I'm surprised you didn't hear me,' she said to June, who just shook her head.

'Anyway, I ran over to him and he was in a bad way – still is, if you look at his ankle. I did what I could, but

39

it's badly swollen and looks very painful. No infection though,' she summarised, whilst Zoe carefully unwrapped the cotton bandages that had been manufactured from a shirt. Toby's ankle was a riot of violent purples and garish greens, and was stuck at an odd angle.

'It's broken I think,' Emily concluded. 'I decided there was no way I should leave him, because it had been an accident that I found him. I had no idea if I'd be able to find the spot again. That's when the real fun began.' She laughed hard at the memory of encouraging Toby to stand up.

'When I found him, he was convinced I was someone else. He kept saying he was sorry for having sex with me,' she broke off and looked at him scathingly, 'as if, and then he apologised about my husband finding out.' The other two women giggled as Toby reddened.

'Oh, that's not the best bit,' Emily paused for her audience to give her their full attention, 'he was very keen to tell me how well-endowed he was and that he'd just been a bit "chilly" when we last met – then he started pulling his flies down.'

Emily laughed as she remembered slapping Toby to get some sense into him and stop him from exposing himself, and carried on.

'We began to make our way back. But he's got to be six foot.'

'Six foot two actually,' Toby corrected with a crack in his voice.

Raising an eyebrow, Emily smiled. 'What's two inches between friends, eh, Toby?' and she took pleasure in seeing him redden a little. He had remembered then. 'And

I'm five feet three. So it was slow-going trying to act as a prop to him, and to get him to walk out.'

'*He* can hear you know.' Toby was mock upset, but seemed to be enjoying the retelling of his rescue, so Emily continued.

'So we walked, sat, walked, sat, you get the picture, and then, just as I was starting to think I'd taken another wrong turn and I'd have to leave him, we came out of the forest – and there you guys were.' She smiled broadly. She'd been so thrilled at seeing the other two her concern for herself had disappeared completely.

'And now here we are,' concluded June quietly, her bare feet scrunching into the sand.

'Yes. And I'm starting to think something has happened.' Emily laid bare the thoughts she'd been having. 'If there are producers on this island, even if they enjoyed seeing us get a bit hungry and thirsty, one – they're not that way.' She indicated the side she'd explored, whilst holding up a finger of her left hand to show her checklist, 'And two – they wouldn't have let Toby get to this condition. He needs medical attention.'

Zoe nodded.

'I agree. There's something else too – have you seen any other helicopters coming in to the island since we landed?' The other three shook their heads. 'Nor me. And I know for a fact that four of the other celebrities were due to be joining us a day later because of scheduling conflicts. One of them wasn't finished in a West End run until yesterday,' she explained, 'so where are they? Why haven't we heard any helicopters coming in,' she paused thoughtfully, 'or leaving for that matter?'

The other three sat in silence, allowing what Zoe had said to settle in.

'So, what does that mean then?' Toby croaked.

The air was heady with an exotic perfume, waves crashed lazily against the shoreline, the sky was of the purest bright blue and the palm trees swayed to their own beat.

It was true paradise.

'I think it means we're fucked,' summed up Emily.

*

'You girls are pretty practical. I'll give you that.'

'Thanks, but we're women,' Emily retorted and continued helping Zoe to make a stretcher for Toby.

'And you're sure we need to move on from here?' he asked plaintively. He was fed up of moving around the island and wanted to stay put so they could be rescued.

June had her hands on her hips as she spoke to him. 'We've gone over this, Toby. We need to make camp in a better place than here. We didn't sleep well last night and Zoe's found us somewhere perfect – we need the water for a start.'

Toby wanted to say that where they were was a huge improvement on where he'd stayed the night before, that the night in the forest would give him nightmares for years and all he wanted was to go home. But he didn't. Instead, he carried on watching the women make a stretcher for him, the outcome of a long discussion between the three women as to how best to get him to the oasis Zoe had discovered.

With the prospect of being carried by an overweight, pale, middle-aged woman with her muffin top hanging over her shorts and Zoe Stenson, a goddess who he'd rather bed than allow to help him, his pride was dented more than the car he'd wrapped around a tree a few years ago after a night-long drinking binge.

'That should do it,' Zoe said proudly whilst all three looked at what they'd created and Toby tried to focus on the now.

June, the morning TV presenter who once, Toby recalled, described him on a segment as 'best to look at, not to listen to', had found two long branches. All three had stripped them of their leaves and Emily had produced a raincoat from her bag along with a T-shirt. The women had pulled them onto the branches to make a rudimentary stretcher.

'Get on then, Toby, let's see if we can lift you,' June commanded, and Toby bristled at being told what to do by her, and the inference he'd be too heavy to lift. Though, in fairness, he noted, he had been doing a lot of weight training prior to the island to ensure he was in peak condition. He might be a bit heavy. But not fat.

Huffing, he shifted his bulk onto the stretcher.

'Well, lie down then – we can't carry you if you're sitting up – can we?' Zoe told him off brightly and, again, he fought the urge to tell them all to go fuck themselves.

Toby decided lying down on the floor whilst being watched by three women was up there in his top three oddest experiences. It made him feel vulnerable. But he did as he was told, lying back and looking up into the canopy of trees, wishing he was anywhere else. Fervently praying the whole experience would be over sooner rather than later and wondering what he'd have to do to stop this making the cut for the day. Even if the girls didn't think there were cameras, Toby was still convinced.

'Okay, Em, you go head end, I'll go feet. I'll carry him this way.' Zoe faced forward and squatted to pick up her end of the stretcher, which, Toby realised, left him with a much more interesting view than the trees.

'Maybe there's a plus side,' he muttered under his breath.

'What?' Zoe looked around and Toby shook his head quickly.

'Nothing.'

Zoe pulled a face.

'Okay. Ready? One, two, three, lift.' The two grunted with the exertion of lifting Toby and then laughed hysterically.

'We can do it. It works,' exclaimed Zoe.

'It's holding,' June agreed. 'See if you can walk,' she told the two women who slowly moved forwards, causing Toby to lurch slightly from side to side. They placed him down after a few steps and high-fived each other.

'So, will you be okay?' Emily asked Toby, who had the odd feeling she knew something about him she wasn't letting on. He was concerned he may have said something when he was delirious, but thought now wasn't the time to ask so just nodded and smiled broadly (the one his mother called his 'plastic surgery face' as it was so fake).

'I'll be fine,' he lied. The stretcher was uneven and very uncomfortable. But it was a large improvement on walking on a broken ankle.

'Well done – a good team effort. So, now what?' he asked, hoping he sounded like he was in charge, not the other way around.

'Now? We go.' Zoe was emphatic. The other women nodded and picked up the small amount of belongings they had. June placed Toby's bag on his stomach and then marched ahead to lead the way.

'Just keep following that path; if I think you're going wrong, I'll give you a yell,' Zoe commanded.

Toby was surprised the other two were happy for the megastar to be in charge. She was so young. What could she know about leading a team? But they did as they were told and, soon, Toby was lifted again and they began to make their way. Pretty quickly though, it was patently obvious how slow-going carrying Toby would be. Emily and Zoe could only lift the stretcher for a few minutes at a time before putting him down.

Every time they placed him down, they banged him, accidentally, on the floor. Every time, they apologised. Every time they picked him up, there was a slight imbalance and he'd wobble in the middle, suspended a metre or so off the ground, and every time they'd apologise.

'I could do with fewer apologies and more walking,' Toby grumbled to himself. There were, however, two things which got him through this most arduous of processes. One was Zoe's butt as it moved rhythmically as she walked along. And the second thing was... Toby couldn't remember the second one.

'Zoe, is it much further?' Emily asked, panting. Toby realised he felt something, maybe pity for her. She had, by this point, now carried his sorry ass all over the island in one way or another. He hoped for her sake it wasn't much further. He also hoped the TV crew would finally rock up and get them off the island. It had gone beyond a joke and although the girls seemed to think something had gone wrong, Toby couldn't, and wouldn't, believe it.

'Just… here,' Zoe panted as June broke through some foliage into a clearing. Toby peered around Zoe.

'Fuck. It's fucking stunning,' he exclaimed as the girls placed him down a little quicker than before. They bumped him on the way down and didn't apologise, because they'd already run to the water's edge of the most ridiculously picturesque piece of Mother Earth Toby had ever seen.

'Last one in does the fishing,' Zoe yelled hysterically and in one motion pulled her shirt over her head and her shorts off, completely comfortable in her own skin – she flicked them onto the mossy side of the pool and Toby watched her as she dived in. Her toned body disappeared into the water and she emerged a few seconds later, with droplets falling from her that glistened in the sunlight. She beamed widely at them all.

'Come in, it's beautiful.'

But, Toby saw, the other two didn't need persuading; they had already shed their clothes. He watched as June peeled off her diaphanous, patterned dress over her head and revealed her incredibly thin frame, then looked away guiltily when she caught him watching.

'No looking, Toby,' she shouted, but not before he'd caught a glimpse of a vivid fuchsia bra and knicker set before she jumped in and gasped with the shock of the cool water. He was relieved she wasn't in a thong – no one needed to see a fifty-something wearing a cheese slice.

'Nor me,' squeaked Emily, who was hiding behind a large fern, and Toby tried not to laugh.

'I'm not looking, you're all safe,' he tried to yell back, but his throat was hoarse from the lack of water, so he ended up coughing like an old man who had smoked sixty a day for the majority of his life. Through his coughing fit Toby spotted Emily by the side of the pool, then watched as she hesitated, turned around and walked to her cavernous bag. She rummaged for something and ran to the water, which caused her pendulous breasts to bounce in their plain and sensible black bra. Toby watched as she bent to the side and he looked away as the matching boring black knickers rose up her arse.

Having completed whatever she'd done, she turned around and walked over to him with too much on display as far as he was concerned. She had a pale, jelly-like stomach covered in stretch marks, her thighs rubbed together as she walked and she wore the most uncomfortable grimace. He suspected she had tried to suck in her stomach but he didn't think it helped. Toby coughed again as she neared him and she bent over, her breasts hanging low.

'Here, drink this. Sorry we forgot to give you some, you must be gasping.' She handed Toby a full bottle of chilled water and parted with the words, 'Drink it, and when I get out I'll refill it for you, hopefully it'll help with the cough.'

Toby watched as she walked away and drained the bottle, painfully aware of the kindness she had just shown, in contrast to his own cruel thoughts.

He continued to follow her route as she entered the water and joined the others. Zoe and June joined her and he watched as they swam and chatted. Emily was smiling broadly whilst she did little circles of breaststroke, June was laughing like a hyena and Zoe was alternating between chatting and disappearing under the water to do handstands. Toby thought they looked like they were at an exclusive resort, not whatever they really faced right now. It was easy to see why, of course, he acknowledged, whilst sipping on the cold water Emily had fetched, as he felt it too. Despite everything that pointed to the contrary ,he had to believe they were still on the show in some way, and that this was all just a test. An extreme one. But a test nonetheless.

Whilst he sat and waited for the three to wash and cool down, the light began to fade, with long shadows casting their spells across the sandy floor, and Toby realised he was worried about the dark coming in quickly, like it had done when he'd spent the night in the forest. Alone. He shivered. He didn't want to dwell on that night again for a very long time.

Just as the thought had crossed his mind that he should give the women a shout and suggest they, as a team, made a start on making a shelter, Zoe pulled herself out onto the side.

She wrung her hair out and released what looked like a pint of water out of it, then wound it back around her head in a large bun, securing it with a thin twig she'd found on the floor. Toby watched, transfixed, as she stood up, her long limbs a burnished chestnut brown, her bottom pert and round.

It was, he decided, unfathomable watching a woman who was so incredibly famous that she went only by her first name, just walking around in front of him in her underwear. She was taller in real life, he noted as she walked over to him, her white shirt tied in a knot under her petite breasts which revealed a toned stomach. She was scrawnier than he'd assumed too. She had an athletic build and fewer curves. He imagined she'd been pushed into a lot of corsets in those films where she'd been a fifties-style hourglass.

'Hey.' She smiled easily at Toby and he wondered how he'd got so lucky to be stranded with her.

'Hey yourself,' he replied as coolly as he could.

'You smell awful. We've voted – we're going to tip you in the pool before we do anything else.'

'Ah. Great.'

*

June's lips were dry and, when she licked them, they tasted as though she'd eaten a bag of ready salted crisps and all the flavour had left itself on her face.

Not that she would have risked a single crisp these past twenty or so years. Certainly not after The Bastard made a point that she'd have to work doubly hard in the gym if she indulged in some, the one time she'd helped herself to a handful at a party.

June smiled at the memory of the party on New Year's Eve. Everyone had worried about the Millennium Bug ruining all their computers. But still they'd stuffed themselves on overpriced M&S vol-au-vents, cheap champagne and posh crisps. Her stomach grumbled at the thought of food and she pushed it from her mind. She'd spent many years teaching herself to survive on very little sustenance; she just needed to stick at it a bit longer, and they'd be rescued and she could have one of her super juices.

And maybe, just maybe, a thick slice of toast with butter melting through it.

Salivating at the thought of carbs and fat, two things she'd avoided for many years, June looked around, cursing herself and the others for not building a better shelter the day before – resulting in two nights on the beach.

Emily's pashmina was acting as a rudimentary shade cover, tied to some branches above them, and they'd all slept on the floor, with just some ferns to act as a barrier to the sand. None of which had meant June had slept any better that night, than she had the one before, even though she ached to her very soul with tiredness and would have assumed she'd fall asleep straightaway.

She hadn't, she realised, walked so much in years and her legs were complaining at being out of high heels, her calves so shortened by thirty years of constant wear her feet wanted to be on tiptoe.

Easing herself up from the ground, she winced as pain shot its way through from her back to her neck, crawling like a line of fire ants. As she stood, her knees cracked and her vision blurred. June acknowledged she did need to have some food soon. More than two days without anything was a bit much, even for her.

'Hey sleepyhead,' called Toby from a tree trunk he was sat up against, 'the others didn't want to wake you, so I said

I'd keep an eye out. Hope that's okay.' He smiled gently.

June walked gingerly over to him, her head still swimming, and sat where he patted the ground.

'Take a pew,' he offered, and she did as he suggested. He passed her a bottle of water. 'The other two refilled our bottles, so you'd have something when you woke. They've gone to the shoreline to see if they can catch any fish, or, you know, see if anyone is looking for us.' He shrugged.

Accepting the bottle gratefully and draining as much of the water as she could, June coughed as the dryness in her throat was eased.

'Easy. There's loads where that came from, so take your time,' Toby advised, amusement flickering across his light-green eyes.

He was a lot fuzzier around the edges than June remembered. She was sure that their last run-in some five years ago or so, when she'd berated him on lunchtime TV for his misogyny, she'd met a hardened version of this Toby in front of her. This one had crow's feet cleaving their way in on the sides of his eyes, and lines emerging on his forehead. It didn't dull his attractiveness; in fact, his light weathering just amplified his looks. Pity that wasn't the case for women, thought June glumly.

'Better? It's hot already, isn't it?' he asked, and June nodded, noticing for the first time how he had a light lisp when he said 's'. It was, she realised, a little bit cute.

'Yes, thanks. When did the other two go? Are they expecting me to join them?' She panicked, the thought that she'd have to do any work in the searing heat filling her with dread.

'Nah,' Toby shook his head, his dark-blond hair lifting

a little as he did so, 'they've asked if we can do anything with those.' He nodded in the direction of a pile of dark-green balls. She looked questioningly in their direction. 'And they are?'

'Coconuts,' Toby explained. 'They're all around here, and if we can hack into them we should find the fruit inside – it'll be something to eat at least.' But his face looked as excited as she felt at the prospect.

'Okay. So we need to bash them then.' June smiled in Toby's direction; she felt better having a purpose. She'd thought she wanted to lie down and do nothing, but having something to focus her mind on was a good idea. Looking around, June spied a sharp, jagged rock a few feet away.

'That might do.' She turned to Toby, who nodded.

'Yep, that's what I thought – but I can't get over there without your help I'm afraid.' He shrugged apologetically. 'I've tried, but it's too painful to walk on still.' He looked down at the swollen mess of his ankle.

'Well of course not. You've broken the bloody thing, you shouldn't be trying to walk on it,' she grumbled. 'Look, I'll help you over there,' she indicated the grey rock, glinting in the light, 'and then I'll grab the coconuts and bring them over to you to break. And maybe, whilst you're doing that, I should try and find some better coverage for our shelter,' she said and he nodded.

Toby allowed June to pull him to standing.

'Lean on me – it's okay, I won't snap,' she commanded, and enjoyed him doing as he was told. The Bastard never had.

Leading him over to the rock, she helped him down and he sat heavily, with a sigh deep-rooted in pain. She left him and walked over to the coconuts on the floor. They were light green and roughly the size of a toddler's head. Noting what an odd thought it would be to watch Toby smash in said coconut heads, June collected two at a time and brought them over to him. He then began hitting them against the sharp, jutting-out rock whilst sitting with his legs either side. He was already breaking out in a sweat.

'Need any help?'

He shook his head and carried on hitting the green fruit, so she decided to look around for some long branches to weave together for a type of floor for their shelter. June knew she needed a lot, and, she admitted to herself, she wasn't sure where she was going to find rope to bind them together, but she wanted to feel like she was doing something.

An hour or so later, June stepped back from her finds and grinned a smile so wide, she thought her face would crack. Using a strength she didn't know she possessed, she'd discovered that by leaning against some of the thinner trees, she could snap them down and had managed to pull together half of the amount they'd need for the floor. She was going to return to the same clearing and find some more, when Toby shouted for her.

'Come here, try this.' He'd had some success with the coconuts and June took in the carnage of broken shells and hairy matting that had come off of half a dozen or so of the fruit spread out around him.

'I haven't quite got it right yet, where I haven't lost the juice from it instantly,' he shook his head a little sadly, 'but I have been able to crack them enough to get some of the flesh out. And it tastes really good,' he enthused, offering her some creamy white coconut which she took gratefully, sitting next to him.

Biting into the hard, white shards, June felt as though she'd never experienced such a powerful flavour. It was creamy, chalky, and yet, crunchy enough to make her feel like she was actually eating something.

'Amazing.' She smiled, looking at Toby, who had been watching for her reaction. 'Really good. Well done.' Her praise caused him to grin too.

'Thanks – and looks like you've had success too.' He indicated in the direction of the branches she'd lined up on the floor.

June nodded.

'Yes, just need some rope and some more of them and we might be a bit more comfortable.'

Moving to walk closer to the shore to find rope, June heard a shout from further down the beach. Getting up quickly and making her way through the trees, she ran across the sand to the two figures walking slowly across, carrying something very heavy between them. Unable to make it out, June ran down.

'What's tha—'

Her words vanished as she spotted what it was.

'Is that – is that a—?' She hesitated. Unsure what it would mean if she put a word to it.

Zoe nodded, pausing to wipe the sweat that glistened on her forehead.

'It's a helicopter door.'

STAR ISLAND HELI CRASH HORROR

HOLLYWOOD A-lister Zoe Stenson is amongst four celebs thought to have been in a helicopter crash somewhere in the South Pacific.

The actor, who recently brought Instagram to a standstill with a naked video, is thought to have agreed to take part in reality TV sensation *Star Survivor*, the first UK series of which was due to be aired this evening but has been delayed by two days.

Accompanying sexpot Zoe is said to be children's writer and ladies' man Toby Masters, *Wake Up* stalwart June Sharp and Instagrammer Emily Chase.

A statement from Edge Productions, the company behind *Star Survivor UK* said:

"We can confirm that four of our contestants have not arrived at the island where the programme is filmed. We still fully expect to find them and ask that people don't jump to conclusions. We are putting all our resources into finding them and will update when we know more."

Matt Chase, husband to influencer Emily .said:

"We have heard there was a crash but we have few facts to go on. They were due on the island two days ago and so far we've heard nothing. It's a very worrying time for all of us."

The crash is thought to have occurred two days ago, during a freak storm in the Cook Islands.

It is believed a search and rescue is now taking place to identify where the helicopter crashed.

Star Survivor is to begin airing in two days' time with the remaining six contestants, including a shunned Royal.

Chapter Three

'We need as much wood as possible,' Zoe ordered of June, who just nodded with a grimace and disappeared into the forest. The realisation they were definitely alone on the island, and no one was keeping them safe, after they'd found the helicopter door, was one which had put the group in a dark mood for the last two days. Zoe had hoped giving everyone tasks would keep them focused but it hadn't worked well.

June had met the discovery with anger and had alternated her last forty-eight hours between stomping around the beach, screaming obscenities at the rolling waves, or sitting far away from the other three and sobbing into her hands.

Not to be outdone, Emily had taken the finding of the door very, very badly, and had stopped talking altogether. She just sat and looked wistfully at the ocean, hoping someone would come to their rescue.

Toby was managing by sleeping most of the day.

This morning, Zoe had taken the decision, whilst staring out at the bay, that the only way to survive was if they thrived.

She had told the group to light an enormous fire and keep it going all day and all night to act as a beacon for anyone looking for them. It was also her idea to give them something to focus their energies on and to build a decent shelter for the four of them.

It was Zoe who had spotted how useful the helicopter door would be to act as a front for the shelter, providing them with protection from the strong winds and sideways rain which appeared in intervals around the severe heat. Along with the door ,they'd found some ripped tarpaulin, and a piece of rope which June used to tie all the branches she'd gathered together to act as a floor.

Gradually the shelter was taking shape, but they needed a lot of wood to keep burning the fire high enough in the hope anyone looking for them would see where they were stranded. However, it was quickly becoming apparent that Toby needed to start contributing more, and as June said she didn't want to tell Toby off, and Emily didn't seem too keen on him, it had fallen to Zoe to have the chat.

'Hey,' Zoe said, as she sat next to Toby, who was up before the sun was at its highest for the first time in two days.

'Hey.' He rubbed his leg absently.

'So, I was hoping we could get you to deal with this.' Zoe pointed to a weathered green fishing net, which was bunched up a few metres away from the two of them.

Toby shrugged non-committedly.

'Why?'

Trying to play down her exasperation, and wondering why it was down to her to encourage a grown man to care, Zoe decided to be honest.

'Because you're doing sweet fuck all,' she replied, her words startling him into looking at her properly.

'Hey. That's not true. I'm in charge of the fire.' He grimaced.

Nodding carefully, Zoe approached the topic again. 'Yes, sort of,' she shuffled across the island debris of driftwood and sticks to try and get herself comfortable, 'you've appointed yourself to look after it overnight. Which just means you sticking some logs on, and then, in the morning, when the rest of us get up at the crack of dawn, you go to sleep – leaving us to find the food, gather water, collect firewood and try and get rescued.' She waited, and cocked her head on the side a little.

'Does that sound like you pulling your weight?'

Toby pursed his lips together, unhappy with the accusation. 'But my ankle,' he suggested, and Zoe nodded in acceptance.

'Yes, we know. It's very sore,' she rushed to continue over his open-mouthed objection, 'more than sore – it's probably broken. But you can walk – you can, Tobes,' she urged. She'd seen him, the night just gone, move from the fire to the forest for a piss, then return to the fire. He had hobbled, for sure, but he could move. More than he'd been letting the others believe.

Breathing in deeply, and trying to remember the chant her yoga teacher in LA would repeat whenever Zoe was getting stressed, she touched Toby lightly on the arm.

'We need all of us working together – as a team. We're

beginning to slowly starve. We need food. And yes, we need to be found, but we need to find more firewood to be sure we can keep the fire going. June is collecting most of it at the moment and she's about a quarter of your size. We're all working really hard despite being worried as fuck that this might be the place we die. We need you to help us too. All for one and all that.' She smiled sadly.

She knew it. She'd gone too far. Toby was quiet, and Zoe had decided she'd managed to push him away completely. She knew she was a terrible leader, she knew she was a follower. Why did she think just because there was no script to follow that she could somehow find a situation she was in charge of?

She stood to carry on with the shelter.

'Okay,' she heard Toby mumble.

'What?'

'I said okay. I'll stop being a useless fucker. Chuck that net over to me and leave me alone.'

She did as she was asked and made her way to Emily, who had returned from a walk along the shoreline to look for useful items that had washed up. They couldn't help but notice what a treasure trove the ocean would bring in on a daily basis. Plastic items of every kind would arrive, from bottles – which they'd begun washing out and using– to toothbrushes, rubber gloves and bags in every colour and degradation imaginable.

There were also many odd things which arrived daily, such as the leather briefcase Emily was carrying with her.

'Off for a meeting?' Zoe asked, getting a rare smile from Emily, which vanished quickly.

'I thought it would be interesting to see what was in

it. Oh, and I've got a few things in here.' She indicated a faded plastic carrier bag from Sainsbury's in her hand.

'How nice, a bit of home,' Zoe commented wryly.

'Just you wait.' Emily walked over with her bags and settled down by the shelter. June arrived out of the forest with armfuls of wood and stopped to drink some water a little way from them.

'June, I've got something for you.' Emily began rummaging in the bag. 'Look – they're not a pair, but you've been barefoot for almost a week.' She handed June two mismatched flip-flops, one a lurid-green Havaianas, and the other a salmon pink, causing the older woman to pull a face and Emily to be crestfallen.

'I know they're not your usual, but they were all out of Manolos,' she said kindly, offering the shoes to June. Turning away from seeing whether the shoes were accepted, Emily looked in her bag again, 'and a pair for you as well,' she said to Zoe, who laughed at hers.

'Oh, they're amazing. Thank you.' She hiccupped at the sight of the baby-blue jelly shoe and red beach shoe, one a size six, the other a size eight. 'I can't wait to wear them.' She smiled and put them on. They certainly made a change from the options of quickly disintegrating trainers or bare feet, and would be ideal when they were on the rocks looking for clams.

'I've got some too.' Emily pulled out her own tatty non-pair of one purple flip-flop and one which used to be white. 'Don't worry, Toby, I haven't forgotten you.' Something about the way she said it made Toby look up with actual interest and his jaw dropped when she produced a 200 carton of Marlboro Reds.

'I think they may still be smokable – see, the plastic is wrapped all around them.' The women had decided some of Toby's high level of irritability had come with his nicotine withdrawal, and with him and June down to their last five cigarettes, this was a miracle find.

'You… star.' An enormous grin cracked Toby's face, and before Emily had a chance to move, he'd launched himself at her with a huge kiss on the lips. 'I think I might need to marry you,' he said with a laugh.

'Hey, I'm married. Hands off – but enjoy the ciggies. If they're dry I may nick one off you. There used to be a time I was a Marlboro Light girl– if these are my last days, I may start smoking again.' Despite the light tone, Emily's words had a sobering effect on the group again.

Clearing her throat, Emily muttered, 'Sorry. Didn't mean to… you know.'

Zoe leaned over and squeezed her hand gently. 'It's okay, we all feel the same. Good finds.'

'Thank you for my shoes, they feel like the most luxurious things I've ever worn,' reassured June, wiggling her feet in her ugly flip-flops and admiring them. 'What's in there?' She pointed at the briefcase.

'Oh, I almost forgot about that,' admitted Emily and the four grouped around it. The fake tan leather was peeling away from the bag, leaving little islands of bare material poking through. It had two locks on the top with numbers which needed lining up to open it.

'What do you think's in it?' June whispered, echoing the thoughts of the other three.

'A penknife would be useful,' Toby suggested.

'Or… chocolate,' Emily guessed.

'Or wine... or gin...' June added.

'Or a working phone,' Zoe hoped.

'Let's open it then, give it here.' Toby took the briefcase from Emily, 'Most people don't set a password on these. I'm sure it'll be something like–' He broke off, lining each of the eight numbers up as a zero, clicking each one in place. On the final number there was a distinct clunk from within and all four took in a breath.

'This is so exciting. I want to call out "Deal or No Deal",' June said, causing them all to dissolve into laughter.

A sound which continued as the briefcase opened to reveal a stack of faded, waterlogged *Playboy* magazines.

'Ah, useful. Very useful,' Zoe guffawed.

Toby closed the briefcase, and drew it closer to him.

'Well if you don't want them...'

*

'You okay?' Toby sat down carefully next to Emily and stretched down to rub his leg. His ankle ached. He had worked on the beach all afternoon and had shifted enormous rocks into position to spell out SOS.

Emily was quiet. Toby hated uncomfortable silences, even those punctuated by the continued racket of bird calls overhead, so cast about for something to say.

'They'd have to be blind not to see that.' He pointed at the enormous bonfire they'd built that evening. In over a week they'd not seen one plane or boat on the horizon, and were starting to panic that no one knew they were missing.

63

'I thought I was, but no, not really.' Emily's confession interrupted Toby's thoughts.

'Want to talk about it?' He knew he was being tentative but he found Emily much harder to understand than the other two. She looked up from where she'd drawn swirls in the sand with a stick.

'Cherry does this when we're on holiday.' She paused thoughtfully. 'Ivy just eats the sand. Or she did last year when we went to Menorca. Every photo of her has a sand beard, or ice cream all over her.' She stopped and Toby watched as a tear rolled down her cheek. She hastily wiped it away and he pretended not to see.

'It occurred to me today that this could be it for all of us.' She looked at him with deep, worried eyes and Toby felt stumped. The man who prided himself on being able to provide a soundbite for any occasion had absolutely no idea what to say.

Before, another lifetime ago, he'd have tried to fix every situation. He'd have given advice, found a solution. But they were in the middle of nowhere with no survival skills and no obvious way out.

'I miss my children so, so much and I realise what an awful human being I've been all this time. Every day when I've been pissed off at them, or upset they've burst in on my me-time or ruined a night's sleep, I've dreamt of getting away from them. Escaping. And now... now I'm... I've... but it's just all... So. Fucking. Shit. Toby, it's all shit. And I don't know what to do.' Emily looked at him again. She looked as tired as he felt, but a lot sadder.

'I'm not whole without them. Why didn't I see that before I said yes to this stupid show? And all for what?

For money? Fame? Where's that got me?' She paused for a moment. 'Can I be honest if you promise not to judge me?' She arched an eyebrow and Toby nodded.

Satisfied, Emily drew in a long breath. 'I said yes on a day when I'd had enough of the kids. Ivy was potty training, I'd spent the morning yelling at Cherry. And I'd had enough of faking how good my life was for Instagram.' She sighed. 'You're judging, I know you are.'

Toby shook his head. But he was. He'd never really understood the appeal of social media, and couldn't understand why people believed the filters and general bullshittery that the feeds came with.

'A bit,' he admitted, the exhaustion of the last week stopping him from censoring his words. 'When I looked at your feed,' he started, then caught himself but Emily had looked up.

'What? Why were you on my feed? Not being funny, but you're not my typical follower,' she looked at him, a frown buried deep in her forehead, 'unless you had a reason to find out who I was? But that... I mean... how?'

Toby shrugged.

'We have a shared agent in Angie. She told me about you when I was signing my contract. Told me—' He broke off, wondering how honest he should be.

'Yes?'

He exhaled. Toby hated uncomfortable conversations. He preferred the safety of small talk.

'Fine. She said Edge Productions – the company that produces *Star Survivor*—'

'I know who you're talking about, I signed a contract too, remember?' Emily interrupted, looking irritated.

'Anyway,' Toby emphasised, 'they said to Angie she could have a sort of buy one, get one free deal. They wanted me.'

'And I was part of a BOGOF?' Emily threw the stick away incredulously. 'No. I'm here on my own merit – I've got a book out later in the year; it'll give great exposure for me.' She looked petulantly at Toby. 'Angie said... and anyway, you're only here because of who you got caught with.'

Toby smarted at how close to the truth Emily was, but he wasn't going to allow her to see she'd hit a nerve.

'At least I knew who I was going to be on the island with – the only surprise is Zoe. I didn't for one second believe she'd be included.'

Emily tossed back her hair haughtily and threw a stone in the direction of the stick.

'It's all a bit of a moot point now, anyway, isn't it? The four of us are stuck here. Together. And it doesn't matter whether anyone has a book out or,' she left the words suspended momentarily, 'they're trying to undo some bad press.'

There was a silence as Toby wrestled with his thoughts. He didn't like being told the truth but Emily had a point.

'You're right,' he smiled a little, 'and look, I don't have kids, so I can't pretend to know how you're feeling.' He gave her a look not to talk when she opened her mouth. 'But I'm very close to my mum and, today, when I was building that SOS. I kept wondering if I'd ever see her again. I've been a terrible son to her and now all I want to do is give her a hug.'

Emily looked up and stared at him.

'What?'

'Nothing. Just…'

'What?' he pressed. She really was irritating.

'I'm sorry. I just. I didn't know you were close to any woman; I'm surprised you're that close to your mum to be honest.'

'Right. I see' He paused and looked ahead, 'What do you think you know about me?'

Emily sighed lightly.

'It's just, when I see the interviews with you, or the articles – like the one with that blonde woman last week– you don't exactly come across as a mummy's boy.' She gave a watery smile.

Toby had no inclination to smile back. He didn't know if it was the lack of food. Maybe it was because for the first time in twenty years he'd been sober for more than two days in a row, but he cleared his throat.

'I'm not a mummy's boy, what kind of thing is that to say?'

Emily looked horrified.

'Sorry, I didn't mean it to sound like that. Just. Oh. You know.' She smiled again.

'No. No, I don't know. You're going to have to explain it to me,' he needled. He could hear himself doing it, but realised he had to know what she thought.

She shrugged and resumed drawing in the sand with another stick she'd found. This time it was a love heart. She didn't look up at him as she spoke.

'I know the sort of person you are. You're a womaniser, Toby. I don't expect you to give two shits about me, or

67

your mum. I do expect you to fall over yourself in getting Zoe's attention.'

As she turned, Emily rustled. The girls had taken to wearing bin liners they'd found caught up in the trees as a way of keeping warm. It was practical, but Toby tried not to laugh when he thought of them all. If the world could see them now. Odd shoes, black bags as coats. June's hair extensions had begun to fall out, which made her look like a scarecrow. Toby touched his chin, absent-mindedly, aware his stubble had fledged into a full beard. They could be anyone.

'You're making some huge assumptions there. How about I make some about you?' Toby replied. He was hungry. Itchy. His head hurt and he felt the beginning of an angry red heat coming down.

Emily was unaware of the anger bristling from him.

'No need. I'm an open book,' she started. 'I'm a mum, as you know. I've got a pretty big Instagram following.'

'Ah, but it's not all about the numbers – are you verified?' he interrupted and saw her face flicker with a hint of irritation.

'Yep, I'm officially me. I've got a big blue tick,' she went quiet for a moment, 'which could, right now, mean I'm officially missing I suppose. People might even be a bit worried about me. About us,' she hastily added.

'I should hope so. I should hope that people would be looking for us – we've got the world's biggest actress here. She alone should warrant a fleet of army helicopters scouring the sea for us,' Toby replied, still absent-minded, thoughts of thousands – no, millions – of people worrying about them. Sending search teams. The outcry in the media…

'Christ, imagine the coverage.' He hadn't realised he'd spoken his last thought out loud.

Emily looked at him, horrified, and he couldn't work out what he'd said that was wrong. Again.

'What?'

The Instagrammer turned around and looked at him. He watched her eyes flashing with anger.

'You have her on quite the pedestal don't you? You know she's just a person – with feelings, and emotions? Added to that she's ridiculously young and she's completely lost. Not just here, on this fucking island. She's lost in her life. Don't you see that?' She sighed. 'Don't keep referring to her as though we have a god amongst us.'

She rustled and returned to looking at the enormous bonfire. Toby did the same.

The orange and blue flames licked ever higher into the inky black sky where hundreds and hundreds of stars were visible. With no pollution and no street lights, it felt like they were on the edge of the universe.

Toby stayed quiet but then realised Emily had finished talking and he knew he had to say something. He couldn't have twenty-five per cent of the island's population ignoring him. He didn't cope well without an audience.

'Not a god... more like a goddess...'

'Toby,' Emily hit him hard on his arm and made him wince, 'shut the fuck up – she'll be able to hear you.' She looked over to where, on the opposite side of the fire, Zoe was getting her palm read by June. The two of them were bent over her left hand and it looked very, very serious.

'Ouch, ah, come on. It was a joke.' Toby smiled and lightly punched her on the arm. 'Emily... Em, come on...'

She turned to look at him, this time with a half-smile. 'Fine. What?'

'You know what. I want to know more about you; how come we have the same agent for example?'

'As I said, I have... I mean... I'm due to have a book out in November, which links... I mean it linked... no, it does still link to my blog, and my Instagram. And the podcast of course.' She smiled tightly. 'It's hard to keep talking about my life as though it's taking place still. Part of me feels like I'm grieving the end of it all. Don't you?'

'No, not really,' he replied. But privately he considered her description of it. He did feel grief for the loss of his life, but he was still clinging on to the hope that he'd be back in it soon. Gazing into the fire, he felt Emily's eyes boring down on him.

'You know what really bugs me about you?' she asked, not wanting a response, and went ahead with carrying on, 'I'm just... I'm shocked. I thought none of us knew who was coming? Isn't that part of the fun of the programme? OUR agent,' she placed the emphasis heavily on the thing they had in common, 'told me I couldn't tell anyone. My mum doesn't even know. She thinks I'm having some sort of operation which meant she needed to help Matt with the kids for a week or so. I wasn't allowed to talk to anyone on the plane in case I—' She broke off.

'Hang on.' She looked accusingly at him. 'Which plane were you on? It can't have been mine because... but...' She started to look increasingly pissed off and he shook his head in confusion, not following the angry train of thought she was currently on.

'You were in First, weren't you?' She pointed her

finger at him. He wanted to lie and say yes. After all, it was, as far as he was concerned, where he should have been. But they were a million miles away from fakery and sometimes the truth was easier to tell.

'No, Business. Why?' he responded, not understanding. 'How did you fly?' It can't have been cattle class, they wouldn't have done that – would they? As if she had read his mind, Emily pulled another sulky face.

'Economy Plus.'

'Hey, at least it wasn't Economy,' he suggested, and immediately regretted it. He sounded like such a dick.

'You're such a dick,' she confirmed.

'Yeah, I've been told that – but in my defence, I didn't have anything to do with plane tickets,' he tried to justify, whilst he ignored the last chat he'd had with his agent when she told him about Emily, and he had made it abundantly clear they weren't travelling in the same parts of the plane. Toby felt a slight wave of shame when he remembered giving the reason to his agent that they'd guess who was on the island if they rode in the same part of the plane, but she and he had known what the problem had been. Toby had already been bumped down from First because Zoe, as it turned out, was there. He didn't want some blogger joining him in Business.

'Still had to have the same helicopter as me though, eh? Or was there some sort of mix-up?' Emily prodded him in the chest. Her finger felt bony and though it wasn't proper pain, it left a light bruised feeling behind.

'The same helicopter which put us down somewhere we're not meant to be and then crashed?' he reminded her coldly. 'Yeah, we were both meant to be on that.'

'Well, lucky us.'

There was silence again which Emily broke with a deep sigh of irritation and then she stood up.

'I wish I'd left you in the forest,' she hissed in his direction, a sentiment lost on Toby as he tried not to laugh when her black bag rustled as she moved, adding a comical sound effect to her conceited departure. He watched as she walked over and sat with the other two women, saying something which caused all three to look in his direction. Toby tried to look like he didn't give a shit and stared moodily at the dark blue in the centre of the fire. He imagined he was at home and he was looking at his log burner, a glass of red wine in his hand.

Distracted by a movement from the other side of the fire, Toby noticed June had got up from the group and was making her way over to him. He paused in lighting his cigarette. As the two smokers, he figured she probably wanted to make sure he wasn't taking them all.

'It's only my second.' He waved it at her and lit it.

'Hey.' She sat in the space recently vacated by Emily and nodded for the cigarette, which Toby gave her and watched as she took a deep pull.

'Terrible things, these. One day I'll quit.' She smiled and then they both grinned at the unlikelihood. They both knew that soon they'd be forced to give them up, whether they wanted to or not.

'Funny isn't it, not being able to just stroll into a shop for a packet of fags,' he said as he exhaled the smoke upwards into the night sky.

June nodded and blew out a long plume of smoke before responding, 'I hadn't realised how much I took my freedom for granted when I lived my "normal" life. Yes, normal meant being papped if I went to a shop, but,' she sighed, 'at least I could just go to a shop when I wanted.'

Toby looked at her and realised he felt the same.

'I know. I was thinking today, I miss everything. I miss the cinema. I miss visiting friends. I miss my mum. I miss the theatre. I miss premieres and parties. I miss pubs. Cafés. I miss grabbing an espresso on my way back from the gym.'

'I miss yoga classes.'

'Pizza.'

'People. I miss seeing people, just going about their lives.'

Toby nodded. 'Yes. All the little background things. I miss TV. Radio. Music. Podcasts. I miss black cabs. Football matches. Concerts. Traffic jams. I crave the noise of real life buzzing around me.'

June looked sideways at Toby, which caught him off-guard, and a light smile played on her lips.

'I miss all that. I do. But I'm starting to think I miss other things too. I want to be able to just get up, decide where I want to go, and just…' She trailed off.

'… Be yourself,' he finished for her.

'Exactly.'

There was a moment of the good island silence he enjoyed with June, not the unpleasant Emily ones. This type was filled with the unseen waves which crashed against the rocks and the fire which fizzed and crackled. The silence of a thousand tiny unfamiliar noises, which Toby loved and loathed at the same time.

June broke it first.

'Toby, try to be nice to Emily. It's hard for all of us – you're missing football and black cabs, but she's missing her kids and her husband. Try and give her a break. Okay?'

He nodded.

She took his cigarette and they took it in turns to smoke in island silence.

*

'Shit.'

Zoe looked at the mess in the net that she and Emily had left out in the sea the day before. Dull, dead fish upon dull, dead fish lay still with their subdued eyes looking forlornly at her. The megastar picked up one of them, the pinkish-green scales faded like the vintage-style furniture her mum loved so much.

'What are you looking at?' she chastised the pink thing. It returned her stare with a disconnected one of its own. It reminded her of the time she'd partied with supermodel Khan at an exclusive club in Paris. Zoe had remained clear-headed; she'd always prided herself on not succumbing to the usual buffet of drugs she was offered at these events. But Khan. She'd said yes to everything, to 'dull the pain', she'd told Zoe, but what pain she'd never discovered. It hadn't mattered of course. The next morning she'd knocked on Khan's door. When it had swung open, unlocked, Zoe had had a bad feeling about what she'd find, but she'd put it down to being tired and overworked.

The rest of that day was a blur. One which, when the media got wind of it, her agent had miraculously kept her name out of. But Zoe would never forget the look on the woman's face, the woman who had been the most beautiful in any room. Dead on her bed. A small trail of vomit seeping out of the fuchsia pink-lipsticked mouth onto the cream silk pillow, the only giveaway that she wasn't sleeping.

'That and the same eyes you're giving me,' Zoe told the fish, screwing her face up at the smell of the rancid flesh, gone off before her and the other islanders could benefit from it.

Wasted.

'Just like Khan...' she whispered, her voice cracking a little, as the sea moved her rhythmically up and down off the sandy floor. She gulped and tried hard not to cry, instead throwing the fish far away.

As she methodically extracted the other decaying fish from the net and threw them aside, watching the birds overhead fight for the remains, she fought to keep the tears at bay. But the frustration at their lack of food and her tiredness began to win against her characteristic determination – the phrase often overused in profile puff pieces – and she allowed a few tears to leak out. It felt good and she gave into it for a few minutes, indulging herself in a moment of sadness and ineptitude. She allowed the fear she was letting her fellow islanders down to surface. They'd soon hate her too. Just like everyone who got close to her.

'No use crying over dead fish,' June called from the shore. 'What happened?'

Zoe rubbed her eyes with the back of her hand and sniffed the tears back.

'Erm, I think we left the net out for too long. We need to be quicker' She paused to collect herself 'We'll have to be quicker next time.'

'Come in, Zoe, you've been working for hours – I think you need to cool off and drink some water,' the older woman replied, her hands on her tiny hips, the remnants of her dress acting as a sarong.

'I just…' Zoe began to protest. She had to keep going. Or they'd all see her for what she was, a complete fraud. She wasn't a leader, she was scared to death about what could happen to them.

'Now, young lady,' June smiled as she mimicked an angry mum, 'I won't take no for an answer.'

Zoe smiled a little at the woman who, until a few weeks ago, she knew only as one half of a famous TV duo. Someone in fact she'd choose to avoid at all costs unless she was promoting a film.

'That's better,' June tilted her head to one side a little and shaded her eyes with her hand. 'Come out of the water for a bit. You're not the only one who can provide, you know.' She looked naughtily at Zoe. 'Come to the shore and I'll show you.'

Zoe allowed the waves to wash her in closer to the shore whilst she tried to ignore the light-headed feeling that came from her sudden burst of crying. By the time the water reached waist height, she was beginning to feel more composed and stood to walk out of the ocean.

'Ursula Andress eat your heart out.' June grinned, causing Zoe to laugh out loud a little.

'What I wouldn't give for her bikini right now,' she replied, 'and the dagger she'd carry that was on her belt.

The luxury of a tool,' Zoe enthused as Toby joined them.

'If you need a Daniel Craig, I'm right here – you don't even need the tiny swim shorts to imagine what I'm packing, you can get a good look already.' He stood with legs spread wide, his hands on his hips. 'I believe this is what the politicians call the "the power pose".' He grinned at Zoe, who was laughing.

'I can't say I'd want to imagine any of them doing it starkers though,' she replied, clutching her side as she laughed hard.

'So,' Toby looked at June and then nodded in Zoe's direction, 'have you told her yet?' June shook her head.

'Not yet, she's been untangling the nets – we're trying for a fish haul tomorrow.' She smiled cheerily at Zoe, seemingly glossing over what the younger woman had felt was abject failure.

'We caught a shark,' Toby punched the air ecstatically, 'and Em is roasting it right now. It smells incredible.' He faked wiping drool from his mouth. 'And honestly, if you decide you're not into eating flesh, I'm cool with that. I will do the right thing by you, and eat your share,' he offered, grinning broadly.

Zoe was gobsmacked.

'You caught a shark? How? With what?' She was incredulous; they'd been swimming and attempting to fish in the waters around their beach for two weeks and because the crystalline water was so clear, they'd been nonchalant about sharks finding them before they spotted them.

A flush crawled up Toby's neck.

'Okay, it sort of got itself caught – June, you tell the

story,' he offered to the other woman, who was smiling at his exuberance.

'Emily and I took a walk out on the rock.' She looked in the direction of the shelf of rock which protruded from their beach, a section of which Zoe had walked out on when she'd made the long and difficult trip round the bay the day after they'd been stranded.

'Apparently they needed some peace and quiet,' Toby huffed a little, 'but who they needed quiet from I don't know.' The three were walking across the blisteringly hot white sand, aiming for their shelter.

'No,' June pulled a face in Toby's direction, 'we went out to see if we could find some of those clam things,' she ignored Toby's disgusted wince, 'and when we got to the farthermost tip, Emily thought we should try and do some rock pooling – apparently she does it a lot with her children,' June explained as they reached the bonfire where Emily was slowly rotating hunks of meat. The smell was rich and overwhelming and Zoe could feel her stomach gnawing at her with hunger as she moved closer to where Emily was sitting.

'Good timing,' Emily smiled at the trio, 'I think we're ready to eat.' She laid out the roasted lumps of meat on a palm leaf. 'Eat up, there's plenty more – go on, Toby, you may as well go first.' She laughed at his whimpers of hunger.

'If you insist,' he replied, sitting down and grabbing a handful of meat in one fluid movement, hungrily wedging the largest piece in his mouth. The three women watched as he chewed with such ecstasy it was though it had been dipped in chocolate.

'First time he's been quiet in two weeks.' June smiled indulgently in his direction as Toby quickly chewed another chunk, and the three women began to help themselves too.

'Tastes... like... chicken,' he forced out between chews. 'Thanks Emily.' She grinned back at his happiness.

'So you can't have caught it.' Zoe nudged Toby to move over and grabbed a piece of shark, took a bite and, though it had been years since she'd eaten anything from an animal, her whole body sang at the iron-rich flavour.

Emily was chewing whilst cooking more of the meat, the smell filling Zoe's senses.

'Nah, we found it – must have got trapped in one of the rock pools – he was alive, though barely,' she added when she saw Zoe hastily stop eating in case it was gone off. 'So, well, June took a big rock and, erm...' She squirmed a little at the memory.

'I bashed him on the head,' June finished, grimacing but triumphant.

'If we were anywhere else but here...' Zoe replied, chewing on her third piece of shark and enjoying the feeling of a full stomach. She felt giggly for some reason.

Emily nodded. 'Yep, I mean, I know where my food comes from – I understand how beefburgers are made, but to kill something... it was...' She trailed off and looked out to the sea.

'It felt wrong but right,' June explained. 'If we didn't do it, it would go to waste and then we'd be another day of not eating.' She chewed slowly. 'We can't be fussy. It's do or die here.'

Zoe hiccupped with laughter, surprising a gaggle of

birds that had settled in the trees into flight, their squawks vibrating through the forest.

'What?' The older woman pulled a face.

'I was thinking back to when I agreed to *Star Survivor* – the various meetings we had before I said yes… my PA giving them my rider,' she saw Emily's look of confusion, 'you know, the list of a celeb's requirements? Tell me you were offered one?' Emily shook her head. 'It doesn't matter anyway.' Zoe covered her face with her hands, trying to hide her embarrassment. 'They told me I'd have a private chef and I wouldn't need to worry about veganism… if they could see me now.' She laughed again and took another swallow of shark. 'I only did it because of… well… y'know.'

'You think that's bad? I said yes to get away from the kids, sure, but also so I could lose two stone. I was going to have a personal trainer – they were going to say we'd all been starving so that's why I'd lost loads of weight. Nothing to do with being on a personalised diet regime.' Emily grinned but the smile didn't reach her eyes. 'Look at me, now I lose the weight and I've got no one to show it to.'

'You will,' June squeezed her arm a little, 'but you should never have felt you needed to.'

Emily shook her head. 'I did though – social media can be pretty cruel. There's a lot of people with a lot of time on their hands, and an awful lot of opinions. My kids are too old for me to have a "mum tum". I need to look better.'

'I hear skeletal is a fabulous look, darling.' Toby emphasised the final word.

'Shut up, Tobes.' Emily laughed. 'Okay, why did you say yes to the programme? It can't have been for the money,' she was silent for a moment, 'though I bet you all got offered more than me.' She shook her head when they all began to talk. 'Not that it's a problem. They offered a life-changing amount for me to do it. I just hope they still pay it, even if I...'

Sensing she was going to become down, Toby picked some shark out of his teeth and cleared his throat to speak.

'Well, I came to the island for love.' He grinned at the women's reactions. June's mouth was agape, Zoe laughed, and Emily opened her mouth to talk. 'Nah, kidding. I came because I fucked the wrong woman, and the only way I could save my career was to say yes...' He wrestled with himself before deciding to say anything else, 'They promised me I'd win. It was going to be my moment.' He shrugged.

'Oh, it was you.' June nodded as though everything had become clear. 'When I got the gig I was told I was being brought on as the "mother hen" type, to keep you all in check, and– no matter how the audience voted – I wouldn't be winning.'

Emily was shaking her head, her hair falling from the makeshift ponytail band she'd fashioned from rope they'd found on the beach. 'I didn't realise it was all set up before we got here.'

June gave her a hug. 'You're a sweet girl, but you have a lot to learn about TV shows. They'll do pretty much anything to get the ratings. Toby winning would have made headlines as he was the one in the most trouble before going into the show. A bad boy turned good?' She looked at him for confirmation and he nodded. 'I thought so.'

'So why did you do it?' Emily pressed. 'You didn't need to lose weight, you didn't have any negative press to handle.' She looked pointedly in Zoe and Toby's directions. 'What did they promise you?'

June looked away at the sea and took a deep breath.

'It's going to sound silly now. Trivial even.'

Toby looked up at the change in her tone of voice.

'What will?'

June sighed. 'They were going to do some "work" on me.' She did air quotes. 'I said yes as they said they could do fillers, Botox, a little lipo – all whilst we were away. Any bruises or odd marks would be put down to various bumps in the jungle. No one would suspect a thing.' She stopped talking and looked at the other three who all looked pityingly at her.

'None of you understand. I'm over fifty and in TV. It's a young woman's game and they're getting younger. I needed to keep my edge and I was going to be paid well for it – enough to really set me up since The Bastard and I divorced and he got most of everything I worked for.'

Toby moved over and put his arm around June's tiny shoulders.

'You're beautiful. Don't let anyone tell you otherwise – don't put that crap in your system,' he told her sincerely. 'I've met a lot of women with a lot of work done and, honestly, they all look like they have. Who wants a seventy-year-old with a twenty-five-year-old body?' Toby leant back against the tree trunk again.

There was a brief moment of silence as around them the waves crashed against the shore.

June sat up straighter.

'Hey, who said anything about being seventy?'

Toby furrowed his brow and sat up a little. 'What?'

'I mean, I wasn't going to say anything.' Emily laughed and Zoe joined in.

'No... I didn't mean you are...' Toby held his hands up in apology.

'You're looking good on it,' Zoe giggled. 'Maybe we should all get Botox.'

'Right, that's it – you're on fishing duty for a week.'

*

'Can't believe I had a bikini wax before we flew out.' Emily scratched the top of her thighs, wincing at the raised red bumps across her skin. Zoe looked from the sea they were wading into and at Emily's legs. Then Emily watched as her gaze moved higher.

'I can't believe you've still got hair there,' she laughed. 'Laser, that's what you need.'

'Hey, now,' Emily paused to catch her breath a little as they began swimming to where they'd left the net. 'One, I wasn't expecting to be walking around naked because I've only got one set of clothes,' she raised her eyebrow at Zoe. 'Two, what's wrong with me having hair? I'm a woman – I'm meant to look like this and, three, there is no way I'm going to lie there and let someone attack my flaps with a fucking laser.'

The two women reached the plastic bottles they'd tied together as a buoy, so they knew where they'd put their net, and pulled it upwards whilst fighting to stay upright as the water was deeper than the day before, then looked with concern at its contents. They were greeted with a mixture of squirming fish, gasping for breath.

'Yes, alive,' Zoe squawked, punching the air, her exhilaration diametrically opposed to how she'd been the day before.

Using all the strength they had, the two half-waded, half-swam their way back to the shore, dragging the net between them. As they walked out onto the sand, Emily stole a glance at Zoe's hairless body.

'So have you had everything done?'

They both began to pick out the fish and throw them into the hodge-podge of plastic bags they'd collected from the shoreline.

'Of course.' Zoe smiled. 'I had it all off years ago. Otherwise I'll be on some shoot and a make-up artist will be trying to put bronzer on my legs and it'll get caught on any hair on them. I need my gleam.'

'Well, of course – you need to do that funny pose for the cameras,' Emily remembered. 'All hips thrust out, leg at an odd angle, shoulder back kind of thing.'

'What, like this?' Zoe, still holding the net, stark naked, pulled *the look* Emily recalled from seeing numerous photos of her over the years. She smouldered at the pretend cameras in the distance.

'Bravo. You've definitely captured the "lost at sea" look, darling; do tell me who your net is from.' Emily laughed.

Zoe bowed.

'Thank you – see, how could I do that without all the hair off?' She laughed.

'Even on your legs though? Fuck. Ouch,' said Emily with a laugh, 'I barely remember to shave mine, and I only do that if I think I'll be having sex with Matt.' The two of them were walking up the sandy beach, trudging through the white hot sand, the heat of the day on their backs but Zoe stopped suddenly.

'What? Why don't you do it just for you?'

Emily was nonplussed.

'For me? Hon, I have no need for smooth legs. I'm very happy with them whatever they're doing.'

'Then why change it for Matt?'

'Just because,' Emily had stopped too, 'you know, I don't actually know why.'

She had a think.

'I tidy the house before the cleaner comes too.'

'What? Why?' Zoe laughed hard.

'The same reason I file my nails and give them a quick paint before any pedicures.' Emily laughed with Zoe.

'Which is?'

'I don't know.'

They carried on walking up towards the shelter. June and Toby were in view; Emily noticed their heads were close together in deep discussion.

'I think I know why.' Zoe looked straight at Emily, giving her the kind of stare which, in another life, would have caused the influencer to admit to anything.

'Go on?'

'You're not true to yourself.' Zoe nodded at her.

'What? No, I'm fine.' Emily laughed, though wondered how someone who'd only known her for a couple of weeks or so would think this.

'Ah, okay, so you clean the house before the cleaner comes because you want a doubly clean house? Sure.'

'No, it's not like that, Zo, it's...' Emily raised her hands up in a show of annoyance, 'oh fuck, you're right.'

'Please tell me you don't cut your own hair before you go to the hairdressers.' Zoe nudged Emily in the side.

'Or do my own teeth before I go to the dentist's?' Emily replied, and thought for a moment. 'I think I might have become a victim of my own Instagram. I'm a hostage to the "tap to tidy" button, Zoe,' she said with a giggle.

'Yeah, I think we might have an age gap on Insta,' Zoe pulled a face 'My stories are more about what fashion campaign I'm in, or mucking about with my friends.'

'But your friends are all beautiful young things, Zo, who live in ridiculous LA mansions that are white and sparkly– it's a different life to the one I lead,' Emily pointed out. 'I saw a story of yours once when you were round at one of the NBA players' houses and you were doing a karaoke thing with basically anyone who's anyone under twenty-five in Hollywood.' She paused for a moment. 'My last Insta story was about how I'd realised I could add a soap dispenser to my sink.'

'Wow, your content sounds fascinating,' said Zoe, smirking, and Emily, always raw to someone's criticism of her, was about to get irritated when she saw the smirk quickly spread to a grin on her friend's face.

'We're quite different, aren't we?'

'There are a few differences. Yes,' agreed Zoe as she waved their catch at the other two, 'but maybe that's why we were being brought together. Maybe you could learn to do more things just for you, and I'll learn to—'

'Fit a soap dispenser?' Emily suggested.

'Exactly. Hey, guess what?'

Emily squinted at Zoe in the sun. 'What?'

'You've just called me Zo – that's a mark of friendship well above the crap on Instagram – Zo is what my family call me.'

Emily smiled at this as June and Toby made their way over to the women.

'Look at you two, a right couple of Bear Grylls.' Toby smiled easily in their direction. He'd been so smiley the last few days, Emily wasn't sure if it was for her benefit. Or someone else's.

'I won't be drinking my pee any time soon though,' Zoe replied quickly, 'but yeah, we've got a good haul here. It helps when they're still alive and less likely to kill you.' She looked at the writhing mass of multicoloured fish.

'Let's get them cleaned up so we can get something in us,' June suggested. 'Why don't you two go for a quick dip to cool off, and we'll give you a shout when they're cooked.'

'Hang on – what was that?' Emily stood still, brought up short by a sound overhead.

'What?'

'I can't hear anything.'

'Shut up,' Zoe hissed, and all four stood stock still. The island sounded to Emily like it was roaring with noise, but there was nothing man-made over the top of it.

Emily shook her head.

'Sorry, nothing. I thought I heard something, a drone maybe? Or a small plane? The sound must have been in my head, sorry, again.' She grimaced. Zoe touched her elbow lightly, and they began walking in the direction of the pool.

'We'll have the food ready soon,' the TV presenter said kindly to Emily, seemingly aware the other woman felt embarrassed about her mistake.

As Zoe and Emily strode through the opening from their shelter to the forest, the air turned damper, and the path underfoot was full of island litter, crackling as their bare feet made contact with it.

Zoe decided she needed to distract Emily from her hopes being dashed of a rescue. 'In the spirit of doing more things for you: if you could live anywhere, where would it be?' she asked as they made their way to the pool, their bodies sticky with sweat and smelling of the fish they'd slopped into the bags.

'A castle. In France,' Emily instantly replied. 'Matt and I holidayed in the Dordogne and there were so many fairy-tale châteaux. In my wildest dreams I see us living in one, maybe running a B&B.' She smiled longingly and, turning to Zoe, said, 'Each girl could have a turret.'

Keeping up with the other woman, Zoe waved her arm in front of her to put off the mozzies swooping in. 'Wildest dreams usually involve something a bit kinkier than bed AND breakfast,' she puffed.

'All right. Bed, breakfast and I'll spank you if you ask nicely,' said Emily, grinning, getting a guffaw of laughter from Zoe.

'Perfect, I would visit.'

'You visit and I'll be guaranteed fully booked rooms for eternity,' Emily replied, stepping into the pool and enjoying the cool water which wrapped itself around her.

'Only if each room comes with a video of me being

spanked,' said Zoe, laughing hard. Emily wheezed with laughter, getting a mouthful of water as a reward.

'Too far, Zoe, I've peed myself now. Bloody pelvic floor.'

'Hey, look, at least you're in the water, no one can tell. It's not like you need to impress any of us. Do you?'

A sound like a boulder hitting the floor distracted the two momentarily. Making her way out to the middle of the pool, Emily turned to talk to Zoe.

'That noise, that's a coconut falling. It's happening all the time and they're huge.' She went quiet for a moment. 'I'm sure we'll be picked up soon but have you ever wondered how we'll actually survive? We've got the fire. The SOS. We're finding food but not much. Everything looks like it could kill us. Even the bloody coconuts.'

She mused for a little longer as she lay on her back in the pool, the water a deep emerald green.

'Tell you what, if I'm ever marooned again, I'm going to make sure I'm very aware of what you can and can't eat,' she noted to Zoe.

'I'd rather you just had the laser hair removal,' Zoe replied, before disappearing under the water to avoid Emily's splash aimed in her direction.

*

'Look at you, hobbling like a pro.' June smiled in Toby's direction. He was walking back from the forest where he'd been collecting wood for the fire. Not that it had made any difference, June considered glumly. It had been close to three weeks since they were left on the island and they'd not seen anything in the sky except for the birds, let alone search and rescue planes spotting their signals.

'Want help?' June made her way to Toby's side, as the effort he'd exerted was beginning to get the better of him.

He nodded. 'Please.' She dove under his arm and propped him up, his right arm leaning heavily along her shoulders.

'You know, I worry whenever you do this I'll lean on you and you'll disappear,' Toby tried to joke.

'I'm not gone yet,' she replied, aware of how painfully thin she had become in the last three weeks.

Feeling compelled to change the subject, she shuffled him back to his seat, or 'Toby's Throne', as they all called it– a car seat that had washed up a few days before. It was padded, and after drying out in the sun, when he sat down on it, the relief of not sitting on the floor was almost enough to render him speechless, which for June, Zoe and Emily, was worth the find.

'That was good. Your furthest yet,' she said, catching her breath by sitting near to Toby. 'You did really well today,' she enthused, stretching her legs out and facing up to the sun with her eyes closed. Her skin was tanned for the first time in years, and with her hair pulled back in a ponytail, the others kept telling her she could be fifteen years younger. Opening her eyes to flick a bug off her arm, she noticed Toby giving her a look and raised an eyebrow as a response.

'What?'

'Nothing. Sorry. Was. Just. Thinking… how… island… life… is… suiting… you,' Toby panted and leant heavily against his throne.

'Okay, hot stuff, I think the heat is getting to you.' June

shook her head and handed him a bottle of water which he drained quickly. They lapsed into an amicable silence for a few minutes. Then, leaning out of his throne to rest his hand on her shoulder, Toby smiled.

'I've been thinking whilst I was collecting wood. I miss home, life, the world. But there is a peace here. There's something to be said about slowing down, shutting up and just listening.' He leant back again after saying his piece.

Smiling to herself, June nodded– she'd been thinking similarly the past few days. The sounds of the island were like something out of a movie – the ocean rushing in over the sand, the sucking sound of it retreating over shells and stones. Fronds of palm trees swaying even on the quietest of days, giving a rustling backdrop of white noise, whilst overhead the birds screeched and squawked and squabbled.

But the noisiest sound was the silence. The lack of everything else was deafening. It felt like she had a permanent ringing in her ears, which acted as a backdrop to the long, silent void.

June heard movement next to her again, and realised Toby was leaning forward, his long, deeply tanned legs protruding over the seat. There was a lot of him. He was all angles, but she supposed that's what it was to be over six feet.

She liked him though; there was something quite straightforward about the way he just said whatever he felt. June appreciated that, though she knew it didn't sit as well with Emily. The two of them were still sniping at each other. Privately June had wondered if it was because Emily didn't get the same response from Toby that Zoe did.

Interrupting her thoughts, Toby cleared his throat.

'The problem with listening to everything around us is that there's a sound I can't block out.' He patted his lean brown stomach which had begun to look like someone had scooped out his six-pack with a spoon, leaving a hollow. 'My stomach is protesting at the lack of food.'

'I know.' June laughed. 'Problem is, there's no easy wins. We work hard for every fish, clam and coconut. If you want to find a croc, you go for it,' she added, not knowing whether there were even any animals like that where they were. They hadn't seen any aside from birds that taunted them from the trees, fish which were often difficult to catch and a few scrawny chickens that moved much quicker than them. Island survival was starting to take its toll on all of them.

June knew she was withering away and it saddened her that she'd not been kinder to herself before. She'd had plenty of time to think back on the so-called discipline she'd kept up, the battle against her body for so many years when she should have enjoyed it more. Should have appreciated her body, her skin, herself a little more and hated herself a little less.

Thinking of the others, June brought the image of Zoe to mind. Beautiful, young, insecure Zoe. She'd worked harder and for longer than anyone else on that island to get them a decent shelter, fought for fish for them and still found energy to collect water when needed. But all that energy being used and not replaced was affecting her too – her collarbone, ribs and arms were beginning to jut out of her skin, painfully pushing through. The last few nights when they'd spooned together for warmth in the shelter, Zoe had found it painful to lie down and sleep because her bones were pressing against the hard wooden floor.

'We should send Emily out looking for a crocodile, she's tough,' suggested Toby, a little bitchily.

June admired Emily; in the past few days she had begun to really show her true colours. She was hard as nails, tough as old boots, whatever phrase you wanted to use – she could cope with the harsh rain and not complain. She could carry litres of water for them from the pool, and June had kept a watch on her when she'd decided to swim from their beach to see if she could reach the one on the other side of the sapphire lagoon. Watched too as she returned when the distance became too far.

She was the only one not to faint. Yet.

'Yes, maybe,' June replied sleepily. 'Have you been okay today?' she asked, remembering Toby's faint the previous day when he'd slipped and cut his hand on a log. It had been a reminder to all four that they had no backup, no first aid kits and no way of combating any infections should they pick them up.

But he brushed off her concerns with a quick shake of the head.

'Yes, fine. You?'

'I think I'm making it a daily occurrence. Get up. Faint. Wee. Faint. Talk. Faint. My head swims and lights of different colours flash past my eyes – like when you watch a film about outer space and the ships zoom past the stars and galaxies. Then I wake up with a racing heart, a bit like when you're really frightened of something. But it stops quickly.'

Toby's eyes crinkled at June with concern.

'I knew it was bad – I didn't know it was that bad, June. Shit. We need to get some food inside you.' He paused. 'I NEED MEAT,' he groaned. 'I've never had a wish to be a pescatarian, vegetarian or, god forbid, a vegan. I need a steak. With chips. And a glass of red wine. Or a bottle. I miss alcohol.'

His monologue stirred something in June, and she remembered what she'd wanted to show him.

'Oh, guess what I found.'

'What?' Toby replied, a little grumpily – she guessed she'd interrupted his favourite pastime of thinking about everything he wanted to eat.

'Well, if you're going to be like that I shan't show you. Or share,' she teased, her face close to beaming. He couldn't help it and smiled in return.

'Okay, I'll play along. Erm, what have you found? Let's think. Coconuts?' She shook her head. 'Not more clams? I can't eat any more of those. Or yam.' She shook her head again which caused strands of hair to unfurl around her ears.

'Close your eyes,' she cooed.

Toby folded his arms across his chest in consternation.

'What? No. Just tell me.'

She pouted at him.

'Don't be a spoilsport, come on. What else are you going to do? Got a lot planned for the day, have you?'

'Fine, I'll do as I'm told.'

June smiled. He always did as he was told. At least, he did for her anyway; they had an understanding, mainly borne out of her being at least fifteen years older than him. She suspected he saw her as a mother type.

'Hold out your hands. No. Together, in front of you. That's right. No peeking!' She was so excited she wondered, briefly, if she was overdoing it a bit.

'What have you found? A flare? Impossible. A phone? Even more ridiculous.'

She stood carefully and allowed the stars to do their usual streak across her eyes, but a few deep breaths brought her back to earth without fainting and she placed a heavy glass bottle in Toby's hands. Liquid sloshed around.

'Is it? Is it…' Toby's throat was hoarse with expectation and June enjoyed looking at his handsome features squeezed together with excitement.

'Say it,' she whispered, and laughed a little, ignoring the light-headed sensation which came with the joy.

'Is it… booze?'

'Open your eyes.'

It was a full, sealed bottle of vodka and the sight of it brought Toby to tears.

THREE WEEKS OF TORMENT

HELICOPTER wreckage has been found in the search for the missing *Star Survivor* celebs.

Wreckage from a helicopter thought to have been the one Zoe Stenson and the three other celebrities travelled on has been found floating in the sea, some 100 miles away from the actual *Star Survivor UK* island.

A spokesperson for the programme said:

"Due to the discovery of the helicopter in the South Pacific, we believe efforts need to be refocused in looking for bodies, rather than survivors. We are doubling our efforts in searching for them, but ask for the families to be given the privacy they need at this difficult time."

Since the announcement of the wreckage discovery was leaked, #prayforzoe has trended for the last two days. It is the longest-running trending topic on social media, with #starsurvivoruk a close second.

International superstar Zoe, who recently made history as the first female Bond, is one of the four who have not been heard from in 21 days. The others include well-loved children's author Toby Masters, mumpreneur Emily Chase and June Sharp, whose disappearance from *Wake Up* has caused the programme to go off air temporarily.

Last night's viewing figures for *Star Survivor* make it the most watched programme of the century so far, with an average of 24.6 million viewers tuning in from the UK – a figure which surpasses the 2012 Olympics' opening ceremony.

Chapter Four

'Quick – over here, oi – hello.' Zoe ran to the shore and jumped up and down, waving in the direction of what she was sure was a plane on the horizon. Emily ran to join her, wafting a stick from the fire, the thick black smoke from the palm leaves wrapped around it causing them both to cough.

'Toby... June...' Zoe yelled in the direction of their bonfire but couldn't see the other two. 'Where are they?' she asked of Emily who was still jumping and waving her hand-made torch, whilst embers flew off and danced around them. She shook her head.

'Dunno, I saw them go off about ten minutes ago. I think they're collecting water – they probably can't hear us from there.' she shrugged. 'We'll have to make enough noise for the four of us.'

Zoe shook her head. It wasn't the noise that was needed,

they needed to attract attention. Toby's SOS. hadn't done the job because the plane hadn't flown overhead– it looked like it was moving further away if anything.

'We need more fire. Grab some more of the branches,' she directed at Emily who ran back to the bonfire and did what she could.

'Here you go.'

Zoe grabbed the branch from Emily and ran towards the trees, ignoring the look of horror on her friend's face.

'Where are you going? What are you doing? Shouldn't we...' Emily's concerns faded away as Zoe ran to the treeline and set light to a palm tree. It was an old dried-up one and it caught so quickly Zoe couldn't help being fascinated by the glow. Regretfully, she looked away to see if the plane had seen them. She looked left and right, scanning the horizon, but all she could see was the endless blue of the sea meeting the sky.

One unblotted line of blue.

'Zoe, I think... I think it's gone,' Zoe heard Emily yell in her direction, just as she was about to light another palm tree. 'Zoe, stop. ZOE!' Zoe pulled up and looked at the horizon too.

'Stop it, or we'll burn the whole place to the ground.' Emily's voice was hoarse but her fear snapped Zoe back to the present, realising the ramifications of what she'd done.

'Quick, Emily, we need to put this out or you're right. We'll be toast.'

Just as the two were running to the lit tree– the fire began to spread across the floor, the dried coconut husks acting as kindling. The two watched as the flames licked towards another tree, a younger, greener one.

'Come on,' she urged her friend on, 'grab anything you can.' Zoe ran and picked up a blue container which had arrived on the shoreline a couple of days ago and ran to the sea to fill it with seawater.

'I need help, Emily, it's too heavy for me to carry when it's full,' she screamed as she watched the smoke billowing above the trees. As Emily made it to Zoe, Toby and June appeared out of the forest and took in what was happening. Zoe and Emily raced to the first tree and threw as much water over it as they could.

'I think this one has almost burnt itself out, but the others need attention too,' Zoe shouted to Toby, who had already hoisted the other water container they were using onto his shoulder and was hobbling towards the patch of forest which was slowly beginning to look as though it was carpeted in flames.

'We've just filled this up,' he yelled, 'but if I don't use the drinking water—'

'We won't be around to drink anyway?' Emily finished for him. 'Go for it, Tobes.' As Toby doused the flames with the water, June began stamping down on any smaller ones in her mismatched flip-flopped feet.

'Be careful,' Zoe called, as she and Emily ran past to refill their container.

After three more containers of water, the four had the fire under control, but the area was blackened and smelt like a barbecue left out in the rain.

'I suppose it could have been worse,' Toby suggested, as they surveyed the scene, catching their breath and taking in the burnt coconuts and frazzled leaves of palms that had missed the arson but were near enough to begin to catch.

'Oh yeah?' Zoe challenged, so upset with herself that she had almost destroyed their island in her haste to be rescued from it. 'How?' She sat heavily on a nearby rock and winced as the stone caught her on her tailbone.

Toby grinned. 'Yeah… it could have been the vodka.' From her perch on a fallen tree trunk, Emily laughed with relief.

'I think tonight would be a very good time to have a drink of that, don't you, June?'

'Yes, definitely,' the older woman exhaled, 'that was… hairy.'

'Sorry everyone. I'm really sorry – I just thought it would get the plane's attention,' Zoe screwed up her face and raked her hands through her hair, 'I wasn't thinking properly,' she admitted.

'Hon, I'd have done the same thing,' June reassured her. 'Did you girls get the fish in?'

Emily nodded. 'We were prepping them when we saw the plane. There's not many, but it's better than nothing.'

'Toby – go and refill the water. We'll sort the food, then we can have a drink.' She winked at him and he smiled broadly, his white teeth emphasised by the deep, chestnut-brown tan he had picked up over the last few weeks.

A little later, the fire burned brightly with flames reaching high into the darkening night sky.

'Ladies and gentlemen,' Zoe paused and looked over at Toby, nodding at him across the firelight, 'I do believe we need to give thanks for our magnificent feast.'

Toby whooped at the now daily custom for one of

them to thank the others for their hard work. It had begun as a jokey thing but had evolved into a serious part of the evening they all enjoyed.

'Well done, Emily, for hauling those fish in. You, m'lady, are a queen.' She curtsied in Emily's direction who in turn laughed, and stood up to mimic her.

'And to you too, m'lady,' she replied.

'To Toby, for fixing the net – again – for keeping the fire lit and for reminding us all daily how naked we all are.' She bowed and Toby laughed hard, sweeping his hand down in a mock bow too.

'And lastly, to June, thank you for finding what seems to be all the wood on the island to burn, apologies for trying to set fire to the supply earlier.' June, Emily and Toby all whooped and hollered but Zoe continued. 'Thank you for cooking our meal tonight and for your incredible beach finds – in particular the amazing discovery of this.' She brandished the full bottle of vodka, and they all roared with approval.

'Encore! Encore!' yelled Toby, whilst Emily stood to give her applause.

'Do you take requests? I'd love a bit of Shakespeare,' she added, making Zoe guffaw.

'Yeah, maybe one day I'll give you my final Bond speech, it's pretty fucking cool – I get to shoot the bad guy.'

'Hey,' Toby was in actual shock, 'no spoilers – huge Bond fan over here, don't ruin the ending.'

'You're confident you'll get back to watch it are you?' Emily challenged, but before Toby could respond, June leapt in.

'I'm sure we'll all get back and Zoe could give us our very own screening – what do you think, Zo?' The actress, having watched the exchange, nodded quickly and sent a silent prayer up that she would be able to do just that. One day soon.

'I believe someone here fancies a drink?' She waggled the bottle in Toby's direction, and he started panting like a dog to make her laugh but shook his head.

'June should have the first sip, she found it,' he explained.

'Sure, June?' Zoe offered the bottle to the older woman, who coughed at the first glug, but went back for a second one, sighing gratefully.

'God, that's good.'

She passed it to Emily, sat on her left, who took a deep gulp and handed it to Zoe, who had settled down but she shook her head.

'I'm okay, thanks, not much of a drinker,' she replied, passing the bottle to Toby who accepted it very quickly.

He gave her a searching look.

'This could be our last few weeks on Earth, are you sure you're happy to do them sober?'

Zoe's mouth fell open in shock.

'Really Toby? You think that's going to encourage me to drink? That's like those guys in shit films who say "the world's about to end, we should fuck".' She did an authentic American Deep South accent and made them all laugh.

'Okay, no vodka. Your call.' Toby took a deep sip.

'Hang on, weren't you in one of those films?' June shouted over the fire to Zoe and Toby, hiccupping. Zoe laughed.

'Oh, yeah, probably. Hard to remember to be honest.'

The bottle started to make its way around again, with each of them taking a sip, and Zoe shaking her head when offered– she didn't trust herself to drink, she never felt in control when she did.

'Look. It's starting.' Emily pointed at the sky and they all sat back watching the sunset unfold.

Breathing in the sight of it, Zoe allowed a smile to creep over her face; it was one of the truest pleasures, even with all the shitty things they had to deal with on the island, and it helped to put the afternoon's fire disaster out of her mind. The sunset never failed to impress them and had become a time when they all sat together to enjoy it. Tonight's was spectacular. Every red imaginable stretched its way across the horizon, from bright cherry, to vermilion, to port, through to sepia. All wrapped up in a dusky rust glow.

It was breathtaking.

'Oops, sorry.' Emily leant clumsily over to June to pass her the bottle and fell to the side. 'Did I hurt you?' She rubbed June's arm.

'No, I'm fine, Em. Honestly.' June put her arm around Emily. 'Y'okay?' Zoe watched her friend nod and hiccup.

'I think… maybe… I shouldn't have any more of that…' She hiccupped again and giggled.

'See? That's why I don't drink,' Zoe said softly to Toby, and nodded indulgently in Emily's direction. 'You lose control.'

'What's wrong with losing control every now and then?' Toby challenged, happy knowing the vodka would only need to be shared between June and him.

Zoe stuck her middle finger up at Toby.

'If you lose control, you lose focus. If you lose focus, you can't keep on being the best,' Zoe replied, more petulantly than she'd planned to, but irritated by how quickly the other three were getting drunk.

'Right. And all of that comes from being in control?' Toby countered, beginning to get argumentative. 'I drink, I allow myself freedom, and look at me, I'm huge. I've sold millions of books. How is that not being the best?' He gestured loosely, and sloshed a puddle of vodka out of the top of the bottle.

'Put the lid on, Toby, or pass it to me,' June called over. Emily had fallen asleep, her head resting on a crooked elbow tucked under her.

The night had already drawn in around them. Zoe looked up at the sky, which looked as though it had been sprinkled with diamonds. It reminded her of a vintage Armani dress she'd worn to one of her film premieres. She smiled when she remembered the dress– it had been made the same year she was born. One of the supermodels had worn it in the early 2000s on the runway, and there she'd been, aged nineteen or so, strutting around in it.

She was surprised she felt a pang for those times.

'Come over here, Juney,' Toby called, 'she's passed out.' June shuffled a little closer to make it easier to share the bottle, and took it from Toby.

'But are you the best?' Zoe asked, turning to face him. The fire highlighted her face, contouring it in shadows and lending an unnatural spark to her dark eyes.

'Of course. Are you?' Toby replied witheringly and in the dark Zoe heard June whisper to be quiet.

'No. And you're not either,' Zoe replied with no flicker of emotion or remorse on her face, 'I'm always trying to improve – I'm not the best yet. But I'd like to be.' She looked into the fire. 'I think it's egotistical to think just because I've been doing well up to this point, that means I'm the very best in the industry. How do you even quantify that? The films I'm in now have done well. But what about the future? Will they be classics? Will people still be showing them in 100 years? I doubt it. I've got so much I still want to achieve.'

'Like?' June prompted, interested to hear from Zoe as she rarely talked about her career.

Zoe looked at her, aware in another lifetime this would have been defined as an interview, with all the gossip attached to it, but the evening and the camaraderie compelled her to share.

'I want to direct. I want to write. I want to keep breaking down the barriers that are put in front of me in Hollywood, and elsewhere.'

She sat and looked at the now limitless expanse of the dark ocean.

June laughed quietly in the darkness, then spoke into the night, her words a little fuzzy around the edges.

'You're killing me; I can't believe the exclusive interview I'm getting and I'll never be able to break it.'

Zoe switched her gaze back to Toby and took in a deep, soul-enriching breath. The air really was so clear here.

'I don't have anything else,' Zoe continued, 'I only have my career and if it's not the best it can be, then... what's the point? What have I sacrificed everything else for, if not for this?' She looked at the other two.

'I have no friends – apart from two from school and since that video came out, which has been made to look like a sex tape, they can't look me in the eye half the time. I rarely see my parents. I can't hold down a relationship because I'm rarely in the same place. *If* I sleep with someone, it makes it to the papers either the next day, or at some point in the future. The longest relationship I have is the one with my PA, Annie. I have… no… life. So, yes, I have to be the best. Because, otherwise…' she broke off and breathed deeply, 'otherwise, what the fuck was the point of it all?'

There was a silence as the other two took in this startling confession.

'Give her this.' June handed Toby the bottle which he passed quickly to Zoe, who took an enormous swig and lapsed into silence, her words left mingling in the air with the sparks from the fire.

'I'm not the best,' Toby started, causing June and Zoe to look at him, confused, as it was the opposite to what he'd said just a few minutes before. 'I don't even write the books,' he confessed and an enormous, unmanly laugh, more like a giggle, escaped from him. 'I don't. Out of twenty books I only ever wrote the first one,' he rushed out. June had just taken a sip of vodka and tried not to spit it out. Instead, she coughed and swallowed too quickly.

'I *knew* it. I KNEW it. There's no way you can churn out as many books as they say you have. Not to a decent standard – and… there have been whispers for a few years,' she added ruefully.

'Well. It's true,' Toby laughed again, 'and who gives a fuck? No one. The kids will still read them, I'm just an aspect of the marketing campaign. I'm not even the best at that.' He nodded in the direction of Zoe, who was giving him a look of sadness at the lies.

'Why?' she asked, scandalised.

Toby laughed again. 'Because I send dick pics, I fuck sexy women– often married, sexy women. I wank over porn on the internet, I have sex with eighteen-year-olds.' June gasped and Toby hastened to clarify his comment.

'I thought she was older in fairness, but still, before you say it, yes, she was too young for me. But I'm a dick… or at least in the real world that's who I am. And that's why I said yes to *Star Survivor*. I HAD to. I had sex with the wrong woman, and to make sure my career wasn't affected I agreed to do this. Free of fucking charge.'

'I had wondered,' June whispered, the vodka slurring her words. 'I saw the coverage of you and that…'

'Woman. Who turned out to be a married woman.' Toby grimaced, remembering the images splashed across the red-tops of him, with his hands all over the breasts of a blonde in the back of a black cab.

'Not just any married woman from what I understand,' June replied.

'Who was it?' Zoe asked, intrigued. 'I didn't see this.'

June laughed hard. 'Well you wouldn't have, darling, you were having your own issues weren't you?' she slurred, slamming her hand against her mouth. 'Oh fuck it, we signed those stupid non-disclosure thingummys to say we wouldn't talk about "you know what" when we were on camera. But we're not now. Are we?' She spoke in a considered way, using the voice she used to reserve for politicians who'd been caught out and were doing the rounds of the talk shows in a bid to prove what nice guys they really were.

Zoe was silent.

'Don't listen to her, you don't have to tell us if you don't want to,' Toby said quietly.

'Hey, at least you didn't shag your boss's wife, Zo. Eh, Toby?' June laughed at her revelation.

'Thanks June. The last person in England not to know, and now you've done it,' he replied. 'Well, okay, fine. Yes. I had sex with a beautiful blonde. Then I discovered she was married to Patrick Roberts.' He took a deep sigh.

'Oh shit,' Zoe replied in recognition of the name, 'how did you… not know…?' She giggled a little and took a sip of her vodka.

'That I was fucking the wife of the owner of Edge Productions, Patrick Roberts? In charge of my book-to-film adaptations Patrick Roberts? Could out me as having a ghostwriter Patrick Roberts?'

'Got you by the nads Patrick Roberts,' June added.

'Oh Toby.' Zoe felt sorry for the man-child, so in need of fame and love and money, he was prepared to pretend he was someone else. Prepared to put his name to books he hadn't even written. Prepared to do a programme to stay in the good books of a media mogul.

At least she'd chosen to do the programme. Rather than being forced into it.

Just then, when she was feeling the most pity for him, he looked at her and his face, she realised, suddenly appeared lighter – younger even, as though the confession had freed him in some way. Leaning in to give him a hug, Zoe wondered properly what the world was making of their absence. What stories were being told, lied, libelled and connived? What secrets were making their way out?

Needing the connection that being close to another human brought, she leant further into Toby, feeling the weight of his body against hers. She could hear his breathing. A deep, slow rumble in his chest and, in an attempt to adjust herself more comfortably, she shifted her head slightly, her movement causing him to turn his face close to hers.

*

Toby winced at the sound of parrots squabbling. Last night was messy. Too much vodka. Too little food. There'd been no further signs of a plane and in the meantime they'd burnt through a lot of wood. He looked over to where the fire was still smouldering and wondered what else they could do to attract attention from rescuers.

He was distracted from his thoughts when Zoe came to sit next to him. She looked as bad as he felt and as green as the coconuts.

'How are you doing?'

'My head is pounding, my eyes itch with tiredness and,' Zoe exclaimed, looking pretty pissed off, 'worse still, what felt like minutes after I fell asleep, I had to get up again to go fishing with Emily first thing this morning.' She shuddered at the memory. 'The sea was so rough and the smell of the fish was so strong, I threw up. In the sea.' She groaned and Toby grinned – even green she was beautiful. He let her continue with her monologue and made a point to listen and nod in the right places. 'I can't remember how last night ended – can you? I can remember us having a row, I think, then... nothing... just waking up in the shelter, my head cracking with the hangover from hell.'

As she talked Toby enjoyed the heat of the day, his eyes closed against the bright sunshine and he took in a deep breath, inhaling the earthy bonfire scent.

'Why are you smiling?' Zoe brought him back to real life and he momentarily stopped the replay of how the evening had ended for him. He opened his eyes to look at Zoe and found her staring at him, her dark pupils looking as thunderous as the clouds coming in over the sea.

'Nothing.' He decided to change the subject, 'Do you know, you've never said why you said yes to doing the programme. Talk to me to keep your mind off of your hangover.' He grinned in spite of her mutinous look.

She folded her arms and looked ridiculously young but Toby realised he really wanted to know.

'Come on, I don't think after last night there's much room for secrets now. Is there? You know why I agreed to the programme. They had me over a barrel cos I couldn't keep my dick in my pants,' he grinned in what he hoped was his most winning way, 'but look,' he pointed to his crotch, currently just about covered by his now almost see-through Calvin Klein's, 'I'm a changed man – dick firmly in pants.' He smiled again. 'I'm a nice guy. Really.'

The silence stretched from a few seconds to quite a few minutes and Toby distracted himself by taking an inventory of all the aches and pains he was suffering with to occupy himself. He licked his lips, keenly aware of how blistered and chapped they were. Despite the ladies sharing out their various potions, Toby knew there was never going to be enough to protect all of them. The heat had made every pore shrivel up, yet at the same time he'd never sweated more.

Toby's lips bled every time he changed facial expression and he had peeling skin all over his body where he'd burnt countless times in the scorching heat. His ankle was on the mend, though he wondered how well it had repaired itself without a cast to set it properly.

'This could be the end of my high-heel days,' he said out loud.

'What?' Zoe looked bemused.

'Ha, sorry. I was, nah… it's stupid,' he said.

'Try me.'

'I was rehearsing the line I'd give about my ankle being broken in interviews. It would go down a storm on any of the prime-time chat shows. Don't tell me you don't think like that?' he asked hopefully.

Zoe ignored him and Toby wondered if he'd shown his crazy side too soon.

'You haven't mentioned *the video*,' Zoe said, interrupting his line of thought and she didn't return his gaze. She chose instead to watch a parrot pecking at the crystal white sand. He followed her stare.

'What video?'

Zoe laughed falsely.

'Very good. One billion views and you weren't one of them? Er, okay.' She threw a stone in the direction of a tree stump and missed it. Toby laughed too. Since last night he felt lighter, more prepared to laugh.

'Ohhh… you mean *that* video… oh, right… yeah… now you mention it… there was something on Instagram. I can barely recall it though,' he added, smiling broadly. 'You weren't really naked were you?'

Zoe laughed again, albeit ruefully. 'Yup, totally topless, nude knickers though.'

Toby shook his head. 'Oh well then, that's no big deal. That billion of people will be *very* frustrated to learn I've been privy to the full-monty version,' he mocked, and nudged Zoe amiably.

'Needs must and all that,' she replied.

'Yes, well, no clothes can—' he started but Zoe interrupted him.

'No – needs must for the show,' she emphasised, 'I didn't want to take part.' She thought carefully before saying anything too revealing. 'I wouldn't have taken part usually, but my agent thought it would be good damage control.' She paused. 'Y'know, because of the attention from *the video*. He told me I was a dumbass for doing something that could get me in this sort of situation and I needed to be smart.'

Toby shook his head in disbelief and in a bid to buy himself some time, threw a stone neatly at the tree Zoe had been going for.

'No, I don't believe that. You're too clever to be marched into a programme against your will, whatever the circumstances were that led up to it.'

She sighed, and Toby knew he'd got it wrong. Again.

'I'm not smart, I tend to hide behind my characters,' she admitted, a little nervously.

Toby smiled again and realised just how much he'd

done that today and placed his arm around her to pull her in. Her head was light on his shoulder and he was suddenly conscious he smelt of last night's vodka, but when he caught a light tang of body odour from Zoe Fucking Stenson, he realised it didn't matter. None of them had access to shower products or deodorants. Or toothpaste. So they smelt, he realised, as they should smell – with no perfumes masking them and he realised he kind of loved it. Zoe appeared to be feeling the same because, somewhat surprisingly, he realised he could feel her relaxing into him.

'Of course you hide behind your characters, you're an actress – a bloody good one at that. But you're meant to embody other people. No one thinks you're being you *all* the time. Anyway, I wasn't suggesting you're the personalities you put across – that would be madness. No,' Toby shook his head lightly so as not to move her, 'I'm commenting on watching you, and how you've interacted with us here. You've been the one with the ideas from the beginning. Cool, calm and collected.'

Toby wondered if Zoe had listened to him. He thought she had. He thought she'd allowed his words to sink in, because she was quiet, her breathing steady. So he waited. He looked out across the horseshoe bay of white sizzling-hot sand and the clearest of aquamarine water, considering the blessing and curse the paradise brought.

Faintly, Toby heard a reply.

'I s'pose I just… keep doing what needs to be done, I don't think about how. Or that I'm doing it.'

They both watched the sky; clouds were forming in

thin wispy lines and the pattern reminded Toby of an outlandish suit he'd worn to a red carpet event a few months ago. What had he been thinking?

'I think,' Zoe started, then moved herself from him and looked directly at Toby, 'I think, I've always listened to others and believed them when they said I wasn't smart. Maybe I've allowed myself to challenge that here.'

'Ah, so the island has changed you too,' he observed as he moved forwards and kissed the top of her head softly. 'I think it's working its magic on all of us.'

'I think you could be right,' Zoe agreed, 'but it won't be any good if we starve to death here.' She leant against him again and Toby realised how good it felt, just to be companionable. 'So I'm realising I'm not quite as stupid as I had once thought and you've discovered you have a heart.'

Toby snapped his head around, causing Zoe to lose her position on his shoulder.

'Hey, I always had a heart.'

'Okay, well. Judging by how you've been keeping an eye on us, I'm guessing you're starting to remember how to use it. And you've not had a chance to sleep your way around us three, so that's given you time to decide what you really want.'

'Was I that two-dimensional just a few weeks ago? What a shit.'

Zoe laughed and punched him lightly on the arm. 'A bit of a shit… but improving.'

Toby laughed a little and went quiet for another moment, when he realised he'd have to be brutally honest.

'Mind you, if we do survive and I'm retelling this in a pub, you were all naked the whole time and constantly throwing yourselves at me.'

'Of course, you had to beat us off with a stick.'

'I could do with beating something off.' Toby gave Zoe the big white-toothed grin that had got him into the top ten 'fanciable' men for the last few years and hoped she didn't punch him again.

He was saved by the weather as the rain that had started as light droplets a few minutes ago had begun to fall heavily with huge sploshes landing around them both, causing damp welts to form in the sand.

'Quick. Shelter,' Zoe instructed, helping Toby up.

'See,' he winked, 'full of good ideas.'

'Shut up and do as you're told.'

*

'Ouch, fuck, ouch.' Emily stopped to rub her foot. A wave had come over the rocks she was climbing across so suddenly she had been slammed against the side, catching her leg but badly cutting her foot.

'You all right?' Toby was a little way behind, a few rocks lower, and Emily swore again under her breath.

'Fine,' she lied through gritted teeth.

'Sure?'

'Yes I'm fucking sure, let's just get on with this.'

Toby nodded and they slowly made their way around the edge to the bay the women had slept in the first night. They had hoped to walk through the forest path, but the storm that had battered the island for the past two days had blown trees across the route, preventing them from taking the shortcut.

Another wave thundered over Emily, covering her from head to toe in foamy water.

'This is more like the cliffs at Saltdean than the bloody South Pacific,' Toby yelled as he too was drenched.

'Wouldn't know, never been,' Emily replied, irritated that Zoe hadn't been able to accompany her on their mission. 'Do you think Zoe's okay?'

'What? Oh, yeah, sure she is,' Toby replied, concentrating on not losing his footing as another wave pounded over the two of them.

Emily was fairly sure Zoe had made up the sudden bout of food poisoning she was claiming and was instead hoping that by forcing her and Toby together they'd find a way of getting on.

'It had better bloody be there, you know.'

'Look, all I said was that I think I had a torch, and it might be on the beach – or it might be back in the forest where you found me. I don't know.'

'You sounded a lot surer last night,' Emily pressed. The idea that they were doing this journey – which they would have to do again when they returned – and all for a torch that may not be there was causing her blood to boil.

'Let's just look; if it's there it'll be useful. No more pitch-black nights.'

The last two nights had been the worst on the island; the weather had howled around the camp, blowing through the shelter and exposing them to everything Mother Nature had to offer. For the first time since their arrival on the island, Emily had really begun to worry she wasn't going to survive.

'I can't believe you forgot it,' Emily said for perhaps the thirtieth time as they both braced themselves against a rock, allowing the wave to crash against it, leaving them with the sight of the next bay in view.

'Look,' Toby straightened up as they found the familiar sensation of the sandy beach under their bare feet, 'I forgot. That's it. Between you finding me in the forest and us deciding to go on to the other bay, plus, y'know, a broken fucking foot, I forgot I'd packed a torch. Well, Mum packed. But as soon as I remembered I told you all.'

'Whatever.' Emily had gone from finding it difficult to talk to Toby because she didn't like him all that much, to being embarrassed to talk to him.

She'd seen them.

It was three nights since they'd enjoyed vodka around the fire. Emily, who was a lightweight at the best of times, had quickly discovered that having an empty stomach didn't increase her tolerance. She hadn't been able to hold her drink and had dozed off pretty quickly. But later, when the sand was pressing hard into her face and the mosquitoes were beginning to bite, Emily had prised open her eyes in an attempt to get up and go to the shelter. And that's when she saw them. Toby and a woman in an embrace.

It could have been either June or Zoe, Emily couldn't recall. They'd been in the shadow of the fire, and the woman's back had been to her. All she knew was they were locked in a long kiss. They'd connected in a way that reminded her of everything she missed.

If only she could have seen who it was.

She couldn't just ask June or Zoe, because whoever it was might be embarrassed at the invasion of their privacy, whereas whoever it wasn't, probably shouldn't know until Toby and the mystery woman admitted it. Or it could have been a mistake. But so far, neither of the women were acting any differently, and Toby was flirting with both of them equally. In fact, if anything, he seemed flirtier with them, but that was no change, he was always hugging them. Except Emily of course.

There was something so frustrating about Toby. So fake. Emily wanted to scream at him to just be himself. There were no cameras, no social media, no phones, no paparazzi, but he still seemed to want to put on this show of machismo, which was quite sad really, when she thought about it. And he didn't like her either, he'd made no bones about that. He'd regularly asked about her work, and made a point of showing how little he thought about influencers, and how insignificant what she did was. As opposed to him.

'Emily – did you hear me? I think we were up here.' Toby seemed to be repeating himself, bringing her back to the present.

She looked around to get her bearings.

'I don't know. None of it looks familiar – there's loads of trees that have come down here too. How can you tell?'

Toby scanned the beach, looking at the forest where she'd rescued him, and the other line of trees where they'd sat out of the sun's reach all those weeks ago.

'Not sure to be honest, but let's try.' He strode off confidently with the slight limp he'd acquired.

Emily followed behind, lost in her thoughts. Zoe couldn't have kissed him, he was too old for her. And he was a well-known ladies' man; she wouldn't fall for his fake charm and floppy hair, would she? But then, she wasn't convinced June thought of Toby in that way either. Certainly, they got on. However, she treated him a little like a pet, or a son. Or both. And he was fifteen years younger than her. Not that Emily thought the age gap was a problem either way, but still. She couldn't decide who would be more his type.

'It's here. Emily, it's here, look.'

Toby was practically doing a jig with happiness as he found his torch, a wind-up one, Emily noticed. She approved of his mum's packing.

'Okay, that's pretty good,' she had to confess.

'Yes it is, look. Wind it up and there we go.' Toby looked so young and excited Emily briefly forgot her irritation with him.

'We better head straight back,' she suggested. She didn't fancy the treacherous rocks in anything but bright sunshine, and already it looked like the sky was darkening for another storm.

Toby nodded and they retraced their steps to the shoreline.

'Fuck.'

'Where's the…?'

The two of them looked to the left, where the rocks had been just a short while before, but they'd disappeared. Completely covered in water by the swift incoming tide.

Emily looked at Toby, anger flashing across her face.

'We can't get back. And all because of your ridiculous torch.'

'You were happy about it a minute ago.'

'That's because… Oh, never mind.' Emily slumped to the ground, her whole body aching from the exertions of getting to the bay. 'What are we going to do?'

Toby sat next to her.

'Think we'll have to wait it out until morning, don't you?'

She looked at him and tried not to cry. The last thing she wanted to do was spend the evening with Toby. Hours and hours of small talk and silence. What she wouldn't give for a song from Zoe or some background chatter from June.

'Let's go back to the treeline. At least we have a few essentials with us this time,' Toby said, trying to cheer her up.

With the precision of a synchronised swim team, the two swiftly found dry leaves and kindling to start a fire with June's lighter.

Toby found a few sturdier branches to push together into a tepee, and Emily helped to bind them together with the vines that entwined themselves around all the trees in the forest. They placed palm leaves inside and she smiled.

'Looks like we've done this before,' Emily noted and Toby nodded.

'Yup, and we've got two bottles of water and there's some coconuts here. It's not much, but we'll cope tonight, won't we?'

Emily smiled tightly.

They sat apart, watching the sunset begin. This was usually Emily's favourite part of the day but she was prickling with irritation. Why did he have to kiss one of her friends? Why was he a flirt? Why did it bother her? She didn't fancy him, she knew she didn't. She just hadn't liked him on first sight and she hadn't adjusted her feelings.

As though he could read her thoughts, Toby cleared his throat in order to approach a difficult conversation.

'Why don't you like me?'

Emily's heart started beating hard. She hated confrontation. She was a middle child with two brothers and never wanted to be in an argument. The closest she got to angry was when the Ocado substitution for hummus was taramasalata and she took to social media to vent her feelings.

He was waiting for an answer.

'Because I know your type.'

'My type?' he pushed, moving closer to her. 'What do you mean?'

She sighed, the weariness of the day, the weeks, the survival, taking their toll.

'Oh come on, Toby, don't be naive. You know what I'm talking about – we've all seen the stories in the papers and online about you. You treat women like shit and move on to the next one, never caring what the outcome is.' It felt good to get that out. Emily knew of Toby, everyone did. She'd seen him on morning shows, comedy panel shows, the Royal Variety, he was everywhere. All the time.

And so were the stories about him.

Toby was shaking his head.

'I'd have thought better of you, Emily. You're the bright one out of all of us.' He smiled, and it annoyed her.

'What?'

'Stories are just that. They're made up.' He shrugged and continued to stoke the fire. Emily could feel her body quivering with rage at how easy he thought life was.

'They're *all* made up are they?' she pushed. 'All of them? I don't believe you.'

He hesitated whilst poking the fire, his body hunched over. 'No. They're not all made up, but a lot are – or a lot are exaggerated,' he calmly explained.

'I don't believe you. All those photos of women you've slept with, it's just disgusting,' she replied, her anger bristling and causing her words to go screechy, not as cool and disciplined as she'd like.

'Not all of it's real. Talk to Zoe. Papers make stuff up,' he began and she cut him off.

'Zoe's not the same though, she's—'

'A woman?' he finished incredulously. 'Shit, Emily, I didn't realise you were sexist. I can be portrayed as a dick in the media, because I'm a man and deserve it, but anything they print about her are lies because she's a woman? Fucking hell.' He shook his head and stared at her.

Emily squirmed. That was what she thought, yes. And it wasn't until he said it, she realised the double standards she was applying.

'I'm not sexist,' she started, then faltered. 'I didn't think I was. But you've got to see the double standards that *you're* applying this with. Zoe gets tarnished by every decision she makes in the global spotlight of the media.

Her body is scrutinised. Her weight discussed. Her life isn't her own and everyone thinks they know her.' Emily began to wonder if it wasn't just Zoe she was thinking of, remembering her own trolls. 'Your stories are…'

'Less important, but more real,' he supplied, a little sadly. 'You seem very sure about that.'

She softened. 'I was more certain about five minutes ago.'

'I'll take the blame for a lot of the earlier stuff, and I've made a lot of mistakes of my own,' he admitted, 'but the last couple of years I've found I've been the victim of set-ups, both on and offline. It would seem the higher you rise, the more people want you to fall.'

She noted the look of sadness pass over his weary face.

'You'll learn that when your book goes stratospheric,' he added, his smooth charm replacing the rawness she'd just seen and she appreciated the switch in emotions. Life on the island often felt extreme, whether it was the swinging of seasons in a day or the toll it took just to stay alive.

'I have to get back to write it first,' she replied, moving closer so they could share the warmth of the fire.

'Here, lean on me,' he offered. 'I promise I won't try anything.'

As she moved closer, wondering how it would feel to sleep in the little shelter with him, after fifteen years of sleeping next to Matt, he nudged his shoulder into her.

'I'm sorry too.' He smiled, making her grin a little.

'I didn't—' she started, and he cut her off.

'Don't ruin our moment. In the morning, let's go back to the girls and tell them we're friends. I think we've been upsetting them.'

It wasn't until she lay down to sleep that night, listening to the rain starting again, she realised she'd forgotten to ask about the kiss.

*

How could so much water fall out of the sky for so long? June would complain out loud but she'd begun to get the distinct impression all comments on the rain, how wet everywhere was, how leaky the shelter was and how incessant it was, were starting to grate on the current island population, so she'd kept her thoughts to herself.

Instead, she'd begun working on an idea for a trap for the chickens that were running in and out of their camp, high-tailing it out any time the islanders approached them. The four had originally assumed the fowl would be tame, as they didn't know about humans. But after numerous failed attempts, including one memorable incident where Emily threw herself on the biggest chicken there, naked as the day she was born, yelling, 'Come here, you mother-clucker,' then falling face first on said bird's puddle of shit, the island's celebrity inhabitants had stopped in their attempts.

Whilst it was raining and they were holed up in their shelter with little to help pass the time, June had come up with a chicken plan. She'd spotted a plastic crate that had washed up during one of the storms, like the ones milkmen use to carry bottles. She was certain if she propped the crate open with a stick and hid out of sight, holding the crate up with some rope, that an interested chicken would wander along to eat the bait she would place there. She thought some chopped clams would work – and then, bang, a trapped chicken.

'Of course, killing it would be a problem,' she muttered.

'What? Who are you killing – not me, I hope?' Toby smiled at her from her side. He'd been attempting to keep her warm by wrapping his arm around her. The camp Emily and Zoe had built was working well in keeping the water out, especially where the helicopter door was. But there were gaps in the roof area, where branches had been placed, along with fronds of palm leaves that with the best will in the world wouldn't withstand the downpours being thrown at them.

They'd all plugged the holes as best they could, but the rain was more insistent than Dorset in February and it was getting through the smallest of gaps. The constant drip, drip, dripping had continued for three days and showed no sign of letting up. None of the four had slept for more than ten minutes at a time and were suffering with extreme exhaustion.

'The fire, Em… Em, the fire,' Zoe repeated to Emily, who had been sitting cross-legged on the floor and who had looked like she was going to fall asleep, face first, in the small fire they had kept alight. Emily awoke and shuffled back away from the flames.

'Sorry,' she mumbled.

Other than keeping as dry as they could, keeping the fire going was their main priority these past few days because, as June had pointed out, they couldn't keep using her lighter – eventually the gas would run out.

At the back of her mind June had begun to wonder

what the four's long-term plans should be. This latest storm had proven how temporary their shelter was. If they were going to be here for much longer, they'd need to look for something more stable.

For now though, the fire had to be their priority. It continued to act as a signal as well as a way of keeping them warm in the evenings when the sun disappeared, and the heat of the day with it.

But this had meant the islanders had spent every moment during the rain-soaked days, and nights, keeping a pot of ashes alight, with whatever dry wood they could source when the rain had let up for a few minutes.

'So,' Toby nudged into June's shoulder playfully, 'was it me you were going to kill?'

Even in the half-light of the tent, even with dark-grey stubbly beard and soot encrusting itself into his crow's feet, even after four weeks of no toothpaste or deodorant – even with all that, Toby was still ridiculously attractive and, as he was way too young for June, she'd enjoyed the pastime of light flirting with him to keep herself amused.

'I'd thought about it, but no, not this time. Though, if we don't get found soon, we'll have to consider killing you – we'll starve to death otherwise,' she replied, pinching him on the thigh as though to test his readiness for cooking. Toby acted flabbergasted.

'Who says I'm the one that gets eaten? You'd have to catch me first.'

Zoe, hearing the conversation from across the shelter, laughed.

'Not sure that's a problem, you're injured – it'll be like taking candy from a baby.'

'Or meat off an injured man,' interjected Emily.

Toby raised his hands out in front of him, as though to stop them.

'Whoa, so, hang on, you're all ready to eat me? You've not got plans to eat any of the rest of you?' They all shook their heads, laughing. 'Zoe, you're a vegan for fuck's sake. Four weeks on this island and now you're a cannibal? Un-fucking-believable.' He sat there, shaking his head.

'Okay, who'd you eat then?' June challenged. Toby looked around and June knew what he was thinking. Zoe and June had lost any ounce of fat they'd had before and their clothes were now hanging off them, and bones that June had only seen at school in biology were showing through them both. Emily, however, was now at a weight which looked just right. She was undernourished, just not as much as the other two women.

'No, you're right. It would have to be me. Think about it logically. You need you three, you each bring something useful to the group – if I could feed you all for a few days, I'd be glad to know I'd contributed to your survival,' Toby suggested, and all the women laughed at his mock bravery.

'Ah, thanks Tobes, but we need the guy. I'm sure there'll be something high we won't be able to reach,' June replied.

'Or a jar we need to undo.'

'Or – a fart joke we've not heard.'

'Seriously. I get stranded on a desert island with you three? You all think you're fucking hilarious… take the piss out of the one man…'

June smiled. It was the first time she'd felt close

to happiness in days; the weather had had the effect of pulling them all down. 'Well, men have been taking the piss out of us for hundreds of years. At least on this island there's no patriarchy to smash.' She nudged Toby back.

'I'll have you know I'm a feminist. I have the literal T-shirt,' he pouted at her. 'I was in that campaign – I hung out with Chris Martin from Coldplay that day,' he muttered. 'That life feels a world away doesn't it?'

Zoe nodded and warmed her hands over the small fire.

'A month ago I had just finished the tour for *Always Say Die*. I was meant to do *Star Survivor*, then I was heading to LA to begin rehearsing for my next film...' She was quiet for a moment.

'I wonder what they'll do about that. Do you think they'll halt production... or... replace me?' she asked, as if it was the first time the thought had come to her mind. June knew as the weeks went past, the assumption they'd be rescued was disappearing. The alternative was too much to consider.

'I was meant to be interviewing Madonna at her house this week,' June added, then tried to work out what date it was. 'I think – though, I'm a bit lost about what date it is.'

'June 28th,' Emily said quietly. 'It's Cherry's birthday tomorrow. She'll be six.' She sniffed and June realised how quiet the younger woman had been that day. She was usually to be counted on for anecdotes and uplifting stories, but today she'd been very distant.

'Shit, we're being so insensitive. Sorry, Em.' Zoe shuffled over to give her a hug.

'Sorry, Emily. We're dicks aren't we?' June added, and looked at Toby who raised his eyebrows. She never swore.

'Yeah, sorry. Of course. Look, when we get home, – I'll give you the whole back catalogue of my books – all signed for her,' he said kindly and, to his surprise, Emily roared with laughter, leaving him nonplussed.

'What?'

'Sorry Toby... I am grateful, but... I'm not sure they'll make up for her mum missing out on her birthday – even if they are signed copies.' Emily hiccupped with laughter and Toby began to join in.

'Not even if I throw in some DVDs of the films?' he asked, wiping his eyes as tears started to cascade down his face.

'Does anyone even watch DVDs anymore, Grandad?' asked Zoe innocently.

'Hang on, what if I brought her on *Wake Up*? Gave her a tour?' June suggested mischievously, starting to giggle too. Zoe had been snorting with laughter.

'Wait a minute, if anyone is going to play the "look what my fame can bring" card, I think I should have a go.' She considered the situation seriously. 'I would buy you a castle,' she smiled at Emily, 'one of the French ones you love so much. I'd buy you a castle, so Cherry could be a princess in her very own turret – and then I'd take her to some sort of martial arts training school so she didn't rely on anyone to rescue her from it.'

Emily gave a watery grin.

'Now that's the sort of gift which says "Sorry I was stranded on an island".'

'It's a deal then. I give you a load of books, June gives

you a behind-the-scenes tour and Zoe buys you a castle. Seems a fair divvying up,' Toby said, listing the most ridiculous gift list on his hand.

'Shush. I think it's stopping,' June said, interrupting Emily's response. All four went quiet and listened, the non-stop pelt of the rain did seem like it was slowing and the drips on the inside of the helicopter door were coming in less frequently.

'I'll check.' Zoe straightened and peered around the door. 'Wow,' she breathed, 'there's an amazing sky – the storm is clearing, look.' The others made their way out of the shelter and looked at the horizon. Where minutes before had been a steel grey of impenetrable weather, a shock of bright blue sky was slicing through.

'Is that–' Zoe broke off, pointing at the trees. All four looked.

'It's a dead chicken,' June finished for her. There'd been no need for elaborate traps it turned out, just a heavy branch from a tree, loosened by the winds, and an unlucky bird.

'It's dinner,' Toby replied and whooped for joy.

Glamour Online

GLAMOUR *magazine has led the way with tributes for the late Zoe Stenson, by filling its social media feeds on a day dedicated to the star.*

Social media was flooded with images of the beautiful star yesterday when she was officially described as missing presumed dead following an accident in the South Pacific a month ago.

The announcement came via Star Survivor's *press office with this statement,*

"We are incredibly sorry to announce that the search and rescue efforts to look for the missing four celebrities have been called off. Despite a huge effort from New Zealand's government as well as numerous local fishermen, no wreckage or bodies have been discovered, giving us reason to believe a freak accident took place. We ask that the families of the stars are given privacy and a chance to grieve."

The day of tributes was accompanied by the hashtag #ZoeOnly, and millions of images filled screens of the stunning actress, with many famous faces sharing their favourite photo of her.

Rapper and fashion designer MYME shared an image of Zoe in just an oversized Lakers top, from two years ago, during the time the pair were rumoured to be seeing each other, with the caption 'I'll never stop following you', in reference to the famous 'unfollowing' which took place around the time of their alleged break-up.

President Michelle Obama posted a selfie of the two at the

White House from last year, during her inauguration with the caption, 'From one woman of colour to another, thank you for everything you did to break down the walls. You leave a hole that no one should, or indeed could, fill. Peace.'

Fans of the actress have been leaving flowers at her home in London and the country house in Surrey she recently bought, as well as at sites across the world which have links to her.

Zoe's most famous role as Jay Bond has been cemented in history following the record-breaking first four weekends at the box office, with takings of over $3 billion, making it the biggest-selling movie of all time.

*

GUARDIAN EXCLUSIVE

GHOSTED BY A MASTER

THE country is in shock today with the revelations from this paper that the late Toby Masters' popular children's book series was written by a ghostwriter.

Following the announcement two days ago of the presumed death of the four celebrities lost in a helicopter crash a month ago, non-disclosure agreements between Toby's agency and his ghostwriter are now no longer relevant, giving the ghostwriter the opportunity to admit she wrote the incredibly popular McMathur series.

In an exclusive interview with The Guardian, Alison May said:

'I've felt very uncomfortable for years that the public has had the wool pulled over their eyes and been told that Toby has written these books. When you think about it, the likelihood of one man writing over twenty books in eight years must have caused some people to think it couldn't be the case.'

Asked why she'd come forward now, she replied:

'As sad as it is that he's passed away, I think it's only right that ghostwriters are given the credit they deserve. We're not asking for our names to be on the front of books for people we've written for, but we'd like to be in the acknowledgments at least, instead of ignored.'

Julian Quanti, author of three bestselling books and a judge for the Booker Prize, took to social media to express his outrage. He said:

'The time has come for real writers to be celebrated, not celebrities just because they sell. The publishing industry needs to be ahead of the game, not lying about it. Readers are not stupid and we shouldn't treat them as such.'

A spokesperson at Toby Masters' agency, Smith, Dean and Wooliss, said:

'We are mourning the loss of one of our most well-known stars, any suggestion that his work was not his own is not something we can comment on at this time.'

The revelations from the ghostwriter have begun a swell of sympathy online, with the hashtag #IWroteFor trending for the last twenty-four hours on social media and many well-known authors being embroiled in the scandal.

*

CONTENT CREATORS

DESPITE a huge push from the families of the celebrities recently lost at sea, the crowdfunding initiative to pay for further search and rescues has not met the target.

The families of Zoe Stenson and Emily Chase had hoped they would gain enough interest from fans to help towards the costs of finding the still missing stars.

It is estimated that a more intensive search and rescue of the area where the four's helicopter was suspected to have been lost will cost one million pounds.

With Zoe's massive fortune unable to be accessed until her will is read, and Emily's family unable to fund it themselves, the two families combined forces to put the request out on social media.

However, despite the crowdfunding pot reaching £850,000, it did not meet its target by the deadline of midnight last night, leaving fans, and the families frustrated and unable to fund the search and rescue.

Emily's husband, Matt, 37, commented from the family's large home in leafy Surrey last night:

'We are dumbfounded at how little help we're receiving in our bid to find the four. We had thought fans would be keen to get them back, but we're beginning to learn there's one thing people say, and another when they actually have to put their hands in their pockets.'

He added:

'I know we all have our own issues, but all my family wants is to get my wife, and my children's mother, back.'

The irony hasn't been lost on Matt that Emily's

following on Instagram as Slummin' It Mummin' It, has now escalated to over ten million followers over the past month since she went missing.

He said:

'I get that it's easy to click "like" and you begin following someone, but you won't get any more content from her unless she returns. The only way we can get her back is with a better search and rescue than what has happened already. That is if it's not too late.'

Zoe's family have stayed resolutely out of the limelight, except for issuing this statement:

'We want our daughter back and we need you to help that happen. Our love isn't going to be enough to find her. Please pray for us.'

However, there are comments on social media suggesting that people are finding requests for money for well-off celebrities a bitter pill to swallow.

Tracey said: 'I've been to her (Zoe's) films and paid for tickets. Why is it down to me to pay 4 her to cum [sic] back.'

Another user agreed, saying: 'If they hadn't been looking to get even richer they wouldn't have been going there in the first place. It's their fault tbh.'

The families are now looking at alternative ways of finding the money, including asking the Government to step in and fund the search attempt.

What do YOU think? Comment below.

*

LOST AT SEA – WHERE HAVE WOMEN OVER 50 GONE?

WITH the loss of daytime television presenter June Sharp from our screens and the subsequent re-branding of her show with a much younger presenter, our columnist Helen Young discusses the disappearance of a certain demographic of women.

When my grandmother was in her fifties, I remember her having lightly permed, greying hair, starched blouses tucked into sensible elastic-banded skirts and flat shoes. That was roughly 30 years ago, and I would have been no older than 10. But at that time, she was most definitely what I would have (and did) describe as old.

Fast forward 30 years, and I know numerous women in their 50s. Vivacious, fashion-forward, blonde of hair, lithe of body and most definitely sexy as hell, these women are not the ones my gran was.

They're the female entrepreneurs who cannily set up businesses, spotting gaps in the market when their children were young, or are at the top of their game as lawyers, authors, journalists and company directors.

What they're not, is old, but, and I need to be careful as I write this as I don't wish to fall foul of my friends and followers in this demographic, they are starting to age.

A little.

There are lines around eyes which have laughed a lot,

jawlines are not as tight as they once were, and there's most definitely more dye than natural colour in their gloriously glamorous lob haircuts.

But this is what aging should look like in the 2020s. It's nice to stand next to someone and know that they too have lived and laughed, and cried, and smiled and screamed and all the other natural, human things that it is to be a person identifying as a woman.

Following the announcement that June Sharp, the well-known TV presenter, is thought to have died in a helicopter accident, as a long-standing fan of hers I tuned into her programme Wake Up, *the day it restarted, expecting to hear a loving obituary to their anchorwoman.*

Instead, following an interlude of two weeks off air, it would seem Wake Up *had done away with any reference to June, or any of the women involved with the show over 30, and had replaced her with a very bubbly 21-year-old who fizzed around 50-something Danny Coleman, the male presenter who appeared to have dodged the cuts.*

Whilst it's unsettling to have a programme change so rapidly, I'm not against moving forwards, it did set me to wondering when it became okay to hide women on TV and films once they hit 'a certain age'. If it's not them being replaced by younger models, as in Wake Up, *it's the astonishing amount of nipping, tucking, polishing, lifting, bleaching and clipping done to women in the public eye to get them to continue to look 'acceptable' for us, the audience – as though we couldn't possibly manage seeing someone age in front of us.*

There is, I would challenge, not one female on TV (unless she's classed as a character actress and allowed an 'unusual' face) who has not had work done to make her look younger.

I won't call out the various celebs who I believe have had work done, it's their choice. But it's also a sad reflection of our society that they feel they need to. I'm happy to see them age. I want to know what I've got to look forward to.

So, my question is, where have all the wrinkles gone? Where is the beauty and grace, and intelligence which comes with a few crow's feet and grey hairs? We know they exist – we see real women in the street every day we know aging happens.

Why, then, is it a mystery on TV and in films?

June Sharp might be lost at sea, but I'd suggest she's not the only one.

Helen Young is a journalist and women's rights activist, and her business Woman Up, teaches people who identify as female how to make their voices heard. Her book, 'The Invisible Female' is in The Times bestseller list, available from all good bookstores, priced £9.99.

Chapter Five

'If we get rescued, what will you do?' Emily asked Zoe, as they lay on their backs in the cool water of the pool. They'd spent the last couple of hours finding wood to make fires along the beach, leaving them both hot and exhausted. Zoe's own worries about not being found were beginning to be amplified amongst her fellow islanders and she and Emily had doubled their energies in trying to build bigger fires to attract attention.

Zoe dipped her head in the water, the chill of it refreshing her body, which she had noticed was becoming more and more weary as the days went past.

'I'd eat everything I could find, drink coffee and sleep in a comfy bed,' Zoe replied and Emily shook her head.

'No, you know what I mean. If we ever get off here, what will your life look like? Your career? Have you thought about it?' she pressed.

Zoe trod water for a while to give herself a pause before answering. She knew what she wanted to do, but she wasn't sure whether she could. She opened her mouth to say it, then closed it again, the action causing Emily to look over, expecting her to reply.

She tried again.

'I'd like to direct,' she said, and looked to see what Emily made of her comment. The other woman smiled.

'That's a great idea. I bet you'd be brilliant at it.'

Zoe grinned widely, getting some of the pool water in her mouth, causing her to cough a little.

'Really?' she checked 'Why?'

Emily laughed.

'Because you're so bossy.' She saw her friend's shocked face, 'Okay, so bossy is the wrong word. But you're great at coming up with ideas – look at what we've all achieved here.' She swept her arms out wide to demonstrate the island. 'All under your direction,' she pointed out.

'Maybe.' Zoe paused. 'Although I'm not sure how much longer we're going to cope for,' she admitted. It had been playing on her mind for a little while, the small amounts of food, the gauntness of her fellow islanders, the lack of any passers-by. She knew her body was beginning to fail her in certain ways as well. They'd been on the island five, maybe six weeks, and she'd not had a period in that time, something she'd always relied on to be every twenty-eight days without fail. It was starting to become very obvious how the four were barely surviving.

Noticing that Emily had gone quiet, Zoe turned round to check on her, only to realise she'd disappeared.

'Emily?' Zoe shouted, her fear swallowed up by the

trees around her, cushioning her words with their fronds. Suddenly the dense forest coverage around them, the subdued light, the lack of birdsong, the sea out of earshot all combined to cause Zoe to gasp with a sense of panic squeezing at her heart.

Panic attack.

She'd had them growing up when she was bullied. Back then she'd go home and her mum would make it all better. Back then, it was schoolkids making fun of her skin colour, telling her she was chocolate ice cream and they were vanilla. Back then it was about being different. Back then it was about finding solace in acting and giving herself a shield.

She'd kept that shield for fifteen years.

But in this moment she'd swap for the panic she knew rather than the one she was facing today. The one where she was entirely alone in a deep pool of water which was threatening to drown her. She swam over to where Emily had been, frantically popping her head under to see where her friend was, but the water was too dark. She couldn't have gone far. Where the fuck was she?

Casting her eyes around, darting from side to side, Zoe attempted to quell a deep, primeval fear, when she saw Emily's body resurface further away, near to the tumultuous thunder of the waterfall. She was making no attempt to move away and Zoe knew something was wrong.

Mustering all the strength she had, Zoe swam the fastest crawl she could across the pool, painfully aware Emily had drifted some fifteen feet from her. When she was fit, Zoe would have cleared it easily, but after weeks of too few calories, she found every stroke took more energy from her, her arms aching with the effort, her breath coming in tight bursts and her legs replaced by jelly. Somehow, she got across.

'Emily... Em... wake the fuck up,' she yelled as she neared her friend who was still not moving.

Reaching her, Zoe threw her arm around Emily's neck, barely daring to see whether she was alive or not, deciding instead to pull her to the side. Drawing on every conversation she and Emily had enjoyed, their laughs whilst fishing, the memories the two had made, Zoe did everything she could to drag her friend across to the side and out of the pool. The other woman's face had gone a sickly blue colour and, looking down at her chest, Zoe couldn't see any movement. No sign of a heart beating.

'Shit. Wake the fuck up, Emily.' She shook the woman. Nothing. She slapped her face. Still nothing.

'Help,' she yelled loudly into the quiet of the forest. 'Help us,' she cried plaintively, aware of how little aid there'd been so far.

'Please. Someone fucking help us.' She threw her hands over her eyes and then suddenly remembered the educational film she'd been in aged eleven. The one where she did mouth to mouth on a dummy. The dummy had tasted like the smell of washing-up gloves and had made her gag – especially when they'd had to do eight takes.

Quickly, Zoe tried to remember what she'd been taught.

She tilted Emily's head back a little, was about to put her mouth to hers, when she realised she had to check her first, make sure there were no blockages. She pinched Emily's nose, and bent down, blowing deeply into her mouth. The sensation of being so intimate with someone was a jolt after weeks of little comfort and she stopped for a moment to see if her efforts had been successful.

Nothing from Emily.

Zoe brought her hands together and pushed down hard on Emily's chest, pushing down for three goes. Still nothing. She returned to Emily's mouth and breathed into her again.

'Come on, Emily. Come on,' Zoe pushed down on Emily's chest, 'think of the girls. Think of Matt. Think of the castle in France. Come on.' She was crying fat, sploshy tears now. 'I promise I'll buy it for you, but you HAVE. TO. FUCKING. LIVE.'

She went to try again on Emily's mouth, when her friend coughed hard and turned on her side to throw up water; heaving, coughing, spluttering and crying. Zoe threw her arms around her and hugged her, weeping.

'Oh thank fuck. Thank fuck you're okay.'

Emily, crying too, lightly pushed Zoe away.

'Hurts,' she croaked, pointing at her chest, where Zoe had been pushing down to restart her heart.

The younger woman sprung away. 'Shit, sorry,' and she sat, shaking her head in Emily's direction.

At that moment, June arrived, breathless with running, a limping Toby immediately behind.

'What happened? We heard shouts,' said Toby anxiously, he and June taking in the scene of the two naked women, dripping wet, both in tears.

Zoe just looked up, exhaustion draining every last ounce of feeling from her. The numbness spreading through her body.

'She died,' was all she could say, turning to Emily. 'You died.'

*

Toby felt rattled after the incident in the pool. Whilst he and the others had, of course, known they were slowly starving and facing day after day of no answer to their SOS. or beacons, he hadn't really considered he might actually die on the island. He was convinced they'd be found.

But Emily's near-death incident had suddenly made Toby realise how much he wanted to live. As he stood waist-deep in the sea, waiting to see if he could catch one of the massive crabs they'd seen waddling past the night before, he thought back to him and June finding Zoe and Emily by the pool. They had both looked so frightened.

Emily wasn't sure what had happened; she only remembered talking to Zoe and the next minute waking up on the bank, coughing and spluttering, so they could only assume she must have passed out through the exertion of building the fires and the lack of food.

Whilst she had survived, Toby and June had noticed how much the incident had cost her and Zoe. Emily was beyond exhausted. She woke regularly at night in the middle of panic attacks where she couldn't breathe and thought she was drowning.

Narrowly missing what Toby assumed was a spider crab, he stood still, hoping the sea life would stop noticing him again and allow him to spear one of them, but because he and June had been taking turns to keep an eye on Emily at night, to soothe her and calm her, his senses were dulled and his reactions much slower. Everything was wearing them down now, but he could only hope that she would begin to get better. It had been five days but Toby had no idea how long it would be before she would begin to heal. All she said was she wanted to go home.

'Fuck. Almost had you,' Toby said to the water swirling with sand after another wasted effort to spear a crab. He wished Zoe was here; she would have known how to do it but she had faded quickly in the last few days. Toby thought the exertion of rescuing Emily, resuscitating her, the elation of her survival, took every ounce of energy from her. These last few days Zoe could barely raise herself up without collapsing and she was disappearing before their eyes. Toby found it hard to see her look as thin as she did.

'Stay. The fuck. Still.' Toby jabbed the spear repeatedly into the water, causing it to froth whilst the sand whipped around him and muddied the clear sea.

'Fuuuuuuuuuuuuuuuuuuuuuuck,' Toby yelled out to the ocean in frustration. With their head angler out of action, it had been down to June and him to keep everyone alive but it was like everything had conspired against them. He tried not to remember their fruitless fishing trip yesterday when they'd discovered, as he and June had reached the shore, that their bastard net had blown away in the storm they had had the night before. He cringed. It had been his fault as he had forgotten to weight it down, the way all the women did.

'In my defence,' he grumbled to the ocean that he'd begun to believe was listening, 'I was in a rush – I was thrilled to have some fish to bring in for everyone and I just walked away.'

He stabbed again. Nothing.

'So that's it. The net's gone, which means we need to be excellent spear-fishers – something I'm clearly not – or we survive on what we find on the ground.' He huffed and looked out to the endless sea.

'And there's slim pickings there as we've been in this bay for something like six weeks.' He thought about June. Brave and fearless June who had taken it upon herself to go ever deeper into the forest to find fruit. She'd had better luck there than he'd had in the water. Toby's mouth salivated as he thought about the mangoes, pineapple and papaya she'd found, which had definitely lifted their spirits. But now, they'd noticed, most of the supply was too high for them to reach.

Walking out of the ocean to dry off for a bit, Toby decided his next plan would be to go out across the rocks to collect the clams and see if any fish had been trapped in the shallow rock pool he'd recently discovered. It was only uncovered at low tide and occasionally held a prize find for them.

Two days ago he'd found a tuna, which had fed them well. He rounded the corner to take a look at the rock pool and laughed out loud. An octopus.

'Thank you,' he told the sea, and hoped it would be edible. There was so little they all knew about the sea life they saw around them, they spent a lot of time hoping they weren't poisoning themselves. Another thing to be continually worried about, he thought as he walked carefully over to the pool to extract the octopus and place it into his bag, narrowly avoiding stepping on something with serious spines in it. He was sure his flimsy flip-flops wouldn't have given much protection.

He returned to the fire, which they continued to feed despite the ever-dwindling resources of wood and palm leaves to burn, and brandished the bag at June in triumph.

'Ooh, well done. That looks great. Octopus for lunch, girls,' she told the other two who remained asleep. 'Wonder how we'll cook this guy then? Spit roast? Is there anything we're meant to remove? I'm sure there's something in these we have to take out.' She looked at Toby who shrugged.

'Erm, how about we chop up the legs and cook those? I'm not sure I want to try octo head anyway,' he suggested and June smiled.

'Good plan. We need more wood on the fire.' She nodded at the small pile of kindling and Toby added it, watching the flames roar a little and then come back down to earth.

'We're running out of suitable firewood, Toby– that's the best I could find this morning.' June continued hacking through the octopus legs with a piece of metal that had washed up, Toby assumed from the helicopter crash, which they'd sharpened by scraping it up and down a rock.

'I've said before, I think we need to move on and find somewhere with more wood, fruit that we can reach and coconuts we've not eaten,' Toby tried again. The women kept telling him no when he'd suggested this lately, and he knew why they didn't want to go anywhere. Zoe and Emily had lost hope and it was affecting their ability to believe they could do anything.

'We could go across there.' He pointed and watched her attempt to prepare the octopus. Toby was sure the octopus was giving him a look, which gave him the heebie-jeebies, and turned the animal's face away. June smiled a little at the gesture and looked in the direction that Toby pointed out across the sparkling turquoise sea, to the bay opposite where a similar beach sat uninhabited.

June shook her head.

'How? Swimming?' She looked meaningfully in Emily's direction. 'I don't think we could,' she muttered just loud enough for Toby to hear, 'and Zoe's in no fit state.'

'It just looks so near.' Toby heard his voice; it was plaintive, but he wanted to offer some suggestion. Then he thought of something else. 'We could make a boat?' he tried and June scoffed in derision.

'Sure, I'll just find a sail,' she pretended to look up and down the beach, 'and a few spare planks of wood.' She laughed. 'Maybe even a motor.'

'Okay, I get it. Ridiculous idea.' Toby laughed at his suggestion– even in their dire circumstances he was convinced keeping a sense of humour had to help. 'But it might be something – we could float our way across?' he tried tentatively, knowing she would laugh again, but she was quiet. Thoughtful.

'Maybe,' she looked at him intensely, her eyes sparkling with the idea, 'maybe we *could* float our way across.'

Toby laughed, then realised she was serious. 'Really?' He was surprised she'd taken his idea. 'We could just, you know, go on our backs and just star-float it across,' he enthused. June stopped from gutting the octopus and laughed.

'Hey, why the intense laughter? No need for fucking raucous laughing. I'm worried you'll cut yourself and not that freaky octopus.'

She looked at him and smiled again.

'What?' He scratched his chin and noted how much beard there was and how little it itched now. In his mind he looked like a shipwrecked Daniel Craig. The girls reassured him it was more Brian Blessed. June's face softened and she leant in to kiss him lightly on the cheek.

'Oh pretty Toby, you are a darling, but sometimes I wonder just how you've coped these last few years in the cut-throat world of publishing. They must have eaten you alive.' She grinned and he pouted a little.

She grinned again.

'It's not a great idea for us to star-float our way across that lagoon – we won't be able to dictate the direction for one thing,' she explained, and although Toby was loathe to agree he decided that she may have a point. 'But,' she continued and looked out to the bay, her eyes shaded by her hand, 'if we found something to hold onto, we could kick our way across and it may not be as much effort.'

'That's what I meant,' Toby started, but June laughed again.

'Don't worry, your secret is safe with me,' she whispered.

'What secret?' he asked, perplexed. Surely not that he'd shagged his way through hundreds of women? That wasn't much of a secret.

She looked at him, the face of morning TV, the one he'd

watched many times in his dressing gown, after sending some woman packing he'd known only for an evening, the face he'd shouted at, cursed at, laughed with, been endeared to and angered by. *That* face smiled indulgently at him.

'The secret that whilst you're terribly clever, you just don't have an ounce of practicality in your genes.'

Toby guffawed; she had him completely pegged – more than anyone else he'd known. He realised he didn't think he'd ever be able to pull the wool over her eyes.

'Do you know—' He paused, not sure if he should say it, but if he couldn't say something to someone when they were on a deserted island, merely days away from death, then when was the best time? She looked at him, expectantly, and raised a thin eyebrow.

'Yes?' she pushed when he faltered.

'You're a really good friend, June. I've never had a female friend before.' He leant over and hugged her. He relished the sensation of human comfort and she returned it tightly.

'Do you know, Toby Masters, you're a really good friend to me too. In fact, I think apart from my very lovely, but patronising PA, Tom, I don't think I've ever had a male friend before.' She looked out to the lagoon. 'And I couldn't think of anyone else I'd like to star-float across a bay with.' She laughed and he cuffed her gently around the ear.

'Look out for the sharks then,' Toby suggested and she squealed in fake horror.

'Right, time to feed our island family. Hopefully this will keep us all going.' June looked down at the octopus which was accompanied by three small fish that looked a little like red mullet.

'I'll take them over.' Toby placed most of the food on palm leaves and carried it gently over to Emily, who was seated on his old throne, and Zoe who remained very still on the sand in the shade.

'Lunch, ladies,' he cooed gently and Emily looked up gratefully. Her face was lined with dirt, her cheeks were sunken and the pashmina June had tied around her for a little sun protection hung loosely off her shoulder blades. The bruises from the CPR Zoe performed, which had bloomed out across her chest and over her ribs the last few days, had begun to recede, leaving patches of light-green islands across her top half. Weakly, she took the morsels of food Toby had brought over and nodded in appreciation. June joined them and had brought water.

'Come on Emily, remember, you need to stay strong for your girls,' she reminded, in a way which was, Toby felt, neither chastening like a headmistress nor to be ignored and it did the job. Emily did as she was told and sipped gently between bites of octopus.

More to keep the thought off his mind that he needed something to eat too, Toby tried to start a conversation.

'Nice eh? I found this one,' he said, aware of the pride in his voice, but after weeks of the other three looking after him, it felt good to return the favour.

'Did you... spear it... with that?' Emily asked quietly, with great effort, and nodded at the large stick Toby had spent the morning unsuccessfully spear-fishing with. Blushing a little, Toby decided he needed to make a confession.

'No, well, no. It was... well.'

'He picked it out of a puddle,' June explained, which made Emily smile.

'Rock pool, actually,' he corrected, 'a big rock pool, and it was still very much alive when I got to it. So it's safe to eat.'

'He didn't like the eyes though.' June nudged Emily, which made her smile again. Toby felt remorseful for being a dick to her in the early days. However, the memory of the octopus distracted him and made him shudder.

'No, he kept staring at me. I'm sure he was pleading with me not to kill him. But a man's got to do, what a…'

Emily interrupted.

'What a woman usually does?'

'Leave him alone,' grunted Zoe, who pushed herself up painfully and squinted at the light. 'He's sensitive.' She smiled at him and lay back down, worn out with defending Toby's honour.

'Nice to see you've woken up.' He sat down and carefully arranged his legs either side of her, pulling Zoe up so she could rest against his chest. She grumbled, but it was the only way he could prop her up easily.

'Here you go.' June handed Toby some water which he dripped carefully into Zoe's mouth, but some splashed over her face which caused her to splutter.

'Sorry,' he said and poured it slower into her mouth as she gulped it down. Eventually, she signalled she had had enough, and before she could say no, Toby placed some octopus in her mouth. He had a horrible suspicion she was trying to avoid food, so the rest of them could eat, but he wasn't ready for that. They were all getting off this island, and to do that, everyone needed strength.

'Come on, there's plenty more. He was a big guy,' he cajoled and popped another mouthful of the octopus in.

'Oh yeah, you should hear the story,' June piped up. 'He had to wrestle the octopus out of the ocean apparently. The size of a grown man it was.'

Emily joined in weakly, 'I hear he had to bare-knuckle fight it.'

In front of him Toby thought he could feel Zoe slightly shake and he realised she was laughing very, very gently.

'All the women in the world and I end up with you three,' he moaned. 'Could have had Julia Roberts, Reese Witherspoon, Kylie. But no. I end up with the three fucking Ronnies.'

'Who?' he heard Zoe ask quietly and innocently, which made the other two laugh harder at his expense.

*

'There's no way you're going to get there, with those.' Emily indicated the island across the lagoon whilst eyeing up the two large blue plastic canisters Toby had found.

'They're light. Empty. If we hold on to them we should be able to float,' Toby repeated whilst Emily shook her head slowly. They'd been having this disagreement for the last ten minutes or so, since he'd dragged them up from the shoreline after fishing.

'I can't see how. Where do you hold on to? They're smooth.' Before he could say anything, she continued, 'What if we get out there and, unknowingly, get dragged out to sea by some swell or something? We have no idea what's outside of this lagoon. We could drown,' she pointed out.

Again.

With exasperation written all over his face, Toby

stayed sat down next to the canisters. The morning's fishing and carrying of wood and water was taking its toll. He rubbed absent-mindedly at his ankle to help with the stiffness and Emily tried to soften towards him. She knew he'd only been trying to help, but after her near-death experience in the pool she'd become worried about everything they were doing, constantly concerned that she would never see her children again.

'I can't,' she started and Toby stopped her.

'I know, you can't see how,' he began, but this time it was her turn to stop him.

'Don't second-guess me, Tobes,' she smiled sleepily. 'What I was going to say was I can't do it. I can't swim out there with a float and risk it all. Not again.' She broke off and Toby waited to see if there was more to come. When nothing did, he ventured a look at her.

'Em, I know. I get it. But the way we're going I don't think we'll be able to swim back for anyone if we end up deciding to stay. You'd be on your own,' he emphasised.

Emily knitted her brow.

'Well, no. I'd be with Zoe, wouldn't I?' She nodded in the direction of the woman who saved her, but who now looked like she could do with saving of her own, sleeping in the shelter. 'She's not going anywhere, is she?'

Looking in Zoe's direction, Toby shuffled a little uncomfortably.

'We're just going to put her on one of the floats and swim behind her. We're not leaving her here, despite her efforts to make us.'

June had been silent until this point, gutting fish and sharpening some wood to cook them on a slight distance from Emily and Toby. 'What if you or I swim over, as we have more energy? Then, if we think the other island is better to live on, we make a fire and the others make their way over.'

This time it was Toby's chance to shake his head.

'No, because we'd been hoping to double up the float for people. If there's just one float for the three of you, I don't think it would work. You'd sink.'

June thought carefully. 'That suggests you think you'd be the one going over on your own,' she pointed out.

'Of course.'

'Because you're the man?' Emily asked, surprised at his return to sexism and machismo.

'Because I'm stronger right now than the rest of you, and if necessary I might be able to swim back part of the way to help,' he said, defending himself.

'But if I went first you'd be able to use your strength to help get Emily and Zoe over,' explained June, who Emily was sure was behind this latest rescue idea, 'and, I think you could have both of those drums, lashed together in some way, for the three of you. I'll use something else as a float,' she continued.

Emily was nodding; she could see the benefit behind what June was saying, but she was worried too.

'What if the other island doesn't seem any better – will you be able to get back to us?'

'Hopefully. With a bit of rest, I'll come back,' she replied grimly.

'I don't like this one bit. Not one bit,' Toby remonstrated once more and this time Emily understood; he had been at the mercy of their care for the first few weeks and felt he owed it to them to help now. She squeezed his hand gently, getting his attention.

'Toby, I don't like it either. But, I realise, you're both right. We haven't got much of anything left here, we need to move. We know we can't go back to the first beach, that's worse than here. We know there's nothing that side apart from more forest, which is seriously hard to get through. Our options are limited and, it would appear, one of them needs to be across the bay.'

She paused and looked out, fighting the urge to cry.

'You'll be helping Zoe a lot if you stayed here to get us across.' She was sure it was Toby and Zoe she saw kissing by the fire.

Then, with a deep sense of realisation, Emily added, 'I don't know how much strength either of us really have…'

She knew she'd been feeling beyond drained these past few days, and understood that a lot of it came from almost drowning, but it was something else too. It felt like her body was beginning to shut down slowly. She felt bone-achingly tired. Zapped of every life source she had.

It had become harder to find the words she needed, too; they'd get lost on their way from her brain to her mouth and more often than not she'd tried to steer away from conversations, choosing sleep instead. She knew her arguments against going to the other island came from her worry that she'd not be able to make the swim and she was sure she didn't have any more energy in setting up yet another camp.

She was done.

Realising June and Toby were looking at her, she laughed briefly.

'Did I do it again?' They nodded as she'd broken off mid-sentence when she'd become distracted. Refocusing, she looked at Toby. 'It makes the most sense for you to help us across, and for June to go alone.'

'Bottles.' The word came from the shelter and Zoe lifted her head.

'What?' asked Emily.

'Plastic bottles. As floats,' Zoe rasped. 'Find enough of them and she can float with them.'

Toby's face lit up with a smile.

'That's genius, Zo, genius. Yes of course. Let's find a load of plastic bottles, some rope and tie them so you can use them a bit like a rubber ring.' He grabbed June and hugged her.

'There are times when I'm incredibly relieved there's no paparazzi nearby looking for some sort of dreadful photo for *Heat* magazine.' She winced. 'A plastic bottle rubber ring... I ask you.'

Emily couldn't help but laugh.

'Well, they already would have had a field day, what with our wonderful footwear.' They all looked down at the latest collection of washed-up flip-flops and jelly sandals they were all wearing. 'And, since we've given up on the bin-liner dresses, the camp's nudity—'

'They were very warm, and can we please not call them dresses?' Toby feigned, covering himself, and laughed.

'Our lack of a visit to a hairdressers for the last two months,' June ran her hand through her hair that resembled straw, 'and, of course, if they got close to us, our incredible body odour and stale breath.' She got the hiccups from laughing. 'Yep, I think *Heat* would have a lot to print. As would *The Sun*, *The Mirror*, *The Daily Mail*.'

'Celebs in hair-frizz shock, that's all the *Mail* would need,' June added. 'Oh, and they'd mention our bodies in various ways too.'

Nodding sagely, Emily agreed.

'Oh yes, there'd be a comparison of how thin we all are, and who'd benefited from this island diet.' She grimaced.

Toby shook his head.

'I didn't realise how bad this stuff was for you all. I'm in the papers a lot, but it's always about who I'm shagging. Not what I'm wearing or how many pounds I've put on.' He looked sad.

'Every female celeb story there is, there'll be a description of what she's wearing or wore at a recent event, who she's been seen with, how thin she is. Or how many children she has. That's how we're defined,' June explained.

'Well, if we ever get away from this place, maybe we can start to change that,' Toby suggested and, for once, Emily didn't want to argue with him.

She liked the idea. It gave her hope.

*

'Ready?' Toby asked, concern in his green eyes. They'd turned sea green that day, June decided, though maybe that was because she was so near to the water it was reflected in them.

'Nope,' she replied, smiling.

He tied one more bottle to her waist 'just in case' and stepped back to admire his work.

She looked ridiculous, she knew she did. She was wearing the dress she'd landed on the island with, hacked back to cover her shoulders and give her a little protection against the sun. Around her tiny waist was tied some twenty plastic milk cartons they'd found, which, as she started to wade out, were beginning to fan out around her, like flower petals. They were floating though. And she was sure she would too. The ones on her wrists were starting to float either side as well.

'Bye then,' she said carefully to Toby and he smiled.

'Bye kiddo, see you soon.' He looked earnestly in her eyes. He would see her soon. She would see them all very, very soon. Nothing awful would happen. She knew she had to believe that.

June carried on wading through the water; it sucked around her waist and pushed under her arms, gradually cradling her upwards so she could start to kick gently. The floats worked, adding buoyancy and ensuring she didn't need to use too much energy when she began swimming. Keeping her head above the water, June ensured she kept the island she was aiming for in front of her.

The water was warm, so similar to body temperature in fact that June felt soothed. The rhythm of the ocean was calming, soporific even, and she felt herself being lightly pulled forwards, allowing the drumbeat of nature to drive her on. Thinking she hadn't gone far, she turned to wave at Toby and give him a thumbs up, only to see he was already distant, the waves of heat rippling around him.

No sooner had the thought occurred to her that she was now completely on her own, then something brushed past June's right leg, causing her to gasp and take in a mouthful of the briny water.

'Don't panic. Don't panic. Just breathe.' The mantra she kept repeating out loud to the empty sea gave June strength. She needed to do this for the rest of them. She was going to find a way out for strong but sensitive Zoe, determined but hilarious Emily and, of course, irritating yet brilliant Toby. The water sloshed over her face as the waves became rockier the further away from both islands she got. June estimated she had to be roughly halfway and although that cheered her, she could feel any strength begin to ebb away as increasingly she had to swim to stay on course, rather than float her way across.

What was that?

She was sure something just brushed past her leg again.

Don't look down.

Don't look down.

June had no idea if there were sharks in this patch of water; she'd never thought to ask when they were prepping for the show as she'd had no plans to get wet. Now look at her, she thought, grinning ruefully, hastily regretting her mistake as she took in another, bigger, mouthful of water. This time it caught the back of her throat, shooting painful spikes of salt into her nose and lungs. Heaving. Coughing. Spluttering. None of these actions helped her to continue to swim, instead upsetting the course she had been taking and causing her to have to swim stronger.

Her eyelids felt heavy. She knew she'd not eaten enough for days to ensure she was strong enough for this, but wasn't that the reason she was trying to get across? To look for more food? To find a better beach where they could build an even bigger fire – one which would have to attract attention. Her shoulders ached. A burning, prickling sensation was making its way down her leg and she wondered, briefly, if it was from overexertion.

Or something else.

She felt like she was having to work really hard when she suddenly realised that around half of the floats had come off her when she'd had her coughing fit, working themselves loose and leaving a trail of plastic behind her. If she did need to come back, how she would achieve it wasn't clear.

Putting all thoughts of a return journey to the back of her mind, June looked ahead and allowed herself a moment of cheer – the other island was getting nearer. Buoyed by the sight, she allowed herself to push her way through the water, noticing the change in temperature as it regained more warmth. She hadn't realised how cool the water had got when she was halfway between the two islands, but now, in the warmer shallows, she enjoyed the feeling of it spreading across her body. Gradually the water receded and she found herself able to touch the floor, the luxury of the sand under her feet bringing her joy.

But as she walked out, where there had been a prickling sensation on her leg, she realised it now felt as though it was on fire. Looking down, June couldn't see the problem as she still had some bottles around her waist. Tearing and discarding them on the sandy beach, so similar to the one she had just left, June looked down and saw an angry red rash making its way up and down her right leg.

Jellyfish sting? Maybe.

She didn't know if there were any here. Hot, salty tears pricked at June's eyes. Why hadn't she asked about this in the programme preparation? Why had she paid more attention to which Manolos she was being gifted than whether there were man-eating sharks? Instead of choosing Temperley gowns, she should have been thinking jellyfish stings and how to fix them.

Her leg was throbbing painfully now and the thought crossed June's mind that it could be one of those fast-acting poisons which spread upwards to the heart. She'd die here. The others would find her body once they crossed the bay.

What a fat lot of good she was.

Lying back on the sand, she allowed the tears to flow. She wished she could have done something more interesting than thirty years on the same programme. Why hadn't she taken more risks? Enjoyed life more? Said yes more. Been a bit braver and a little less mean to herself?

'I promise, if I live, I will make a better life for myself,' she whispered to the azure-blue sky.

The combination of heat from the sun's strong rays, the exertion from crossing the sea, and whatever was happening in her body from the sting she'd received was pushing her deep, deep down into a fog of exhaustion. If she closed her eyes, she could sleep here forever, she realised. Sleep for a thousand years.

Giving in to it all, June closed her eyes. It felt good to have peace. Lying there, listening to her breathing, she

felt calm. If this was it, she'd done her best. Breathe in…
breathe out… breathe in… breathe—

June sat up quickly, the world snapping back into
vivid, technicolour reality. What was that? She could hear
something.

Music.

The Sun Online

STAR SURVIVORS

*The world is in shock today as four celebrities, thought to
have died in a helicopter crash almost two months ago,
have been found on a desert island.*

*The four, which includes Bond megastar Zoe Stenson,
disgraced former children's author Toby Masters,
Instagram Mumpreneur sensation Emily Chase and ex-
Wake Up presenter June Sharp, were all discovered on the
uninhabited atoll of Manuae in the South Pacific.*

*It was only the bravery of Ms Sharp which ensured the
rescue of the four after she swam from one side of the atoll
to the other, looking for resources, when she was discovered
by a science expedition.*

*The scientists only visit the atoll every four years
to monitor the wildlife, and it was their temporary
encampment that June stumbled into a day ago, which
quickly brought about the rescue of the other three stars.*

A spokesperson on behalf of Star Survivor, said:

*'We are unbelievably relieved that the four have been
found. We cannot begin to imagine the circumstances they
found themselves in and are thrilled to say that, whilst*

they're in need of a lot of looking after, they're all in good health.

'Due to the severe circumstances they've been surviving in, all are being treated for heat exhaustion, dehydration and starvation and are in hospital being monitored until such time as the doctors believe them to be well enough to return to the UK.'

They added:

'We request that they, and their families, are all given the respect and privacy they so desperately need at this moment.'

It is thought that the youngest of the four, Zoe, is suffering the most after losing a third of her body weight.

The families of the stars have all been contacted and are hoping to see their missing loved ones at a date to be announced shortly.

Chapter Six

Zoe stared at the mirror, unable to square the image confronting her with the one she'd seen a thousand times over.

Starting at the top, she took in the wild, untamed mass of wiry, dark hair. Two months of heat and saltwater had combined to ensure her naturally coily hair had, with no access to products or care, transformed itself into a knotty and tangled jumble. Despite her plaiting it and tying it back as best she could whilst on the island, Zoe knew her hairdresser would have a heart attack when he tried to put her back together again.

In the meantime, Zoe felt the answer would be to crop it tightly to her head, and allow everything to start over, though she knew it would mean wigs and extensions for the next couple of years if she went back to the film production schedule she was signed up to.

She appraised herself. Her usually tawny-brown skin had turned to a burnt sienna under the strong sun, with hints of rose-gold highlights. Smiling uncertainly at this stranger, Zoe stood back a little in her hospital room to get a look in the full-length mirror.

Still wearing the mint-green hospital robe she'd been in since their rescue, Zoe reached slowly to the back of her neck and pulled at the string to untie the bow. She stepped lightly out of the gown and looked up.

'Fuck.'

The sound broke the stillness of the private room she'd been in the past two days. She'd been hooked up to a drip since her admission, and fed carefully with small, but nutritious meals to begin to fatten her up. She'd noticed the look in the nurses' eyes when they came to tend to her, but she assumed their concern was a well-worn attitude to anyone in their care. However, on seeing herself properly for the first time, Zoe had to admit she did look like she needed looking after. There wasn't an ounce of fat on her body and though she usually was a slim person, the woman staring back at her screamed for ice cream. Her collarbone pushed painfully against her skin, accentuated by the sticks that had replaced her arms.

Never one to have large breasts, Zoe looked down at the pitiful mounds hanging limply and wondered if she'd ever see them again. She could count all her ribs. But it was her hips which were the biggest surprise. Zoe had inherited her Mum's pear shape and was used to a thin layer of fat sitting across her thighs. But this woman's hips jutted out like a coat hanger and when she turned to check out her behind, she realised she was even more upset at the loss of definition in that than she was her missing breasts.

But she was still alive. She knew everything she was looking at was temporary. They'd survived almost two months, and they'd all been rescued.

The flashing lights across her eyes had started up again and Zoe knew she had to get her gown on and get back into bed. She still had little energy and the sparkling across her vision was an indicator she needed to sit down.

Sitting back into bed, Zoe allowed herself the joy of resting her head back on the plumped-up pillows, breathing in the smell of clean sheets. The first night, two days ago, when she'd been allowed to settle in this room, after the numerous check-ups the doctors had insisted on doing on her to be sure she was okay, the bed had felt so luxurious compared to sleeping in their shelter night after night. But although she'd been shattered, she couldn't sleep. The sounds of the corridor outside her room, though muted, were different to the ones she'd been used to going to sleep to. No more shrieks from the trees. No more waves crashing along the floor. No more Emily snoring gently next to her.

Zoe had realised she'd become used to sleeping alongside a warm body and having that sense of companionship. Her lonely room and single bed served only to make her long for someone even stronger.

'Lunch.' The day nurse who'd been tending to Zoe was back, this time bearing something that smelled delicious and, for the first time, she reached out for the tray.

'Well done, ready to feed yourself are you?' asked the older woman who'd been helping her the past two days as she'd fought through feverish nightmares.

'Please.' Zoe smiled and took the tray, hesitating when she saw it was some sort of beef stew. She'd been vegan before the island, she needed to return to that, but she was salivating at the scent of slowly roasted meat and vegetables in a thick gravy. Gingerly she dipped her spoon into the sauce and enjoyed the heavenly sensation of it. She took her time over each mouthful, savouring the sensation of chewing it, the rough texture of it moving down her throat, the gradual filling up of her stomach. It was so satisfying.

'Eat up now, we've plenty more,' the nurse reminded her as she offered Zoe a hunk of bread to mop up the gravy, watching as the actress gulped down a large glass of cold water.

'Sorry, s'delicious.' Zoe's words got lost in the last mouthful of lunch and her nurse laughed.

'Well I'm glad, love, I was worried when you came here – I didn't know if we'd lose you.'

Zoe nodded. She had given up on all hopes of rescue the last week or so on the island. She'd hoped she'd die in her sleep, then the others wouldn't have to keep worrying about her.

The day they were rescued felt like a dream now. She'd been lying on the beach and it had been hours since June had gone. Zoe had decided to just lie on the sand and allow the sun to dry the life out of her. She was, she realised now, still in shock after Emily's near-death incident and, according to one of the doctors, may have been suffering with the trauma of it.

When the helicopter landed on the beach, Zoe allowed the doctors and nurses to tend to her cuts and bruises, to bandage the ones which had become infected. She'd watched lifelessly at the hospital as they'd hooked her up to an IV, taken her blood pressure numerous times and given her countless pills. Zoe had allowed the nurses to bathe her gently, watching in horror at the colour of the water coming off as they washed her. Allowed them to trim her nails, wash her hair. Feed her. She'd been docile and undemanding, dazed by the onslaught of people and how clean and pristine the hospital was in comparison to the riot of colour the island had offered.

She'd not seen Toby, June or Emily the whole time she'd been here.

'Where are the others?' she asked, aware her voice was no longer cracking due to dehydration, but retaining a slight huskiness, brought on from swimming in the salty sea every day.

Her nurse smiled.

'I'm glad you asked – I was beginning to think you'd forgotten about them.' She chuckled and took Zoe's tray. 'You're all in the same hospital, in fact you're all in this corridor but' she began as Zoe looked as though she'd get up, 'we need you all to stay in your own rooms for one more day; three of you have infections in your cuts and we need to make sure we've treated you before you expose your fellow survivors to anything they may pick up.' She nodded gently at Zoe who mirrored the nod in response.

'My mum? My dad?' she asked, suddenly aware she'd not given a thought to anything except deciding she was going to survive.

Smiley nurse grinned again.

'We've called them and they know you're safe and well but you had so many delirious moments the past forty-eight hours, we thought it better for your fever to pass before you spoke to them. We thought they'd been through enough without hearing you talking about attacking chickens.' She laughed at Zoe's confusion. 'We got to hear a lot of strange chatter from you, but I think you're through it now.'

Zoe yawned and the nurse took that as a sign to leave her. She closed the shutters to her room, casting deep shadows across the white walls, allowing the megastar to sleep peacefully for the first time in days.

Stopping at the door, the nurse looked at the globe's most well-known actress and hoped she would be okay when the real world came knocking soon. She looked so fragile and young, so unlike the healthy woman in the films.

The hospital had been besieged by members of the press from all over the world since it was announced the four had been found, and it had become something of a security nightmare to keep them all out as they vied to get the first photo. The exclusive would be worth hundreds of thousands to whoever secured it.

The only answer had been to shut down an entire ward and post security personnel at every door with just-cleared medical staff allowed in and out of the rooms.

Shutting the door to Zoe's room carefully, she nodded at the security guard outside.

Not for her the life of a celebrity, she thought to herself, making her way down the quiet corridor.

Far too complicated.

Toby stared at the TV screen in his room without seeing. It didn't matter because he couldn't watch it as it wouldn't turn on. He'd been staring into space for what seemed like hours, rigid with boredom.

He'd been in the hospital for two days and still only saw the nurses and doctors when they came on their rounds. There had been little conversation with them and he had begun to wonder what the point of the rescue was. What was even more unnerving for him was the distinct impression they were all in on something he wasn't. The furtive glances. The raised eyebrows. He was sure something was going on, but with so many of them in masks and other PPE he couldn't see their faces properly to be certain.

One of the only things Toby had learnt was that out of the four, he and two of the women had caught infections from the cuts they'd picked up from the coral when they were fishing and swimming. He'd noticed he had a cut on his side, but with everything else that had happened the last week or so he'd not taken much notice. The masks and the PPE were all precautionary, to be sure they'd not picked up any infectious diseases. Toby thought it was more to protect the health of the staff rather than him. Realising now how lucky they'd been, part of him was annoyed he hadn't listened to the safety briefing before they'd left for the programme. Had he known about their poor chances of survival at the outset, he wasn't sure he'd have been that gung-ho about it. Especially in the later weeks.

After much discussion between themselves, the doctors had decided Toby's ankle had healed relatively well, and although he'd complained of it being a little achy, they had told him it was best left alone. But Toby sighed moodily and threw a balled-up sock in the air to the ceiling– his ankle wasn't the only thing being left alone. He seemed to spend hours just waiting for something to break up the monotony of the day with no news from the outside world. He caught the sock and threw it up again.

If he was honest, he'd have thought the discovery of four missing celebrities would have been something people would want to talk to him about. He'd assumed he'd be inundated with interview requests. But he'd received nothing except for one call from the *Star Survivor* production team telling him to get better and they'd be briefing him soon.

But no one had told him on what.

Throwing the sock ball up and down, Toby's thoughts moved to that of his fellow islanders.

He wondered how they all were.

He'd been deeply worried about Zoe the day they were rescued. She had been strapped firmly onto a stretcher and hoisted up into a helicopter which had flown away quickly. Emily and Toby had been helped carefully onto the scientists' boat which had then headed to the mainland where they were brought to the hospital. He didn't even see June, but they had promised him she was okay.

Toby stood up and looked out of the tiny square window which let in a small ray of light. He could smell the sea but couldn't see it. He felt trapped.

Closing his eyes, Toby imagined being able to finally talk to his mum– another luxury that was being kept from him. Every time he'd asked for a phone it was like he'd asked for the moon. Apparently dead people aren't expected to need their number anymore, he thought. Or bank accounts. Everything had been frozen.

'Food, Toby?'

The nurse who smiled all the time was back and Toby's smile was of genuine warmth.

'Have I ever told you you're lovely, Rosemary?' he said as she brandished a huge bowl of something beefy and stewy which made Toby salivate.

'Over here now, we need to get you built up again, don't we?' She grinned.

'Rosemary?' Toby tried to be careful as she busied herself around his room, not meeting his eye.

'Mmm?'

'What am I not being told?' he asked tentatively but noticed her reaction. Her body stopped, briefly still, and she hesitated before speaking.

'N... nothing,' she replied.

'I don't think that's true...' Toby chewed carefully for a moment and watched her for signs. 'Any more bread?' he asked and she nodded, relieved, he thought, to avoid his questions, then disappeared for some extra food. He chewed in the silence, contemplative.

She returned a few minutes later, and Toby assumed she was going to continue pretending he wasn't there when she popped the bread roll on his tray. Then she did something unexpected. Instead of walking away, she paused, then withdrew a silver mobile from her pocket.

'Your agent has asked you hear it from her, but I think you need forewarning,' she admitted and typed something on her phone, then held the screen in front of a confused Toby.

'Here, you take a look. I'll come back for it in a few minutes and then this evening I'll suggest it's okay for your agent to call as you're much fitter now. More able.' She smiled sadly at him and backed out of the room.

'Hey, wait,' Toby shouted to her as she closed the door, 'what the fuck is going on? Why is me living – no, surviving for fuck's sake – not to be celebrated? Why all this cloak-and-dagger bullshit?'

With no response, he looked down at the glowing blue light of the screen and started to make out what she'd been keen for him to see. The headline quoted online read *'Ghosted by a Master'* and Toby's heartbeat quickened as he began to read an account from his ghostwriter. The one who had signed her life away to protect his series, took the money and stayed quiet for nearly ten years.

'All you needed was for me to die, wasn't it,' he muttered. 'Just after recognition were you?'

Under the first article was another, then another. Toby quickly scrolled and saw that a huge online movement appeared to have gained momentum due to his ghostwriter having unmasked herself. There was even a hashtag with #IWroteFor trending for two weeks whilst authors who Toby respected were outed as being ghost-written. His apparent death had caused the destruction of at least twenty well-respected and lucrative authors' reputations and their books.

'Shit.'

Toby looked up from the phone and considered the situation. Him being alive wasn't the good news people had wanted, as he'd originally thought; instead there appeared to be a lynch mob prepared to tear him to shreds. He'd shattered their illusions about what an author should be and, if he believed the thousands of comments, had ruined many of their childhoods.

He read out loud some of the comments.

'A talentless moron, nice. A waste of space, excellent. Would have been better off dead, right. Oh, I shouldn't have survived and am a disgrace to my family. Thanks. Thanks so much. You actually would have preferred it if I had died.' He was shocked at the level of abuse and the trial by social media without his side of the story and shook his head, catching sight of his forlorn appearance in the mirror across the room. A shell of a man stared back at him.

He resumed looking at the comments and news articles, then pulled up short when he saw that people had graffitied the side of his house. The papers had reported on it, but underneath the story links were the comments where people praised the vandalism.

They declared him as deserving to die in the helicopter crash.

They'd even sprayed 'liar' on his mum's fence.

'Oh Mum, I'm so sorry,' he whispered.

Then a thought occurred to him. There'd been very little response from his agent whose idea it had been to have a ghostwriter in the first place. The same agent who'd made a fuck-ton of money out of Toby and his ghostwriter. Very, very quiet. Merely a statement on the company's website to say the films would be no longer in production, the books no longer printed and his name posthumously removed from their lists of authors.

So that was it.

He didn't exist.

*

Emily stared at the mobile in her hand. In the week since they'd been rescued, she'd been through two days of total inertia in the hospital where she'd finally, completely, relaxed. She'd slept. She'd been fed. She'd had as much water as she could drink. Her injuries had been looked after and she'd allowed the nurse to bathe her. Every part of her body had been in pain but the sleep and the care had helped her and everything had begun to heal, but she was desperate to talk to Matt and the girls.

When she'd been awake, the nursing staff had explained time and again she couldn't see her family yet just in case of infectious diseases. But she needed the warmth of her girls in her arms, wanted to see their smiling faces. They, and Matt, had been all that had kept her going.

And then reality had crept in.

Slowly, fingers of anxiety had worked their way into her thoughts. What if, when she called, Matt wouldn't want to talk to her? What if, in the last two months, he'd decided he was better off without her? What if the girls were frightened of her? She couldn't explain it but the anxiety was so strong, she felt as though she was strangled – she couldn't form sentences.

Her nurses had told her she'd had numerous calls from well-wishers, from her agent, from Matt, but she'd refused all of them, just in case she started crying and didn't know when to stop. Flowers filled her room, from zingy orange lilies which made her sneeze to calming cream roses, and armfuls of cards were piling up, unopened, on the cabinet next to her. Emily had no idea who was sending these to her, but she didn't have the energy to look. She'd survived, but how would she put into words just how painful every second of every day had been?

Looking around the room, as if with fresh eyes, Emily noticed gifts were piled up too. Numerous boxes stacked according to size.

'What's in those?' she asked the nurse who'd come in.

The woman looked around.

'Ah, I think you have a few fans.' She smiled, unsure how much Emily knew. She looked keenly at her. 'You know there's a bunch of photographers just waiting for you all to come out, don't you?'

Emily pulled a face.

'Really? Why?'

The nurse laughed.

'Because you four surviving is the biggest news story of the year. You've made headlines all over the world. You must know that?'

Shaking her head, Emily felt a bubble of nausea and excitement.

'I had no idea. No one told me,' she started, distracted by a woman pushing through into the room, holding a pink helium balloon which bore the word *'Congratulations'* and a picture of a teddy.

She saw the look of confusion on Emily's face and looked up at the balloon.

'Ah, yes, sorry. They don't have many "well done you didn't die" balloons in the gift shop so I thought this would do.' She laughed throatily and then, to ensure Emily fully understood, added, 'You're not pregnant, it's okay.'

Emily grinned a little awkwardly.

'Thanks, though I think I'd know that—' She broke off. 'Sorry, who are you?' she asked of the impeccably dressed blonde with porcelain-white skin and the sharpest bob she'd ever seen.

The nurse looked concerned.

'You said you were her agent, I checked you out. If you're another of those journ—' Her worries were dismissed swiftly by the blonde with a quick wave.

'I am her agent, she just hasn't met me yet.'

Turning to Emily, she fixed a piercing blue-eyed stare at her.

'I'm Angie – the person who sent you to *Star Survivor* before, well—' She stopped, aware what she was implying.

'Before I didn't make it?' prompted Emily, recognising the clipped tones of the woman who she'd only ever spoken to on the phone before and trying to reconcile the squat woman she'd somehow assumed Angie to be.

Her agent smiled tightly.

'Exactly. Now, we need to get down to business, but before we do, I need to know how much you know.' She tilted her head to the side, as though to get a better reception, and Emily shook her own.

'About?'

'About you. About Slummin' It Mummin' It?' Angie said the words with such meaning, but Emily couldn't make out why.

178

'Er, I know a lot about me. I am me.' Maybe this was some sort of test to see if her mental capacity was screwed? 'I know about SIMI because again… that's me,' she replied, and raised an eyebrow.

'Yes, yes, I know that. I know that you know that. What I need to understand from you,' at this point, Angie came over to Emily's bed and sat carefully on the end of it, causing Emily to shift her feet a little at the extra weight, 'is whether you know what's been happening whilst you've been playing dead.'

Emily was aghast.

'I've not been "playing dead", I've been very much alive. And WE'VE been trying to survive, whereas everyone else appears to have decided to leave us to die,' she exclaimed loudly.

'Shh,' the whisper from Angie was patronising, 'calm down. I didn't mean for you to take offence by it.' She rushed on to stop Emily talking again. 'Have you spoken to Matt yet?' Emily shook her head and Angie nodded lightly. 'Good, he's done as he's told. Then you know nothing.'

Before she could open her mouth in protest, Angie explained.

'Ever since you four went missing, there's been a lot of interest in you all. The first two weeks were chaos. If there was a post with yours or any of the others' names in it, it would go viral. If there was a mention on the news of any chance of survival, the phone lines would be jammed with people offering condolences or titbits of advice.' She looked to check Emily was listening and, happy, continued.

'Anyway, the *Star Survivor* lot paid for a month of search and rescue and they found nothing, so they – as in the programme,' she clarified as Emily was getting confused, 'called off the search and rescue and declared you all as dead.' She waited to see what, if any, reaction Emily gave. Seeing nothing to worry her, she continued. 'But Matt, well, Matt, bless his heart, didn't believe you'd died. He couldn't.' She pressed Emily's hand with her own – warm despite its cool appearance. 'He began a crowdfunder with Zoe's family to pay for more rescue missions and that's when things really took off.'

Emily drank some water.

'What took off? The funding?'

Angie shook her head.

'Oh fuck no. The funding campaign was awful. Turns out a lot of people don't want to give money to celebrities. Think you've all got plenty – whether you're dead or alive – no, the crowdfunder was abysmal and Matt was really downhearted. No, he'd been wearing a T-shirt with a phrase you'd written on the last photo you added to Instagram and people began asking for one as well.'

'What did it say?' Emily could only remember a slightly washed-out photo of her bags, being careful not to say what she was doing so she didn't get in trouble with the producers of *Star Survivor*.

'At least you can say I tried.'

'Is that what I said?'

'Yep, but Matt just abbreviated it to "I Tried".'

'That's nice.'

'Better than nice. The hashtag #ITried became a mantra, a way of living a...' Angie struggled to sum up the wave of public outpouring towards Emily and the gorgeous Matt, 'a call to arms. It was a way of expressing everything we do as women, as mothers, as people in just two words.'

Emily wasn't sure what to say; it was nice to inspire people though.

'Emily,' Angie tried to get her currently most important client to look at her, 'look at your Instagram page.' She passed her phone to Emily who stared.

'There's got to be something wrong here? I had 1.5 million followers when I left for the island,' she started, quietly.

'There's nothing wrong, you've got 18 million followers now, and it's going up by the day – especially now you've survived,' Angie enthused. 'You'll have 20 million by the end of the month.' Her excitement was palpable. 'Don't you see? You have a voice bigger than we ever thought you would. Your book has already pre-sold a million copies.' She beamed.

But Emily knotted her eyebrows together in confusion.

'I haven't written it yet.'

'Doesn't matter, the people want you. They're baying for you and we need to get you out there ASAP to make things happen. You need to start back on social media as soon as possible, thanking your followers for their love and commitment – you need to be riding this now.' Angie's words tumbled out as though they'd been stored up, ready for the moment.

'Now?' asked Emily, scared, excited and worried beyond belief. What had she done? What had Matt done? What was happening?

'Now.' Angie was firm.

June stared out of the window of the plane, watching the wisps of frothy cloud go swirling past. Two months ago she'd slept through as much of her flight as possible, to avoid talking to anyone. Today, the experience felt unreal. Ethereal even.

'Champagne?' the impeccably dressed steward leaned in and showed her the Veuve Clicquot La Grande Dame she'd dreamt about on the beach.

'Just a little glass,' she replied. The bubbles were quickly going to her head and, after two months off the booze, June was surprised to learn she wasn't all that bothered about going back on it.

'June – have you seen the size of the bed?' Emily had poked her head into June's First-Class suite and was beaming at her. 'The lovely flight attendant, Sahara, made mine up for me.' She squealed a little. 'I'm sort of pleased it's going to take us a day to get home.' She giggled. 'Not that I don't want to see the kids of course, but this is quite fun.' Emily looked concerned at June, who didn't seem to be reflecting her enthusiasm.

'What's the matter? Aren't you happy?'

June smiled. 'Of course, who wouldn't be in a place like this?' She smiled more widely, expanding her arms to take in the stunning First-Class suites aboard the plane they'd all been put in for their return to Heathrow.

Emily smiled back. 'Guess what happened when I went into my suite for the first time?'

June shook her head. 'No idea, what?'

'You see that there,' she indicated a compartment in the

suite, 'it's a wardrobe. I asked Zoe to film me getting in it so I can share it on Insta,' she giggled, 'so I got in, and I fit – I'm only five feet three aren't I, but then Zoe closed the door on me – I was in total darkness.' She giggled again. 'She recorded it all – you'll have to come and see. I got her back though. I got her to lie down on the floor to show how big it was at the same time Sahara came in with our coffees – he took it all very much in his stride to be fair.'

June laughed. 'I see, so that's the new way of measuring is it? Out with metres and in with people?'

'It's amazing though – I swear my first flat was smaller than this. Zoe and I are going to have a pyjama party in my suite – have you seen we get free pyjamas? Temperley ones?' Emily's eyes were wide with awe, then she looked around June's suite.

'June, we've been on board for two hours – you've not opened anything. Look, we've got loads of lovely products too – there's a gorgeous face mist, some body lotion, face cream – Bulgari perfume, you should open it. We can keep them all too,' she urged. Sensing June wasn't as enthusiastic as her, Emily shrugged her shoulders a little. 'You should come over for our PJ party, Sahara is making us some grown-up hot chocolates,' she winked. 'We've got face masks, and,' she poked her head back to the aisle so her voice would carry, 'if Zoe stops being embarrassed, we're going to watch one of her films too.'

Realising she wasn't going to be able to ignore the onslaught of an enthusiastic Emily, June nodded. 'I'll be down in a bit, let me get changed and I'll join you – make sure my hot chocolate has marshmallows.' She grinned.

Appeased, Emily left the suite, pulling the doors

closed behind her, muffling any sounds from outside the cabin. June exhaled and enjoyed the peace and quiet, something she realised she was reluctant to give up. Closing her eyes, she allowed herself a moment to recall their island. The swim to the shore. The rescue. Days spent in hospital. She still felt in shock by their change of circumstances.

'First timers, eh?' Now it was Zoe's turn to open the doors and June shook her head; she wasn't going to get much time alone on this flight. But, she realised, she loved the other two women so much, she didn't mind. They were, she realised, like a family now.

'Bless her, she's enjoying it. Never been in First Class before.' June hadn't either, but she had travelled in Business so often she felt she could take it in her stride a little better. She considered her friend. Emily had emerged from the hospital as incredibly hot property. Not as big as Zoe, June acknowledged, but Zoe was already stratospheric before she went missing. But Emily was in higher demand than herself or Toby.

Poor Toby. She sighed quietly.

'You all right?' Zoe was rubbing some cream into her face. They'd all found their skin kept peeling after the amount of sun exposure they'd had and the only answer was to regularly reapply the thickest cream they could find. She was in tapered black jogging bottoms and a red hoodie, accompanied by some chequered Vans trainers. It was the sort of outfit June would only have worn at home, but somehow, with her gawky nature and affable girl-next-door charm, Zoe owned it.

'Just feeling guilty.'

'About Toby?'

June nodded. Zoe came further into the suite and sat opposite her on one of the sumptuously soft cream leather seats. All the women had been given a double, made for a couple, so there was plenty of room to spread out. She looked keenly at June.

'I've seen the coverage. He's lost a lot of fans hasn't he?'

June nodded. 'I know his name isn't exactly a popular one at the moment, but I hardly think that warrants splitting us up for the return home. Does it? I can't believe they've put him in Economy and us in First.'

'I know. It's shit. I offered to pay for him to be bumped up but they kept saying there wasn't any more room in First,' Zoe replied, causing the two of them to raise their eyebrows, both fully aware the only guests in the First-Class section were them.

'It'll be that guy from Edge Productions; he'll be doing it to make a point to Toby,' June theorised.

'What? Patrick thingamy? Oh, was it his wife who Toby slept with?'

June nodded and saw comprehension dawn on Zoe's face.

'That would make sense I suppose. Probably annoyed that Toby didn't do the show. Toby said that had been the deal, he wasn't even going to be paid for it.'

'Poor Toby.'

The two women were interrupted by Emily in the doorway, wearing some midnight-blue satin pyjamas. 'They've got them in my size. I don't know how they've done it, but these are just the most perfect PJs I've ever had.' Her face fell. 'I get to keep them... right?'

Zoe laughed. 'Yes, you get to keep those,' and Emily beamed.

'Phew, they make a change from M&S. I wasn't sure I could go back,' she giggled. 'What were you talking about? Did I hear mention of poor Toby?' she asked, with a little concern.

'Yes, because we're here with all of this luxury, and he had to be in Economy,' June explained and was surprised when Emily laughed.

'Come on. It's a bit funny, don't you think?'

'Why?'

'Oh, just, it is a bit.' Emily looked at both the women. 'I came to the island in Economy but return in First, he went in Business and comes back in Economy. I know it's not great, but I'm sure he'll be fine,' she added, then her face changed back to happy. 'Come on, pyjamas,' she demanded of Zoe and June, then left.

'Best do as she says.' Zoe grinned and left too. Absentmindedly, June also did as she was told, remembering at the last minute to change into the soft slippers that had been placed in her wardrobe and realising she may never put a pair of heels on again. She vowed to only wear things she was truly comfortable in.

She made the short journey to 1A, where Emily's suite was, and laughed out loud when she walked in. The staff had made a huge effort for them, with piles of pillows across the bed and plenty of room for the three of them. There were face masks, as Emily had promised and—

'We're having pedicures. Sahara insisted.' Emily smiled at the flight attendant who, it appeared, was a master in all arts as far as June was concerned.

'Of course you are.' June smiled, settling next to Zoe, now dressed in matching pyjamas to Emily and June.

'Chocolate?' She offered a small plate of delicate truffles to June, who took one and savoured it. Clothes she was comfortable in, and allowing herself treats every now and then, she vowed. It was the least she owed to her body.

A little later as the three watched a much younger Zoe in a rom-com called *For The Love of God*, where she played a nun who fell in love with a, now June watched it properly, way-too-old-for-her reverend, and sipped on hot chocolates, Emily spoke up.

'I think the Toby thing just shows how fickle all this,' she flapped her hand in the general direction of First, 'really is. Which is why I intend to make the most of it – I have no idea when I'll ever be on First again – if ever.' She grinned. 'Let's get some photos – my followers will love this, we look pretty cute.' She held her brand-new iPhone up to take a selfie of them in their matching night-sets.

June watched their faces reflected back at them. She didn't have any make-up on. She should care, she realised.

But she didn't.

Zoe laughed and held up a V for victory sign.

'She has a point – Toby will be fine, and he's done this before. When we land we'll all be in the photo together – we've all got the press call together. If there's a bit of male posturing from Roberts, then there we have it. It's Toby's fault in the first place – he could have had sex with someone who wasn't married.' She smiled at June.

Nodding, June agreed, although she still felt sorry for him. She went to take a sip of hot chocolate but it left a bitter taste.

'So Emily is going to be a multimillion-selling author, I'm sure I've got a few job offers to wade through.' Secretly June thought Zoe enjoyed being blasé about her popularity. 'What's your plan when we get home?'

'I don't know. Even though it was so hard, I think island survival has made me want to do more. You know?' She looked at Zoe who nodded.

'I've been so worried about going back to normality and returning to the *Wake Up* sofa. I keep thinking how I'll just be trapped in the monotony of life from before. But, after seeing that article,' she referred to something Emily had shown her about *Wake Up* being described as an "under 30s only" joyless programme, 'I know I've lost the *Wake Up* job anyway. So I suppose it's down to me to decide what I do next.'

'Isn't that exciting though?' Emily replied, unpacking some Bowers & Wilkins earphones. 'You've got the chance to shake things up and start again. The clean slate everyone craves. You can do anything.'

'Or you could go back to presenting and just, you know, being the old June. If that's what you'd prefer,' Zoe added kindly.

'Can we keep these?' Emily asked, holding up the earphones.

Zoe shook her head. 'I'm pretty sure you're not meant to.' Emily frowned as Sahara came into the cabin.

Noticing they had a few hours before they landed, June got up. She needed to have a sleep in her own suite.

'Can you make my bed up please?' June asked, just as Emily spoke.

'Can I keep these?' The headphones dangled from her finger and the flight attendant laughed.

'Yes, I'll make your bed up. Would you like some chamomile tea?' he said gently to June who nodded.

'Perfect, thank you.'

Just before he turned out of the room, he winked at Emily.

'We usually say no, but as it's you…'

Emily grinned and clapped her hands together. 'Matt will be so thrilled – he's always wanted a pair of these.'

June began to leave the suite, then turned to face the other two.

'I don't want to be the old June,' she replied quietly.

Zoe was immediately apologetic.

'Oh, fuck, sorry. I don't mean *old* old, just the previous June. The one who was all glamorous and presented morning TV,' Zoe said, hastily trying to make amends, causing June to laugh.

'I know that. I mean I don't want any of that stuff. The heels. The early wake-up calls. Making an effort for other people – it's so tiring, don't you think?'

Zoe smiled, but as June left the two younger women to chatting and taking selfies and generally mucking around, she felt the age gap widen. They'd all been on the same level on the island but their return to real life was beginning to show itself in little ways. The hierarchy of the plane. The interest from the press. The age gap. She still didn't give two hoots about social media and enjoyed instead recalling the time on the island.

Back in the peace of her own cabin, she sipped on her tea and looked at the dark sky, feeling deflated. Compared to the kaleidoscope of vivid colours that etched their way into her memories of her island living, the muted skies and dark buildings she was returning to now filled her not with a longing to escape to her Dorset home, but to get on the next plane out to a new adventure.

In the cabin the TV screen was on mute, but someone had handily left the subtitles on. She watched as a BBC news special report flashed up.

'Their loss shocked the world, but now their discovery has made even bigger news. The four celebrities including Zoe Stenson...' At this point a video montage of Zoe in numerous red-carpet looks was aired, whilst the newsreader continued talking, '... after being rescued from a deserted island in the South Pacific just over a week ago, will be holding their first press conference later today.'

Today. June had lost all sense of time but would have preferred an easing into the timezone, rather than being leapt upon by the media.

'I'm sure there'll be lots of questions, not least how they survived, and whether – as some commentators have suggested – it was all set up. And now the weather and travel where you are.' He threw it over to the local London news and June looked out of the window again.

Set up? Surely no one would suggest what they went through was a set-up? June thought of the severe hunger they'd all experienced. What about the injuries they each received? She still shuddered when she thought how it could all have been very different if the sting from the bluebottle jellyfish she'd been caught by had been its similar-in-size-and-shape cousin, the Portuguese man o' war.

No. It wasn't a set-up. What they'd gone through was true endurance.

Now they had to learn how to survive the press.

The Sun Online

PLANE DRUNK

DISGRACED children's author Toby Masters has been arrested today at Heathrow on suspicion of being drunk whilst in the air.

The author had been returning home following the discovery of him and three other celebrities living on an island, after it had been assumed they were killed in a helicopter accident.

Masters, 47, was, according to one fellow passenger, "absolutely off his face" whilst on board the flight to London.

Witness Maddie Spencer, added: "He had no idea what was going on. He kept yelling at the air hostesses to bring him more booze, but when they refused he got really argumentative. When I recognised who it was, I was really shocked."

Another passenger, David Enright, said: "Toby kept asking everyone if we knew who he was and kept demanding that he was taken up to First Class – saying it was where he belonged. He was effing and blinding. He was so smashed, the place he belonged was in the hold. With the suitcases."

Videos of the incident have surfaced on social media and show Masters swaying as he walks up and down the plane aisle.

Masters was due to be part of a press conference this afternoon, along with Zoe Stenson, June Sharp and Emily Chase, but whilst his co-survivors were driven away from the airport in a stretch limousine, he was taken away by the police.

Chapter Seven

'Okay, time to shine.' Zoe smiled brightly as two security guards held open the creamy white-French doors for the three women to walk through and make their way into the opulent Lancaster Room at The Savoy.

As they took the two steps up onto the blindingly white stage, Zoe looked at the 400 or so members of the press packed into the beautiful room and stood briefly on the stage to allow those that wanted to grab a photo of her before she perched on one of the white stools that had been set out.

'Thank goodness I wore the jumpsuit,' Emily whispered to Zoe and she smiled back in agreement. There was nothing as uncomfortable as a constricting dress and being forced to sit down.

'Very wise.' June grinned, walking carefully to avoid her Jimmy Choo trainers catching the back of her very wide trousers. Zoe smiled to herself about the demands June had made as they'd prepared for the press call, eschewing the high-heel Choos for sneakers, telling the stylists she'd decided on flats for the future, but they still needed to be fabulous.

The three sat in the places marked out for them, each with a narrow see-through table beside them, and arranged themselves, waiting for the chatter from the press to calm down.

Zoe, on the pretence of shuffling to get her microphone more comfortable, looked around the room and took in the enormous *Star Survivor* logos projected behind them.

The *Star Survivor* producers had pulled out all the stops for the press conference by holding it at The Savoy, the quiet buzz of the press subdued by the ornate soft furnishings and tastefully designed lighting. They wouldn't know, of course, but the blue and gold in the carpet reminded Zoe of the sea and sand back on the island. Even the ceiling seemed to have an effect of white puffy clouds painted across a deep sky blue.

Everything oozed old-school glamour and Zoe applauded them for the choice. She had done her fair share of press calls, including one infamous occasion when Robert Downey Jr jumped on the table she was sat at and it broke, but so often the calls were in brash and bright function rooms in large hotels with no personality.

She didn't expect today's to be quite so energetic, as the three of them were feeling the effects of the travel and the onset of jet lag, not forgetting that they were still trying to recover from the ordeal of being away. Looking to her right, Zoe noticed Emily fiddling with her water bottle and remembered not everyone had done one of these before.

'Welcome all,' came the voice of Patrick Roberts, owner of Edge Productions and owner of *Star Survivor UK*, a black South African in his mid-fifties who wore a self-imposed uniform of crisp white shirts and slightly too tight grey trousers. He spoke with authority into a microphone set on the side of the stage and commanded the attention of the press much like a vicar to his flock.

The camera bulbs flashed and Zoe remembered countless premieres where she'd barely even blinked at them. She felt Emily stiffen next to her and reached for her hand to give it a squeeze of reassurance, knowing she was doing it as much for herself as her friend.

'We have half an hour, which should be more than enough time for you all to ask questions of Zoe, Emily and June. Please keep your questions limited to their island experience, no enquiries of a personal nature.' Patrick smiled, his gleaming white teeth an ode to his dentist, and Zoe hid a grimace. There was something very untrustworthy about him. She'd heard rumours about him that he was calculating, driven and would do almost anything to ensure he was successful. He was so precise, the rumour was that he scheduled in visits to the loo. She wondered how someone this controlling would be able to cope with Toby's disappearance.

Before she could dwell on how Toby was doing, Patrick cleared his throat and smiled broadly at the assembled press.

'You will have noticed we are missing the fourth

survivor.' He allowed a theatrical pause. Zoe knew it was all over the news why Toby hadn't arrived at the event, but she wondered if Patrick was enjoying his further fall from grace. Toby had said the programme was meant to redeem him for sleeping with Patrick's wife. Maybe Patrick was mad at Toby for not making it to the correct island.

'Toby, unfortunately, appears to have been detained,' a few members of the press tittered, 'and is not up to speaking in public. We're reassured by his representatives he'll be back when fully recovered. Now, who would like to ask our survivors a question?'

Hundreds of hands shot up and Zoe was relieved they only had half an hour. She could already feel her eyelids getting heavy and regretted turning down the coffee she'd been offered before.

'Zoe – Lance from the *Daily Mail*, hi,' an overeager, slightly greasy-haired reporter, with a pale pallor and simpering tone, waved in Zoe's direction.

'Hi, I would like to know how you managed to stay in such good shape whilst on the island.'

Trying not to shudder, Zoe smiled tightly.

'Well, Lance, it had a lot to do with coconut water and trying not to die,' the room sniggered a little, 'but seriously, we had very little to eat so what you see here is what we saved,' she indicated the three women, 'and it's amazing how much muscle tone you can create when constantly fishing, cutting down wood or making a shelter,' she finished. She knew by this evening the headline would be something like *Zoe's Coconut Water Diet Secrets*. They'd have all missed the point of course. On the island it was nothing to do with diet secrets. It was drink that. Eat that. Find that. Or die.

'Thanks Lance. Yes – Debs.' Patrick smiled at the round-faced, jolly woman from *The Times*, whose demeanour belied that of a journalist whose barbs ran rings around any of the celebrities she took down online.

'Emily, how are you coping with the enormous amount of attention you're all receiving and did you ever dream you'd be as popular as you are?' she added, getting a mimed mock scolding from Patrick for asking more than one question.

Emily was quiet and Zoe looked to see if she was okay. She smiled lightly and cleared her throat: she'd already confessed to Zoe that her heart was hammering in her chest and she was convinced she'd be sick if she said anything.

'We. I mean, I,' she stuttered, 'well. It's a surprise, but I'm flattered that so many people want to know about me. The gifts are good too,' she added, enjoying the smattering of laughs from across the press.

'We're all amazed at the attention our survival is receiving – though I totally get how weird the situation is. We're still coming to terms with it ourselves,' she admitted, and looked to Patrick – Zoe thought for reassurance that she hadn't gone too far with her honesty. He nodded and Emily continued.

'It never occurred to me I'd be this, how did you describe it?' She paused and looked at Debs to remind herself and half a dozen camera phone flashes popped in her direction. '*Popular*, but I think it's less to do with me personally, and more about this incredible story we've found ourselves in the epicentre of. I'm just thrilled to be back with my family.'

Debs appeared satisfied and Patrick searched the room again, this time finding one of the writers for *The Guardian*.

'Yep, Tamsin, you're up.' He smiled at the redhead in the front row in such a way Zoe wondered if something had gone on between them. The thought was compounded by the smile the woman returned before looking at the three on stage.

'My question is for all three of you. How do you feel knowing *Star Survivor* did better without you, with viewing figures reaching,' she looked at her notes, 'approximately 30 million a show. Do you consider yourselves dispensable?'

Zoe cleared her throat.

'I'll take this one, ladies, if that's okay?' She looked at June and Emily who nodded, clearly taken aback by the less than light-hearted query they'd been expecting.

'Thanks. To answer your question, Tamsin, I would suggest that none of us feel as though we owe the company behind *Star Survivor* anything,' she looked confrontationally at Patrick. 'They did, by all accounts, send out search and rescue teams, which is good. But whether our disappearance benefited them or not is entirely out of our hands.'

She took a sip of water and noticed the journalists scribbling on their pads.

'We don't think we're dispensable, no one should *ever* feel that about themselves,' she put heavy intonation into her words in case Toby was watching. 'That's why we did everything we could to survive. Everything. And it would do well for everyone to remember that. Two months of survival can't be distilled into a half-hour press conference.' Zoe delivered her words with precision in Patrick's direction and wondered how much of this circus was going to continue.

June nodded and took up the mantle.

'We lived. That's the story. We survived with very little knowledge about how to do it, but we did and I thank all the gods every damn day that we were blessed with each other,' she smiled at the women next to her, 'including Toby.' There was an intake of breath and she smiled. 'Yes, I'm saying his name. He survived too. We were a team and there's nothing any of you can do to change that.' Zoe grinned next to June who continued.

'Whatever has happened here whilst we were away – whilst you all moved on and grieved and whatever.' She flapped her hands as she got carried away with the words she'd been bottling up. 'We. Kept. Going. And yes. You want the salacious details? Yes, we spent a lot of the time naked, know why?' The journalists were scribbling furiously, others held phones up to record.

'Have you ever lived in the same clothes for two months?' The room laughed. 'And don't even get me started on Manolos – no good for fishing with, I can tell you.' More laughter. 'But a bra makes a good foot cover when you're trying to walk along stones to fish. Though,' she was on a roll now, 'not Zoe's, bless her,' and Zoe laughed loudly at the clear description of her tiny tits.

'Oh, and no. We didn't all roll around fucking and whatnot.' Zoe raised her eyebrows at *The Guardian* reporter, who blushed lightly. 'Come on. Aside from various age gaps and aside from one of the group being married,' she smiled at Emily, 'have you *tried* having sex on a beach, even once? Sand gets everywhere. Now imagine you've lived in that sand and the sea for weeks on end, your body constantly tightened by the salty water, your scalp itchy with sand granules which have embedded themselves within your hair, and other bits of shellfish and whatnot all ground up and in your fajango?' She intimated with a look at her nether regions.

Emily joined in.

'Not so much crabs, more like oysters in your crotch.'

The room roared with laughter and Patrick jumped in before they went any further. Zoe got the impression this wasn't how he'd wanted the press conference to go.

'Okay, I think that's about it, ladies and gentlemen, I suspect you have *plenty* to go on with now.' He smiled tightly at the press.

'You've got a chance to take photos and that'll be all. If you have further questions, you can contact my office, thank you.'

Patrick sat down and the women got down from the stools. Zoe noticed Emily was holding her head a little higher than before the conference had started, and June looked like she was going to laugh. She linked arms with both of them and stared ahead at the press and their cameras.

It was Debs that started it; a one-woman clap, joined quickly by the woman from Ents 24 next to her, followed by the three-man team from the BBC, then ITV joined in, Sky, *The Telegraph*, *The Guardian*, and so it continued.

One after another, after another, hard-bitten, no-nonsense, seen-it-all-before journalists, standing up, clapping and cheering the three women.

'We're back, ladies.' Zoe smiled brightly.

*

'Where am I?'

'Why can't I move?'

'Why is my head pounding?'

'Ah, Mr Masters, you're awake.' A voice replied from somewhere to the left of Toby, but either they were hiding, or his sight was blurred, because he couldn't make out what they looked like.

'Who are you?' He couldn't move his head and wondered, briefly, if he'd somehow ended up being put in a psychiatric hospital.

The bodiless voice replied calmly, 'You took quite a nasty tumble, but we'll get you fixed up.'

Toby felt like he was suffocating and his heart pounded as he tried to get his bearings. He could smell bleach. He could hear machines bleeping faintly. A sheet, or whatever it was, was tucked in tightly around his body, stopping any movement.

'Emily?'

'June?'

'Zoe?'

'Shush, shush. Don't get up, Mr Masters, you need to stay where you are for now. We'll have you patched up and right as rain in no time, just you wait and see.'

Toby tried to encourage his thoughts to catch up. Who was talking? He decided it had to be one of the girls. No, they didn't like being called that. Women. No. Friends. It had to be one of his friends.

'June?'

'No love, not June. I'm Wendy, I've been keeping an eye on you. You took a bad trip but you're gonna be okay.' The woman moved into his line of vision and although his left eye remained closed as he blinked the right one, Toby began to make out the outline of a generously sized person to the left of him.

'How did I...?' He couldn't place where he was. Or how he got there.

He could see Wendy shaking her head.

'I expect it's to do with the amount of alcohol in your bloodstream, Mr Masters. You drank enough to sink a rhino.'

'Is my hand...?' His wrist was throbbing so much, it reminded him of when he broke his ankle on the island.

The nurse interrupted his thoughts.

'We bandaged your wrist, Mr Masters. It's not broken, just a bad sprain but you're lucky – if you'd landed any differently it would have been a bad break.'

'Oh. I see. I think,' he replied absently, whilst he tried to piece everything together.

Wendy cleared her throat and he blinked to pull his vision in properly, only the right one continued to do as it was told. He could see she was dressed in light-blue scrubs, a bright-pink hairband was squashed onto her mass of curls. It didn't look like it was doing much to hold her hair back.

'If you're up to it, there's a policeman here who wants to talk to you?'

He shook his head, wincing at the pain.

'No.'

'You have to at some point y'know and I can't put them off for much longer. You're not concussed anymore, Mr Masters.'

'Fine.'

She smiled.

'That's the spirit.'

Toby heard Wendy leave and tried to open his eyes fully. The right one was okayish, but he felt like he was prising open the left one – it felt sticky and the room had a hazy quality to it.

What he could see was white. Very white. That, along with the bleeping sound he heard regularly, the smell of disinfectant and the nice, if a little offhand manner of Wendy, meant if he was a betting man he'd take a punt he was in a hospital.

Again.

'But where?' he growled out loud and winced at the pain in the side of his face. The last he remembered was when the police released him without charge after his lawyer intervened in the drinking-on-the-airplane drama. They'd got him off by saying Toby had been more deeply affected by the booze because he'd been off it for the past two months and he wouldn't usually be as much of a dick.

Toby wasn't sure they had said the last bit, but it was something along those lines.

The nurse came back into the room and he closed his eyes, not wanting to be bothered by her whilst he figured out what had happened. He could remember he had walked out of the police station into… where was it… somewhere… the jet lag had taken its effect by then, and the drinking, he acknowledged.

There was a pub opposite the police station and Toby recalled thinking what a marvellous and terrible idea it was as a location.

So he'd gone in for one.

Then he was going to call for an Uber to take him home to Brighton as *Star Survivor* hadn't organised anything for him.

Unlike the girls.

He'd seen them doing the press conference at some swanky hotel on the pub's TV whilst he downed another pint. They'd all looked sensational and the press had lapped it up.

After that it was all a bit foggy.

'Mr Masters?' Wendy had come to his side.

'Hmm?' He tried to seem asleep.

'This is Sergeant Mike Constanza, he'd like a couple of words. Okay?'

Toby hoped he didn't groan out loud. He felt spaced out and couldn't be clear on what was real and what wasn't.

'Sure.'

'Mr Masters—'

'Please call me Toby. I'm going to close this eye if that's okay.' He didn't wait for permission, it was much easier if he shut everything out.

'Mr Masters, can you recall how you received these injuries?'

'No.'

'Mr Masters, do you remember being at The Parrot in West Street, Brighton, last night?'

'I'm in Brighton?'

'That's not quite what I asked.'

'No.'

'Do you recall—'

'Look, can we just cut to the bit where you tell me what a naughty boy I've been? My head hurts. A lot. And I think we can both tell I can't remember anything.'

There was a sigh and the bed creaked as Mike took a load off by perching on the end of where Toby lay.

His voice had a hint of an Italian accent and Toby found his mind wandering, thinking how he should take his mum to Italy.

'Mr Masters. I know you've been through a lot and we need to spend our time catching proper criminals.'

'I'm a criminal? But I wasn't arrested for the plane thing.' He peeled open his one goodish eye and saw Mike looking concerned at him.

'Not the plane thing, Mr Masters.'

'Toby, please.'

'Toby. The press have dubbed it "the Waterstones Scandal", y'know, like Watergate—'

'I get it. I had a knock to the head, I haven't lost my knowledge of modern history or shit headline-punning,' Toby said, cutting him off.

'Mr Masters, you were caught urinating in public.'

'Oh.'

'Against the window of Waterstones in North Street.'

'Ah.'

'In broad daylight.'

'Right.'

'Whilst singing, and I think I've got this right,' the sergeant consulted his notes, 'the words "All I am saying is give me a chance".'

'I see. A sort of version of *Peace* by John Lennon then?' Toby grinned, stopping quickly when he realised how much his jaw hurt.

'I don't think that's quite the point.'

'No. Quite right.'

There was a silence only punctuated by the sounds of a hospital during the day; machines bleeped, people talked quietly somewhere and, ever so faintly, the call of some gulls. He had to be in Brighton, Toby decided.

He reopened his one good eye and looked at the police officer.

'Up against a window?'

'Yup, of a display of children's books,' Mike added.

'That's… erm, I'm afraid I don't remember doing that.' Toby smiled in what he hoped was a redeeming way, but his face hurt so much he was convinced his skin might crack.

'Rather a moot point I'm afraid. There's plenty of video footage that could be used as evidence you did do it.' The officer produced a phone out of his pocket and within a couple of seconds had thrust the screen in front of Toby's right eye, which stung with being open for so long. He watched the video of himself as though it was someone else. There was a very drunk man pissing up against the window of Waterstones, as the police officer had said.

'What did I say just then?' The words were muffled and Toby's head was throbbing. He wondered if Wendy would be back soon and whether he could ask for something to take the pain away.

The sergeant looked uncomfortable.

'Ah, you said, I think, "Fuck you all",' he confirmed, looking at his notes.

Toby nodded.

'Sounds about right.'

There was a pause and Toby was about to ask how he hurt his head and his wrist, when the officer seemed to think it wasn't worth waiting for a confession from someone who couldn't remember the incident.

'Waterstones have said they won't press charges but they've asked you to stay away from all of their stores. If you go against that, they will sue you for "anything and everything",' Mike quoted from his notes.

Toby had continued to watch the film of him pissing. He didn't know he could urinate for such a long time. There was steam rising around him like a noxious cloud and passers-by had gathered around him like an audience. Just as he was wondering how much more he had left in the tank, the question mark over how he hurt himself was soon answered.

He watched as police officers arrived on the scene just as he was zipping up. He saw them, saw himself yell 'Fuck you, pigs.' He watched as he tripped, went tits up in the air, landed heavily on his hand and thumped his head hard on the pavement.

It was funnier in cartoons.

*

Emily waited in the wings, listening. She was certain her heartbeat would be heard on the microphone.

'My guests tonight are, quite frankly, the only people we're all talking about, but let's get them on stage to find out what really happened.' Graham Norton looked into the camera and smiled broadly, 'She's been on TV longer than I have, and that's saying something,' he chuckled, 'Please welcome June Sharp.' He held his arms open wide and June, offstage, was told to walk on.

Sauntering out in her black Gucci wedges and full-length black dress with a thigh split almost up to her waist, she held herself taut and tall and beamed at the Irish presenter, greeting him and air-kissing both cheeks. He indicated for her to sit on the red seat, and she took the place she'd been allocated in rehearsal.

Graham looked down the camera once more and Emily took in a deep breath. *Be cool. Be cool. You might have watched this programme for years but be cool.*

'My next guest has gone from slumming it,' he hadn't got any further when the audience erupted into a cheer. 'That's right, it's Emily Chase,' he ad-libbed, knowing it was better to get the guest on stage straightaway.

Emily felt a slight prod in her back and the runner with the headset told her to go. She walked out onto the stage, as in rehearsal, but this time the lights seemed much brighter and felt as though they were burning her retinas. She went to put her hand up to shield them but remembered her recently acquired manager, Charlie, had told her off for that. Walking as well as she could in the four-inch Louboutins she'd forced her feet into and painfully aware of the Spanx pinching her everywhere so that her midnight-blue satin dress clung delicately to her hips, she kept Graham in her sights.

As she neared him, he leant in and whispered, 'It's okay, they love you,' and indicated for her to sit next to June who was smiling broadly at her. Emily looked for the first time in the direction of the audience and couldn't believe the beaming smiles she was getting.

Assured his slightly anxious-looking guest was settled, and aware the production team were shouting at him in his earpiece to move things along, Graham returned to the camera.

'And finally, she's the woman with more films under her belt than she has years to her name. It's Zoe, everyone.' The black-clothed runners held up the prompt boards but there was no need; by now the audience was roaring with excitement as the megastar took to the stage.

Emily watched her friend looking as though this occasion was no different to a stroll along the beach. She strode confidently out in a white Stella suit, on extremely high heels, but she looked like she was gliding rather than stomping. She walked over to Graham, air-kissed him, blew kisses to the audience and received whoops from them in response, then sat down next to Emily, leaning over to kiss both the women on the cheeks and whispered,

'Deep breaths, ladies, here we go.'

Graham sat in his chair, allowing the audience to continue clapping and smiling. June waved at a few with banners saying *'We wish they'd Wake Up'*, in reference to her being dropped by the show and Emily laughed as she heard the chant 'I tried, I tried, I tried' ringing out around the auditorium. She looked to Zoe who was grinning from ear to ear and, on catching her eye, Zoe put an arm around Emily and hugged her tight. The audience roared again and Graham began chuckling.

'Okay… okay… ladies…' He broke off as the noise of the audience resumed, with stomping feet, clapping and cheering reaching such heights that the three women and the presenter could do nothing except soak it all in. Emily felt for Zoe's hand and held it tight; she needed the reassurance that this hysteria wasn't spreading to her steady pal. She got a squeeze back and Zoe saw Emily looking awestruck at the sound now threatening to deafen them.

Emily, on receiving the reassuring squeeze from Zoe, knew she needed to pass it on to June, and took the older lady's hand in hers. The three sat with their hands clasped across each other, causing the audience to roar even more. Distracted by a movement next to her, Emily saw June hastily wiping away a trickle of a tear which was making its way down her cheek. She knew she was thinking of the fourth survivor, and how cut off he'd been.

Seeing the tear, Graham, the ever-gracious host, leapt up and in an entirely unprecedented move swept over to the seat and produced a lilac hanky from his pocket.

'It's not just for show, you know, these things come in terribly useful.' He crinkled a smile at June who took it a little shakily and dabbed at her face carefully, trying to avoid removing the make-up which had been plastered across all three of them.

'Ladies.' Graham attempted to attract the attention of the three women. Emily was dazed by the response and searched out the familiar outline of Matt sitting in the front row with her mum. Both waved and Matt did his usually geeky, but right now very much needed, two thumbs up at Emily, the normality of which calmed her.

'I would suggest you all take a big gulp of whatever drink you've asked for,' Graham nodded in the direction of the champagne June and Emily had requested, and the glass of water Zoe was sipping, 'and we'll reset a little. When this lot have calmed down I'll be able to have a chat with you.'

He moved in front of them, protectively, Emily felt, and raised his arms to the audience.

'Ladies and gentlemen, I think we can all agree that that is quite a rapturous welcome to our wonderful stars,' the whoops began to die down a little so they could hear what he was saying, 'but unless you lovely people don't shut the fuck up,' the audience tittered, 'we won't be able to find out anything about their two months. Like, is it true you were all naked all of the time?' He did his trademark chuckle as he turned back to the women, winked and sat down in his chair. It was only Emily who noticed the very large gulp of wine he took.

Finally, the audience settled and Graham sat back, shuffling his cards.

'Well, I think it's fair to say that's the first standing ovation we've had at the *start* of a show.' He chuckled and the audience laughed, with a few shouts of encouragement. 'Thank you. Right, now ladies,' he looked and smiled at Zoe, Emily and June, 'you're all looking gorgeous this evening, aren't they?' The audience applauded. Emily wondered why she'd been nervous; all she'd need to do was sit there and be celebrated for her looks.

'Er, now, Zoe, I did just mention it and I need to know – is it true you were all naked on the island?' He smiled encouragingly.

Zoe rolled her eyes in mock exasperation.

'Well, you see…' she looked at Emily and June who grinned at her, 'if you only have one set of clothes with you, after a few days they can get a bit… unpleasant, and so, yes… we were naked a lot of the time,' she admitted ruefully. There were catcalls from the audience and June laughed.

'I see, so, Emily, tell me, what was it like living with a naked Zoe Stenson? Did you spend moments on the beach just thinking "Oh, that's Zoe Stenson, I've seen her movies"?' Graham laughed.

June felt Emily squeeze her hand, which she was still holding and she returned the gesture to reassure her.

'I—' she had a catch in her throat, 'sorry, I'm not used to this.' She laughed to deflect the nerves paralysing her words, and Graham smiled.

'No, well, I don't think many of us would be – would we?' he asked the audience, who in response whooped and yelled.

She smiled.

'Thank you and, yes, in answer to your question there were numerous times I'd catch myself in a situation with Zoe and just for a moment I'd remind myself who she was – well, is,' she paused to look at the woman on her right, 'but she's just a human being, and we, well, we made friends for life on that island, didn't we?' she asked of her.

Zoe beamed, flashing her pearly whites, and pushed a little loose hair out of her eyes.

'I can say, hand on heart, I never want to lose this woman,' Zoe indicated Emily, 'either of them. We survived this… this…' She faltered and Emily knew she was remembering her almost dying, their nets breaking, the starvation at the end, the dehydration.

'Ordeal?' Graham offered, breaking her thoughts.

'Yes, exactly,' Zoe breathed out, realising she just needed to take her time. 'We went through something so out of the ordinary, so unprecedented. There was no protocol for what we needed to do. No script for us to follow. It was just…' She forgot her train of thought again and June picked it up.

'Living.'

Graham turned to June.

'I am so in awe of all of you. Tell me, June, when did you realise something had gone wrong? How did you feel?'

The three sat there remembering the find of the helicopter door and their fear which had took hold that evening. They recalled crying around an enormous bonfire, knowing that they had just themselves and an injured Toby to rely on. They remembered toasting their unknown pilot with precious water and hoping he'd survived. But the producers had told them to keep it light, so June smiled tightly.

'We didn't know for a day or so; we kept thinking we'd see a camera or someone from production. But yes, after a while we just realised that there was no way this was right.'

Graham nodded to encourage her to keep talking and, after taking a sip of bubbly, she continued.

'It was frightening. But we thought the best thing we could do was to stay positive and build the biggest fire we could – to attract attention. We hoped help would be on the way.'

The presenter nodded gravely. 'But it was two months before that happened. If you'd known you'd be surviving for eight weeks at the beginning, do you think you'd have believed you could?' They all shook their heads truthfully, and caught each other doing it.

'No way, Emily,' Zoe shrieked and hit her playfully, 'you kept saying we'd all get through it.' She laughed and Emily joined in.

'Well, you can talk – you said there'd be help.'

Emily turned to June.

'June. You kept telling us before you swam away that we were strong enough to survive anything,' she accused cheerfully, before the memories of seeing June leave the shore came to mind again. She shook her head gently at the memory.

'This woman is the only reason we *all* survived,' Emily emphasised, because despite the trial by media Toby was going through, he too had also almost died and needed to be remembered. She turned to Graham.

'She was the strongest, in the end. She was the one who swam away from us to see what she could discover, and she found help. June is the only reason we're here today.' Emily turned to June and did something she'd wanted to do since their rescue, but had not found the opportunity.

'Thank you for saving my life.'

The whole audience gave a resounding 'aw' and Emily realised how much fun being famous might be.

Graham looked at the camera.

'And now, music from Cyan.'

*

'June,' a voice whispered into her ears and June wondered if she was asleep, dying or daydreaming. She was so tired she couldn't remember the day or time. All she knew was there was a cool breeze and the scent of sweet peas, which made her realise she had to be in her garden.

Slowly she pieced together where she was.

'June, do you need anything?'

Shading her eyes and squinting at the shock of light dazzling them, June blinked rapidly and smiled to buy some time.

'Ah.' She coughed, realising how thirsty she was.

'Water, here you go.' Tom knelt beside June with a tray, upon which lay a glass of water with a generous handful of ice. Droplets of condensation sped down the glass as a reminder of how warm it was already in the garden.

'I think I—' She broke off as she sipped on the freezing water and savoured it. Never again. She would never take any of this for granted again.

'Fell asleep?' Tom finished and smiled. 'Don't worry, I cleared your diary – did a bit of reshuffling.' June smiled at him and noticed he'd moved a parasol over her at some point in the past couple of hours to keep the sunshine off her. So thoughtful. She placed her hand on his.

'Thank you, Tom. You are far too good for me.'

'Well, I'm relieved I have a pay cheque again. Got to keep the boss happy, don't I?' He grinned and June laughed.

'Right. Lunch, then I think we'll need to go through some emails. You're in high demand and you need to tell me what you want me to do with all the fan mail and, well, stuff, which keeps being delivered,' Tom grinned again. 'Not sure how your address has been found out, but you've got a lot of free stuff coming your way.'

June shrugged. She realised back on the island none of the 'stuff' meant anything to her anymore. She could still have a look though. Only right.

'Do you fancy a giggle?' Tom asked, with a paper behind his back.

'Depends. Is it at my expense?'

'Have a look.'

He handed her a copy of *The Sun* with a twinkle in his eye. 'If there's anything you want to tell me, let me know, okay?'

She took the paper with raised eyebrows and watched as he walked back to the house.

'Come in soon for lunch. No more snoozing or you'll never be back on British Summer Time,' he shouted over his shoulder.

'Yes boss,' she shouted back, smiling.

Turning to the paper, she flicked over a couple of pages until she found the one Tom had marked with a neon-pink Post-it note, with the words *sounds fun* and some love hearts scrawled across it.

June looked at the article.

ISLAND SURVIVORS' LOVE TRIANGLE

THE celeb survivors have praised their rescue but are staying quiet over the alleged three-way fling which took place.

Ever since the stars were rescued two weeks ago from desert island paradise, rumours have been rife within the hospital where they stayed, as well as on their return, regarding a love triangle between June Sharp, Toby Masters and Zoe Stenson.

An aide who worked in the hospital said:

"All the celebs were kept in their own rooms in the hospital, but there was a lot of sneaking out of rooms and into others. It's easy to see that something's going on with Toby, Zoe and June as he was in and out of their rooms all night."

On returning to the UK all three have stayed quiet on the subject, with only married Emily saying "no comment".

Despite putting on a united front for *The Graham Norton Show* which aired over the weekend and was recorded last week, it's said that there have been angry clashes between megastar Zoe and ex-television presenter, June, behind the scenes.

A source close to Zoe said:

"When they were on the island, Zoe and Toby became really close, and although there's an age gap, she felt a real connection with him. They made loads of promises to each other about what they'd do if they survived, but now they're home she's struggling to get any response from him. He's gone into hiding from the rest of the world, but she'd hoped that wouldn't include her."

Disgraced author Toby, who was not present at the press call last week and hasn't been seen since, is thought to be living with his mum whilst he attempts to salvage his career. Friends of the author are concerned. One, who wished to remain anonymous, said:

"He's gone through a lot both on and off the island, but he's used to getting his way and always gets the woman. This time, though, it looks like even that's not enough."

Meanwhile, although June is staying quiet about any torment, her social media channels have begun to be used, and late last night she posted the following on her Instagram – "Thanks for all the support – let's all stick together xx" along with a photo of a seashell.

June sipped on her water thoughtfully. Slowly she got to her feet and made her way to the house.

'Did you see what they said about Instagram?' she asked of Tom who was busy making her a chicken salad.

He laughed. 'I know. If they knew it was because you and I had a couple of margaritas and you just wanted to say thanks to the fans – amazing how they can twist it all.' Not looking up, Tom sliced a few yellow tomatoes and placed them on a plate.

'So was the rest of it made up then?'

June looked up from rereading the article.

'Pretty much.'

Tom returned her gaze but she wasn't giving anything away.

HELLO! Magazine

At home with mumpreneur Emily Chase after her two-month survival on "hellish" island.

It's been a busy time for Mummy Blogger Emily Chase– after surviving on an island with three other celebrities for two months, she shot to global fame overnight with an Instagram following of over 19 million and has spent the last month settling back into home life, juggling parenthood with writing her book.

In an exclusive Hello! interview we caught up with Emily at her home in Surrey to find out how life is treating her since the island and what is in store for the girl next door.

Emily opens the door of her beautiful rambling Victorian home to us, with a mug of steaming coffee in one hand and holding her delicate daughter Ivy. She's beaming with excitement, and explains "I've just found out I'm up to 20 million followers now, isn't that amazing?" as she lets us in to the cool white interior and ushers us into the living room.

The space is filled with black-and-white photos, mainly of her children, interspersed with interesting trinkets displayed across salvaged shelving.

"Sorry it's a mess, it's been a busy time." She shrugs, displaying her now famed underplaying of the extreme success she's seen on her return from surviving in the South Pacific with little more than the contents of her handbag.

Sitting back in a sumptuous orange velvet chair and sipping at her coffee, Emily lets us in on what her life is like now.

"It was really surreal returning home. The main thing for me was seeing my children," she smiles peacefully at the family photos on the wall. "I missed them and Matt so much. There were times when I was on the island I really didn't think I'd see them again," she confides, her eyes beginning to brim with tears.

Composing herself, Emily smiles bravely and continues, "When I got off the plane I gave them the biggest cuddle. I couldn't believe they were there – in the flesh. It gives me goosebumps just thinking about it," she admits and pushes up the sleeve of her light-blue cashmere jumper to show us.

Since her return home, Emily has found herself at the centre of a lot of attention, alongside her island survival celebrity friends, Zoe Stenson, June Sharp and Toby Masters. A-lister Zoe mentions Emily daily on her social media feeds.

When we mention this to Emily, she smiles beatifically, "Zoe has a special place in my heart. When we were on the island we spent many hours discussing everything from our childhoods and what we'd do if we survived the island, to favourite music and clothing brands."

She looks as though she's remembering their talks. "Nothing was off-limits, and I think when you connect with someone like that, in a very different situation to what's usually normal for you, yes, you create a bond that's like no other."

What about June? Whilst the TV presenter currently being celebrated as a pin-up for women over 50 is all smiles, there are rumours her and Emily never saw eye to eye on the island.

Emily laughs and pushes back her still sun-bleached hair from her eyes. "June deserves every accolade coming. Sure, we had our fall -outs," she admits, "but we were in an extreme situation. I'd suggest any group of people surviving in those sorts of conditions for that length of time will suffer some frustrations. We got on a lot of the time and that's all that mattered."

She finishes her coffee and puts her head on one side. "I'm really proud to say I survived because of June. She's so strong. She's an incredibly warm and charming and witty person and I hope she continues to have the most exciting life. I can't wait to see what happens next for her."

Asked about the fourth survivor from the island, Toby, the shunned author who has gone into hiding, Emily firmly shakes her head.

"I'm sorry, I don't wish to comment on that. As far as I'm concerned, he's just a really nice man. I wouldn't want to discuss his career. I just hope some slack is cut for him; he's not the only person in showbiz to be saying one thing and really meaning another."

With three women and one man on the island, a lot has been made of potential romantic entanglements, but when we suggest this to Emily she shakes her head quickly.

"Oh no, nothing like that happened. We all got on and spent a lot of time together of course and bonds were made but no romance as far I'm concerned. I always thought I'd come home and make my way back to Matt."

Since her return from the island, many questions have been asked about what happened, but Emily says she is none the wiser. "We're just as confused as everyone else. All we know is that there was a storm and we got placed on there; we're assuming the pilot was mistaken due to the conditions. We just hope the pilot is okay, though he's not been found apparently." She looks sad and stares out of the open double doors, where the slate of her floor leads straight out onto the mature garden.

Looking to the future, it seems Emily's life is going to continue to be busy, especially since the phenomenal response to her Instagram account, Slummin' It Mummin' It, whilst she was away. At this suggestion Emily laughs. "It's amazing; it turns out going missing was the best thing to happen to me. I can't thank my followers enough for finding me and sharing my words. I had no idea anything I'd say would mean that much to people."

Emily's husband, Matt, comes into the living room and asks if we want another drink. Before allowing him to disappear though, we ask him how life is with Emily back and he kisses her hand, saying, "I'm so thankful she's come back to us. I don't know what we'd have done if she'd not returned. The girls and I missed her terribly."

It was Matt's idea to put one of Emily's quotes on a T-shirt, which was quickly picked up across the world. Now the duo are looking at extending the range to include more designs for adults and a line for kids to be launched imminently.

Pre-sales of her book of the same name as her Instagram handle have reached one million, despite not being due out until October.

Emily shakes her head. "I'm so overwhelmed by it all. It's a bit much to be honest!"

Emily was styled by Marco Jeski, photographed by Alan Dmitro. Words by Amy Winchester.

Chapter Eight

Miss you.

Zoe pressed send and threw her phone to the side, distractedly picking up another script. Whilst the island and their ordeal was a huge experience to manage and understand, Zoe knew she needed to begin to get back into the swing of her new normal.

There were aspects of it she was keen to embrace, such as being able to pop out for an espresso from the little Italian deli that was incongruously positioned in the bustling village near to where her house was, its red, white and green bunting fluttering exotically, standing out from the twee tea and antique shops that littered the main high street. Zoe had enjoyed, too, the opportunity to visit the cinema and watch her own movie, in disguise of course – something she had always done to get a feel for an audience.

She was thankful the Bond movie had received such acclaim as it was still running in the two-screen cinema in the small town a few miles from her home so she was able to revel in people's reactions. She'd enjoyed one of the audience member's responses a lot, he'd actually whooped at the end when she fought a twenty-five-stone wrestler. That sort of reaction was usual in the States, but unexpected in the UK, so she'd had a little giggle.

Some of what she'd enjoyed on the island though she missed now. No noisy traffic, or planes overhead to interrupt her thoughts. No phones to be distracted by.

As a woman who always thought she was more inclined towards the city than country, it was a surprise to like the quieter life. Things had been much simpler during their eight weeks. But, she acknowledged, at least here she wasn't trying to avoid dying on a daily basis. There was something refreshing about not keeping any eye out for a stonefish whose sting could kill you.

Casting an eye over one of the scripts, Zoe sighed loudly.

'Annie, look at this one.' She flung a script across the vast ocean of grey carpet to her assistant, its pages fluttering in the air. Reaching down from her position on the teal sofa, Annie went to read it.

'Don't, it's utter shit, we'll save it for the fire.' Zoe laughed and looked at the next one her agent had sent.

'This one opens with "a young woman is bent over a desk".' Zoe faked gagging and grimaced in Annie's direction.

'Why am I being offered roles where I'm either a stripper turned good, a cop with a heart of gold – fuck, there's three of those here,' she looked at the scripts and giggled. 'Oh, now, hang on, what about the old tried and tested *Pride and Prejudice*? I see Sky want to do a full-blown remake – bringing it into the twenty-first century. That could be good.' She stopped to look at the part, her eyes quickly skimming the text.

'Scullery maid? Are they fucking kidding me?' she scoffed, shaking her head and flinging it across the room, adding its weight to the numerous others stacking up in a small paper mountain.

'I think they're all a bit unsure about what to do with you,' Annie suggested. She was curled up on the other sofa wearing black dungarees over a Led Zeppelin T-shirt. She looked at Zoe and gave her the stare, the one which unnerved the star.

'You're doing it again,' she said, lightly chastising Annie, who shook her head and rearranged her features.

'Sorry. It's just… You're here. You're really back – and you're alive. I still can't take it in,' she explained. 'I always believed you were alive, but two months is a long time. Everyone kept telling me I should just let you go and begin grieving for you.'

Zoe looked up from the script she'd been looking at and saw Annie's face. Her chin-length bob was dyed pink, which further emphasised the blue of her eyes that were currently filling with tears.

'I'm so sorry, I don't know where these are coming from. I can't seem to stop doing this.' She laughed snottily, wiping her face with her hand. Rising from her sofa, Zoe crossed the carpet and sat next to Annie, pulling her in for a long hug. Despite the obvious relief at being rescued, Zoe had spent more time the past two weeks mopping up other people's tears than her own.

'Thank you for not believing I was dead,' she said, kissing Annie on the cheek. 'I didn't give up on getting home, though it did get a bit close here and there,' she admitted. Annie hugged her back and sniffed hard.

'We need to fatten you up, you've lost so much weight,' she scolded.

'Well, there's a lot to choose from.' Zoe thought of the piles of cakes and brownies and other delicious items which had been sent to her ever since she did an interview with *The Times* and said the worse thing about the island was not having something sweet to eat. She'd been inundated ever since.

Annie had got up and was busy arranging a few deliciously tempting vegan chocolate macarons, then made them both a coffee and returned bearing the goodies. Both the women munched in a companionable silence.

'We're taking all those to the care homes down the road later,' she nodded at the stacks of patisserie goodies. 'They'll get through them.' Her kindness made Zoe smile.

'Yes, of course. And I've been sent books too, after saying I missed those. We could give them away too.' Annie nodded as though she'd already thought of that.

'You know…' Zoe started, a little hesitantly.

'Yes?'

'I was thinking. I don't need to wait for the perfect script to find me. I could just, well, I could write my own. Couldn't I?'

Annie smiled.

'Your own film? Of course you could do your own – you could write and produce it – maybe even direct it if you wanted to. You've said for years you wanted to be more in control – maybe this is your opportunity.'

Sitting forwards in the chair, Zoe was excited. 'Yes. Yes, it's my opportunity. Although, I've never written anything before though,' she admitted, and Annie gave a soft laugh.

'And when has that stopped you? You'd never ridden a motorbike before being Bond, now you own two. You hadn't done more than buy flowers and then you taught yourself floristry for your part in *Roses*.'

Zoe grimaced; that film had flopped so badly six years ago she'd considered an actual job change to a florist, hoping she could hide away from the scathing reviews.

'Now, I wonder what you could write about,' Annie mocked Zoe, her eyes glinting in the morning sunshine which now flooded the living room.

'Would people want to watch it though?' Zoe pondered, her hands wandering to the plate which had mysteriously become bereft of sweet goodies.

Annie laughed.

'You're kidding, right? Of course people would want to watch it. You could make it more salacious if you wanted to, as long as the others don't mind of course, or you could do it from, I don't know, a bird's eye view or something, but you could base it on your experience on the island. My guess is a lot of people would enjoy it.' She gesticulated wildly, sending cushions onto the floor.

Zoe nodded.

'Oh, I'm going to enjoy telling Richard this.'

'I think you should ditch him too,' Annie suggested, tentatively, as though Zoe's agent had been on her mind for a while. 'He was wrong to send you onto *Star Survivor*.

Even if you had got onto the programme they'd have just spent the time filming you in a bikini and edited it so you looked dumb. At least, that's what they did to the other female celebs who were on. That Royal has been in therapy – she's been ripped apart by the press.' Zoe found herself nodding slowly to Annie's surprising monologue.

'He's been steering you badly for years – just because he's the one who took you on originally and saw the star potential. Everyone knows it and right now you're hot property so why is he sending you crappy scripts? He's not even the one who got Bond for you – that was you, turning up at the closed auditions for the role and refusing to leave until they saw you,' she reminded Zoe.

'You're right. I need a clean slate,' Zoe acknowledged. 'I need to take control – I keep saying I need more control and when I was on the island, I realised I could be in charge. Toby would say I was the leader of the island, you know,' she said warmly and Annie looked up at the change of tone.

'You talk a lot about him.' She nudged Zoe playfully in the ribs and she blushed.

'Ah, well, I talk about all of them. They've been my life this past two months, my family. It feels odd not being with them all the time – they all mean a lot to me. I miss them all,' she qualified.

'Of course,' Annie agreed, 'but Toby is right, you can lead. You can definitely be in control, you just need to make the decision to do it. I bet you could have your pick of agents.'

'Actually there have been a few calling and asking for a chat. I've just been a bit reluctant to do anything yet.'

Annie was already typing something on Zoe's phone.

'What are you doing?'

'Calling Richard.' She handed the phone to Zoe who laughed.

'I'm very lucky to have you in my life you know,' she said to Annie who smiled knowingly as the phone clicked and Zoe's agent picked up.

'Zoe darling, how are you? Have you decided on the next script? I was thinking I quite like the one which opens with you at the desk...' He trailed off as Zoe spoke over him.

'Two words, Richard – you're fired.'

*

'Hey June.' Toby smiled at the familiar face on the video call.

'Hiya, everything okay?' June replied, as she finished one of the yoga moves she'd taught Toby on the island. He thought it was the 'warrior' pose maybe.

'If this is a bad time, I can call back?' he asked. One of the problems with coming back from the dead was, he'd found, his whole life had to be restarted – which would no doubt be hard if you're a normal human being, but it was a whole lot harder when you were a well-known face with a career in tatters.

'No, it's okay. How's it going?' She went into some sort of 'sun salutation' pose and he watched, thinking how much fun it had been doing the same moves on the island. Even if they'd been starving at the time.

'Not brilliant. Put it this way. I've quickly discovered

that I am Person Undesirable. Whereas you're all being invited on every panel show under the sun and I can't open a magazine or paper without seeing at least one of your smiling faces, I am *persona non grata*. In fact, it's like I didn't survive.'

'Oh Tobes. Don't be so dramatic. Okay, the ghostwriting thing is a bit of an issue, but you rather buggered up your own reputation when you went and got drunk, no one will go near you in case they get tarnished with the same brush.' June breathed calmly through her 'asana' pose as she delivered this speech and Toby felt furious.

'So it's true then. No one will go near me? I knew Emily and Zoe might struggle as they're with the same agency, as I hear Zoe's fired that other guy. In fact, if I know Angie well, I should think her and Emily's manager Charlie will have her in a communications lockdown. I have no idea who Zoe's agent is, she'll have someone on the actor's side of the agency, but I thought they might see how I was doing.' Toby went quiet and watched June drain some water. 'Is the only reason you're talking to me because you've made the audacious decision to be your own boss and not be looked after by anyone?'

June stopped and picked up the phone, her face a pinky-warm hue from her workout.

'You have no idea do you?'

'I know that online and in the press you're all toeing a relatively similar line, with little to no reference to me. I'm assuming to save your own careers rather than associate yourselves with the car crash mine has become.' Toby looked away from the phone and tried not to show how angry he was. He'd been looking forward to speaking with June, now he just wanted to end the call.

'When did I do that?' June asked, looking very upset.

'Look, June, I understand. I suppose I'd do the same. But I feel let down. We survived together but somehow I'm being left on a new island by myself.'

'Goodness me, Toby, you are indulging in a bath of self-pity, aren't you?'

'You just don't understand,' he muttered. He wanted to tell her how lonely he was. All he had was his mum who had insisted on staying at his flat. Toby didn't know if it was because she'd been frightened since people started throwing things at her windows, or because she thought someone should stop him from pissing on a bookstore.

It was like growing up again. But this time it was just him and her; not because his dad had walked out on them, but because he'd fucked everything up. Again.

'I just – It's nothing. Don't worry, why don't you just, y'know, go back to your interviews and job offers. Leave me behind. It's fine,' Toby stuttered out, between mouthfuls of cold coffee.

'You really have no fucking clue do you? I'm right here, Toby. I'm here and we're talking, but you're not even trying to listen. Are you?' June replied, but Toby couldn't focus on the words and she just grimaced before hanging up on him.

Toby looked at the blank phone screen. Too removed to care.

He flicked through *The Times* as he sat on his bed, wallowing in his dressing gown and having a – what did June call it? – a self-pity bath.

'Yeah, well, so what. Fuck you, June,' Toby said to

the still-blank screen, 'any pity is good for me right now.' He was distracted when he spotted Zoe's beaming face in *The Times* and the headline *I'm A Survivor*. She'd been shot by an artistic photographer and styled a bit like Beyoncé with a vivid orange dress which swirled loosely around her.

If he had any mind to, Toby considered screen-grabbing it and sending it to her to tell her she looked hot. He didn't though.

He just looked at the photo.

She was stood on some sand – he assumed she was in a studio and wondered if she hated the feeling of it just like he did now. He wasn't sure he'd ever be able to go to a sandy beach again. 'Give me Brighton's pebbles any day of the week,' he told the photo.

Almost as a reminder of life outside of the four walls, a gull squawked on his window ledge which made him smile. At least he could be thankful his beautiful flat in this seaside city hadn't been sold. His mum had refused to allow anything to happen as she'd been convinced he would be found alive.

She regularly told him that despite being an ardent atheist she had prayed to 'as many gods as possible' for Toby to be found. She'd had words with the *Star Survivor* team as well when she thought they weren't doing right by the four of them, including harassing Patrick Roberts on social media and bombarding him with emails.

Having skim-read the article about Zoe and taken in the photos where she looked, he decided, beyond sexy, Toby threw the paper on the floor and considered the row he'd just had with June. Why hadn't she listened to him?

Understood the issues he was having? He thought she, of all people, would have been more understanding.

Smiling a little, Toby thought back to the island. It was hard to imagine they'd all been walking around naked in front of each other just a few weeks ago. He wondered if any of them would have considered it possible, their survival; whether that would have changed their minds about their behaviour. Possibly. Possibly not. Who knew? He had been as naked as the rest of them. As honest as they had been. Especially that night with the vodka when things were said, things were done.

That kiss though. Toby never discussed it with any of them. Maybe he should have done. Maybe he should have spoken to Emily, she'd have told him what to do. Whether it was a bad idea or not.

As he continued to look out of the window on to the greying skies, Toby lit a cigarette with the end of the last one, took a puff and watched the clouds that rose to the ceiling, replaying the call he'd received out of the blue from Patrick Roberts yesterday. That had been something he'd meant to talk to June about.

It had been an odd conversation. Brief. Toby had never spoken to him directly before; it had always been via his agent. Though, he acknowledged, as he was agentless now maybe that's why Patrick called.

Toby scratched his beard trying to recall what Patrick had said that had made him feel uneasy. He'd mentioned something about his wife said hi. That was an icebreaker if Toby had ever heard of one. He'd asked him what his plans were and when Toby had said he was considering writing an island memoir, pitching it a bit like a manual 'how to survive on an island with three women', Patrick had laughed. Hard. Then wished him luck with getting it published. All relatively normal. But he knew there'd been an underlying tone of something else which Toby couldn't put his finger on.

The screen on his phone lit up and for a moment Toby was relieved that June had changed her mind that quickly, but soon saw it was a withheld number.

'Fuck's sake,' he grumbled, 'that's the tenth one today.'

'Toby, are you awake?'

'Yes.' He could hear the teenage him, petulant, irritable. But his mum chose to ignore the tone, preferred instead to come into his room with a mug of tea in one hand, a packet of chocolate digestives in the other and a ridiculously pleased look on her face.

'What?' Toby asked, as she placed the mug down on the shelf next to him, removed the used one, swept some rubbish into the bin and opened a window above his bed seemingly in one move.

'I've done something.' She smiled excitedly.

'What?'

'When you went missing, I drew down on my pension a little as I thought I might fly out and…'

'Look for me yourself?' he asked, teasingly.

'Well, something like that. But no. Anyway, I never did it because the day I was going to book my flights the call came that you'd been found.' She stopped to ruffle his hair and kissed his forehead. 'Anyway, I promised myself that when you came back we'd go somewhere you could recuperate. Somewhere away from all of this.' She waved her arms around as an indication of the madness she'd experienced.

'So I used that booking app,' she smiled, pleased with herself, 'and I booked a house in New Quay, in Wales. It's just for a week, but I bet no one will know who you are there. And we can just relax. It's even got a hot tub,' she added in a small voice.

Toby's instinct, as always when told someone had organised something on his behalf, was to want to do the opposite. But when he looked at his mum, he realised she looked old. She'd aged ten years in two months and Toby was well aware it was his fault. He realised she needed the relaxation and a chance to work back from the stages of grief she had begun to go through, even if he didn't want to leave the safety net of his own home.

Toby looked up and saw her waiting for his response. She appeared anxious and he wondered why he'd never noticed he had this effect on her. Why would she be worried just because she'd done something without checking with him? Was he really that much of a dick?

He took a sip of tea, wincing at the sugar she still added despite the fact he'd not taken it for thirty years.

'Sounds great, Mum. When do we go? Next week? Next month?'

She leaped like a six-year-old girl and sloshed tea over herself.

'Tomorrow,' she replied with relish.

'What if I'd said no?' he called after her, shaking his head whilst smiling at the way she'd played him.

*

'Muuuuuuuuuuuuuuummmyyyyyyyyyyyyyyyyyyy.'

Something about the way Ivy was yelling this moniker made Emily wonder if it wasn't the first time. But she was lying so comfortably on the large cup-like sofa in the lounge, its sides holding her, as if willing her to stay put so she couldn't move.

The last week had been such a whirlwind, Emily could barely remember how to breathe she was so tired. When she'd been dropped off by the driver that afternoon, she'd managed three steps into the house and would have fallen if it hadn't been for Matt scooping her up and placing her on the squashy orange sofa, where she'd stayed for the last hour. He'd brought her a cup of tea, a large glass of water and a slice of toast with loads of salty butter on and then left her to it. She'd no sooner drunk and eaten everything than she'd fallen fast asleep, enjoying the dark emptiness which came with finally being able to relax in her own home.

'Muuuuuuuuuuuummyyyyyyyyyyyyyyyyyyy... Muuuuuuummyyyyyy, MUMMY.' Ivy's voice carried through the house and Emily tried to work out where her youngest was. Wherever she was, she'd definitely called for her. And Emily would get up. She would. But oh fuck, her body tingled with tiredness, her limbs loosening after a week of high heels and sky-high tension. She was thirsty too, not as dehydrated as island living, but she needed water.

And the loo. Time to kill two birds then, she thought begrudgingly. If only she had some sort of Shewee device, she'd never have to get up. The prospect of never having to leave the sofa was too delicious.

'Ah, thought you might be playing dead.' Matt came into the living room with a big grin.

'Sorry, I did hear her. I was getting up, I promise.'

'Liar. But you've missed out.' His smile was huge as Ivy came running in, a Barbie in one hand and a plastic saw in the other.

'Really? What happened?' Emily shuffled up so she was sitting. It made her need a wee even more but she was ready to listen.

'Do you want to tell Mummy?' Matt asked a shamefaced Ivy, who stood a little way away from her, head down.

'No.'

Matt shrugged gently and smiled.

'Okay, I'll explain. Mummy,' Emily winced as she always did when he called her that, 'Ivy went for a wee in the big girl toilet,' he started and Emily clasped a hand to her mouth.

'Did you? I had no idea you could do that,' she exclaimed and felt sad as she thought of what else she might have missed over the last couple of months.

Laughing, Matt stopped her from carrying on with a hand held up, to show he had more to say.

'Ah, well, Ivy has been doing that for a few weeks now, haven't you, poppet?' He patted the little girl on the head, and she nodded seriously.

'But Ivy didn't have the little girl seat on. Did you?'

'No, Daddy,' she twiddled her curly hair, 'forgot.'

'So what happened, Ivy?' he gently prompted.

'I fell down toilet. Got stuck.' She pulled a sad face at Emily who was trying very, very hard not to laugh.

'Oh Ivy. Darling… you poor thing, that must have been… quite… a… shock,' she managed, her lips quivering, cheeks puckering in an attempt not to guffaw.

'My bottom got wet.'

'I'm sure it did, oh dear love.' Emily kept it together until Ivy had left the room, then laughed hard, her sides squeezing with mirth and her pelvic floor working overtime in a bid to not let her down. Matt had been laughing too, and he knelt down so he was on her eye level.

'You have no idea how good it is to hear that sound again.' He smiled sadly at Emily. Ever since her return he'd been keeping her at arm's length, as though afraid she was some sort of mirage. He'd insisted on sleeping in the spare room to allow her to settle back into life, but she'd found his insistence on being apart cold and a bit isolating. She'd even begun to allow seeds of doubt to wind their way in and suggest he didn't want her back.

But by the way he was looking at her now she could see she had been wrong.

'I've missed you,' he murmured, leaning tentatively into her. She could smell all the things that were Matt, the hint of peppery cologne mixed with a trace of minty shower gel and the sweet chalky smell of the hair wax he used, all amalgamating into a familiarity that meant home as well as love.

She kissed him lightly on the lips, very aware that she was in need of a shower to wash off the travelling and hotels she'd clocked up the last few days. She'd only been home for three days in the last month since her rescue, despite her repeatedly explaining to anyone who would listen that she just wanted to be welded to her children for as long as possible. But as Charlie, her manager, was keen she didn't miss out on maximising the publicity her return meant for SIMI, she was scheduled onto every radio and TV programme that asked for her (and some that didn't).

The problem was, of course, she'd spent more time out at hotels than she had in her own home this month. Ironically, she even had to schedule being 'at home' for a *HELLO!* interview. She was there for less time than the journalist was. She'd arrived just in time for Matt to hide all the dirty washing and usual life crap under the stairs in the hope they wouldn't notice and thrust a mug of tea in her hand.

She continued to be grateful for Matt. He was rising to the challenge of 'husband to island survivor Emily Chase' pretty well and he knew how to make her melt with a kiss.

Relaxing into a snog which was more than just a welcome home, Emily felt her body ease for the first time in weeks knowing she wasn't expected to do any public appearances for the next four days. She moved away a little to stop kissing and ran her hands through Matt's hair. Emily looked deeply into his eyes.

'I stink,' she said, fully aware that she needed to freshen up.

'Well, I didn't want to say anything.' Matt's eyes crinkled up with humour and she walloped him with a cushion.

'Thanks, well, I need to have a shower,' she added, and saw the look of hopefulness in his face disappear into a slight shimmer of disappointment.

'Ah, yes, okay. Of course,' he said haltingly and moved a little to let her unfold herself from the chair.

As Emily strode away, she realised he was still kneeling on the floor where she had been just moments before and she grinned broadly.

'Plenty of room for two in there as I remember,' she called, laughing as he almost fell over in the speed he got up and dashed past her.

'I'll meet you upstairs – just going to put *Frozen* on for them and chuck a bag of crisps in their direction. That should buy us a bit of time.'

'You think a lot of yourself… it's a ninety-minute film,' she called back, but grinned again and ran up the stairs, shedding her clothes along the way, her aches and pains quickly forgotten.

*

'Would you believe this?' Tom was unpacking another box of freebies 'It's the Tiffany necklace you've been dribbling over for months,' he was exclaiming excitedly and June smiled.

'I don't think I need it. You can have it if you want,' she offered.

'What? No way. I'll pack it up and you can come back to it, you know, whenever you need to.'

June replaced the weights she'd been using in their rack and wiped her forehead.

'I don't mind using these, but I miss just hauling logs around, or swimming to get fish. It was a much more enjoyable way of being fit. Not that I'd want to be quite so cut off from civilisation just for a workout,' she explained to an enthralled Tom. Her assistant hadn't left her side since her return and had hung on to her every word.

'I could ask at the farm down the road whether they

need a labourer,' he offered, laughing, and she threw her sweaty towel at him.

'None of that, you,' she chastised and got in position to do her plank. Tom looked at her and took in the transformation. Gone was the bony, skinny, label- and body-obsessed woman. Replaced was someone who was strong both in character and body, eschewing all beauty efforts apart from moisturiser and a regular shower.

'You look stunning you know,' he said for the millionth time since she'd returned. 'You're glowing. I mean, I know we're still getting some meat on those bones,' he indicated her sparrow-like arms which would take more than a month to heal years of disordered eating, 'but stripped back, no make-up, hair just in a ponytail, I mean it, you look sensational.'

Grimacing at the final ten seconds of her two-minute plank, June allowed herself a moment to catch her breath before replying.

'That's enough gushing now, Tom – okay?' Her assistant reddened and nodded. 'But it does feel good to say that I'm over all the,' she flapped her arms around to indicate the house, 'extras in life. All the peripheral crap that we just don't need. I look in the mirror now and I see,' she smiled at Tom who was listening enrapt, 'I see just me. I don't see areas I need to fix or change or blur. Just me. June, the island survivor. Before that, June The Bastard survivor. I'm me – no more, no less and I want to just enjoy myself.' She thought back to the argument with Toby and stiffened a little. She'd had enough of people not being in charge of their own lives.

'I want to do more of it you know.' She nodded, and Tom had to press her.

'More what? Exercise?' She could see the concern in his eyes that she would make this her latest weight obsession, but she shook her head.

'More travelling. Tom, I haven't seen anything for most of my life and for two whole months I saw everything. We used to watch crabs – huge great enormous horrors of shellfish – just waddling past our camp. Massive spindly legs, ugly eyes.' She shuddered and smiled. 'At least a metre wide and they'd just sidle past our shelter giving us no space. They were awful and I'd be worried they'd hurt us, but they just got on with their lives.'

Tom looked horrified. 'That sounds so scary.'

But June shook her head. 'No, it was beautiful because,' she paused to make the point, 'we were just guests in their space; they owed us nothing and we got to take from them this wondrous, horrible sight.' She smiled happily and Tom shook his head.

He returned to the pile of gifts that had been sent for her, looking wistfully in the direction of the Hermès, Mulberry, Tattinger, Mont Blanc, Tiffany and many, many more goodies, teetering in a pile just waiting to be enjoyed. It seemed such a waste now June wanted nothing.

'I've got an idea. What if we give these gifts away on social media? Say that you had a spiritual awakening on the island but want people to enjoy these as you have no need for them?' He looked excited about the idea but June was unsure.

'I don't know. What would be the point?' she asked and Tom screwed up his face, then realised the answer was brilliant.

'You said the island you were found on was a haven

for scientific discovery? Right?' She nodded. 'But you also said the scientists who rescued you were no longer being funded because the government didn't support their plans anymore?'

June nodded again. 'Yes, it's very sad because the wildlife there is beautiful. Did I tell you about the geckos?' She was about to go into detail and Tom stopped her.

'What if you do an online auction? We won't look in the boxes, we don't know what they are, but assuming they're like this sort of beauty,' he indicated the diamond Tiffany necklace hanging from his fingers, 'people could get some true stunners. All proceeds will go to your rescuer scientists, how does that sound?'

For the first time since their return to the UK, June felt genuine euphoria.

'Oh, I love that idea. Brilliant. Well done, Tom. Yes. And I bet Emily would share it for us,' she enthused and Tom's face lit up.

'Yes of course, she's got millions of followers, bet they'd love something – in fact, I wonder if she's been sent stuff too? We could gather as much of it that you and the others want to give up, and you could raise a load of money for them?'

June bounced up and kissed him on the cheek.

'That's a brilliant idea and calls for a green tea. I'll make them.' She disappeared out of the room, leaving Tom brimming with plans for how the auction would take place. He was relieved she'd perked up. She'd had some sort of falling out with Toby a week back and Tom had been concerned. June popped her head back in.

'On second thoughts, maybe I should hang on to this

one.' She scooped up the Tiffany box which made Tom smile, and brought it into the kitchen with her. There was still a bit of the old June there, she acknowledged, and that was no bad thing.

She hummed happily in the kitchen as the water boiled, clattering spoons in the mugs and enjoying the process of making a cup of tea. Electricity and water – she'd never take them for granted again. She heard a dull thump as the post arrived.

'Want me to grab it?' Tom called through from the sitting room. There was a lot of post at the moment and he was tending to respond to the fan mail.

'No, it's fine,' June answered as she walked back through the door, two mugs of tea in one hand and a handful of post in the other.

'Tell you what, I'll open them, you tell me what to say,' Tom offered and she nodded with agreement, sitting down cross-legged on the floor, tucking her feet up in a yoga pose.

Tom started going through the post.

'Autograph, autograph, this one wants you to know you inspired her.' He carried on sifting through and June smiled.

'I'll respond to her.' She took the letter.

'Oh, Tom, you've given me two. Don't worry.' June pulled away the envelope which had attached itself to the letter Tom had already read out, and stiffened in recognition of the handwriting on the front of it.

'Tom…' She showed it to him. He looked up and his smile disappeared.

'Just ignore it, June,' he said quickly. 'I'll get rid of it,' he offered and outstretched his hand.

'But it's from… y'know. I should really read it.' Her voice wavered.

Tom shook his head and tightened his lips.

'He's sent three others this week. I'm sorry but I've binned them without opening them,' he admitted. 'He's not known as The Bastard for nothing, June.'

'Tom, that's not your decision to make,' June admonished, irritated that The Bastard could make her feel so small so quickly just by the sight of his handwriting.

'Open it then,' her assistant suggested, a little sullenly, and June softened.

'Sorry, it's just a surprise. Eighteen months of nothing, and now this.' She held up the light-blue envelope and shrugged in apology.

'You should open it. This is the fourth this week. Maybe he's got something useful to say,' Tom suggested, not believing a word. June slid her finger in the envelope and took out the note, scanning the few words on the paper and dropping it to the floor.

Tom quickly picked it up and read it too.

Dear June, I've made a huge mistake. Take me back. I love you, x.

Chapter Nine

Six months later

'That's incredible, I'm so... pleased for you.' Toby had had to search for the word which would sum up the enormous amount of happiness he had for his friend, whilst enduring a certain amount of jealousy he couldn't get rid of.

'Oh yes, you sound it,' Zoe replied and her grin was so wide, her smile so incredibly genuine, that even though it was over WhatsApp, Toby knew she was letting him off as only a true friend would. He shook his head in a form of apology and smiled properly this time.

'No, I mean it. I'm thrilled. Tell me more, when does it all start?'

He watched as Zoe replaced the cup of coffee on her desk in her new rental in Los Angeles. She'd moved over a few months before, with her PA Annie in tow, in a bid to escape the British press and since then her feet had barely touched the ground with the amount of work she'd been offered. But she'd turned the majority of it down in favour of crafting her own independent film based on their island adventure.

'As we thought, it's much harder to turn people down in person than over a video call so I've got the film backed,' she began.

'Helps if you're Zoe though – I should think that got your name through a few doors.' Toby grinned and she smiled.

'Yes, but they had to like *pause* enough to want to put their money where their mouths were though,' she pointed out, 'and it's still really tight. If production overruns I'll have to find further backers, but as of today, I have permission to film on our island.' She laughed, clearly relieved.

'Well done. And you've got that Ben chap signed up to play me?' Toby checked and Zoe smiled in acknowledgement. 'Amazing. If I could have picked anyone in the world to be me in a movie, it would be him,' he gushed and then laughed at the egotism of it.

'I think the other two will like the actors playing them too. I'll be me of course.'

'Of course. This is huge, Zo, well done.'

The megastar smiled at Toby again but even that couldn't distract him from comparing the sparkles of sunlight pouring in through the massive windows in her office, which overlooked lush grounds and a huge kidney-shaped pool she'd shown him when she'd first moved in, to the dark and dreary cottage he was living in in Wales. With his mother. Still. He realised Zoe was staring at him over the video with a concerned look.

'Hello? Zo? Are you... have you paused?' He pulled a face as he'd been hoping to discuss a few more things with—

'Hello? Toby? Sorry, I think something happened there.' Her face was reanimated again and Toby laughed with relief.

'Where was I?' She shook her head, 'Anyway, yeah, so Ben is going to be you. He was hilarious when I offered it; he kept saying how he couldn't think of an easier job than one involving living on an island. Remind you of anything?'

'Er, just exactly why we all said yes to that fucking programme in the first place,' Toby winced. 'I hope you've set him straight.'

'Well, yes, I've told him I want it to be authentic, but of course nothing they endure will be like what we really went through. The only way that could work is if I cut them off. Do a *Blair Witch* on them and just leave them with a camera and a small amount of supplies – see what transpires.' She laughed at the horror of it but Toby just raised an eyebrow.

'Actually. Funny you should mention that. Remember we talked about that odd call with Patrick Roberts?'

'Yeah, he creeped you out but you put it down to talking to him sober.'

'Ah, yes, thanks for that reminder. Anyway, for weeks after we got back I kept getting calls from a withheld number, which I ignored. Obviously.'

Zoe nodded.

'Anyway, a couple of months ago, I finally got intrigued. They'd been trying to call me for weeks and I figured it couldn't be the press as they've run out of shit to sling at me. For now.'

'Right. So, what happened?' Zoe asked, her head on one side. It reminded Toby of the island and any time they were telling each other stories. It was as if she heard better. Tuned in.

'They hung up.'

'What? They call for weeks, you answer and they hang up? That's quite the long game to play.'

Toby cracked a huge smile.

'Ah yes, but the next day they called again and this time I answered it quickly and they spoke to me.'

'And said?'

'You were framed.'

'You were framed?'

'Yep.'

'That's it? Not much to go on.'

'It was a woman.' Toby grinned.

'Okay, but, and I hate to break this one to you, so is approximately half of the globe, give or take.' Zoe raised her eyebrows back at him. 'I think you need more than that.'

'I have,' Toby began, but just then Annie came into shot, the ends of her hair dyed a vivid orange to contrast with the ice-white-blonde bob. Toby envied her individuality. Pink hair one week, orange the next. He wished he could be so confident. 'Oh, hey Annie. You okay?'

'Hi Tobes, great, cheers. Just got to have a word with this one. Hang on.' Toby watched as Annie turned to Zoe.

'Your mum and dad have just phoned, they're due to leave Heathrow in about half an hour. I've said I'll send a driver to collect them from LAX but your dad is sure they'll just get a taxi. I've told them to call when they land.' She smiled and placed a glass of something green on the desk, then leant down so she was at the same height as the seated Zoe. Toby watched as she brushed a strand of Zoe's curly hair away from her eyes, and gave her a light kiss on the lips.

'Don't be on the phone much longer; we still have a lot to do. Speak soon, Toby – come and visit us before the end of the year, you will love the view on the beach.' She grinned.

'Cheers Annie,' he replied, grinning in response as she disappeared out of the screen. He watched as Zoe looked to the left, watching her girlfriend go.

'Do your folks know yet?'

'I don't think it'll be as much of a surprise to them as it was for us,' Zoe acknowledged. 'Mum was the one who'd said how in bits Annie had been when I was away – much more than a typical assistant relationship, I think was how she put it.' She raised her eyebrows and grinned broadly.

'Did you know? Before you came to the island?'

'That I was bi? Or in love with Annie?'

'Both I suppose. You never really discussed any of that stuff with us,' Toby probed gently. If he'd learnt one thing these past few months, it was that women opened up to him if he asked the right questions. And didn't stare at their tits.

'I've known for years I was bi and when I got back from the island, those months after, the only times I was truly happy was when I was with Annie and we were just laughing and hanging out. It took a little while to hope she fancied me too though.'

Toby laughed.

'C'mon, who wouldn't?'

'Ah thanks, but I have trust issues. The only boyfriend I had sold me out to a newspaper.'

'Ah yes. I remember that. It'll be his fault you agreed to do the show, because you did that video in response to the article didn't you?'

'Sort of. I did the video because of the article.' She nodded, then shook her head. 'I shouldn't have been on the same helicopter as you though. That must have been a mix-up.' She looked embarrassed.

Toby didn't follow. 'Why shouldn't you have been on the helicopter?'

'Well,' Zoe looked a little uncomfortable, 'I'd made a bit of a fuss about doing the programme in the first place, and said the only way I'd consider it was if I had a private plane there and back as I didn't want people taking my photo. I'd underestimated that video and how obsessed people had become with taking photos of me.'

'Wait, hang on. But you were on the same plane as me though?'

'Yes, I was in First, you were in Business because they said they couldn't do a private plane. But they were making it up to me by chartering me a separate smaller plane to where *Star Survivor* was being shot.'

'But you got in the helicopter with us?' Toby was confused.

'Yeah. The producer told the driver to go to some

airfield, I didn't catch the name, and I suppose he brought me to the wrong one? But I still arrived with you guys.'

'Huh,' Toby was thoughtful, 'don't you think that's a bit weird?'

'Well. Not really. I mean, they fucked up even more when the helicopter dropped us on the wrong bloody island didn't they? I'd hardly complain about a plane slash helicopter switch,' Zoe explained in a matter-of-fact way.

'No. I mean, isn't it weird that you were never meant to be on that helicopter?'

'Maybe? I'm glad I was though. I made some good friends.' Zoe smiled and Toby beamed back.

'And now I have to go because I'm hoping to spend some time with my very gorgeous girlfriend in my own pool, before my mother and father turn up and I get told all the things that are wrong with my hair.'

'Sure. Speak soon. Have a great swim.' Toby hung up and looked thoughtfully out of his window which showed a bleak Welsh moor.

It was only much later he realised he hadn't told Zoe what he'd found out from his mystery caller, but sleep was calling and he decided it could wait.

He settled on his bed, wrapping a blanket around himself, and allowed all thoughts to drift away.

*

Dark fog was swarming over him. It pushed him deeper and deeper down into water. No. He realised. Not fog. More water. Thousands and thousands of gallons of water pouring hard, keeping him under the surface. He couldn't breathe. A face peered through the ripples but he couldn't reach her. Everything was muted. Dark.

Toby gasped as he woke up. It was so dark wherever he was he realised there was no difference between his eyes being open or closed.

This wasn't his room. Where was he?

Wales.

It turned out his mum had known exactly what he needed. Total isolation and a chance to work in peace. They had found a small stone cottage on a cliff to rent for a few months. They had loved the Airbnb and had settled into a quiet, contemplative routine.

Until tonight.

Toby realised he was soaked with sweat, wrapped up in his sheets and, like a child, had been having nightmares.

Again.

'You okay, love?' His mum was at the door, wrapped in a fluffy pink dressing gown, the hall light streaming around her. Toby felt like he was eight again.

'Fine. Go back to bed.'

'You were yelling. Was it that dream again?'

Yes, Toby thought to himself.

'No. Just a bit hot,' he lied.

She didn't seem to believe him but smiled nonetheless.

'If you're sure.'

He wasn't.

'Yes. Fine. Go to bed.'

'I've just made myself a hot chocolate as I couldn't sleep – you sure you don't want one too?'

Toby softened, she was only trying to help. 'Actually, yes please, that would be nice.' He watched as she disappeared from the doorframe and he noticed he was shivering now the sweat had turned cold. Toby flicked on the bedside light and hesitantly stood – his ankle still gave him trouble sometimes. He stripped his damp clothes off and looked around for some tracksuit bottoms and a hoody to fling on, the light from the bedside lamp casting long shadows across the reflection of his torso in the ornate dressing-table mirror that came with the rental.

Funny. When he'd agreed to take part in *Star Survivor* it was to make amends for shagging Patrick's wife. But he'd also planned to get fitter. However, it turned out that moving to Wales, eating healthy food and running every day across the hills had done it for him. He was looking pretty good. Unfortunately the only person to appreciate the change was his mum, and she didn't count.

He heard her call through and Toby made his way to the cosy living room where he found his mum sat in one of the comfortable armchairs by the dying embers of the fire, leaving him the worn leather one. She was sipping on her drink, staring into the fire, and when Toby sat down she looked up at him, a faint smile on her face.

'How come you couldn't sleep?'

She was so quiet Toby began to wonder if she'd heard him. 'I've been thinking how to tell you that I need to go home, Toby,' she replied, looking sad.

'Why?'

'I need to go. I never meant to be here this long and I, well, that is, I have a life back home. And I'm missing it a bit. Not that I haven't enjoyed this time together, darling,

I have,' she rushed out, 'but I think you're ready to be on your own again.'

'I meant why didn't you think you could just tell me? Have you been staying here against your will for weeks?'

'Don't be silly. You've not held me captive – it's just the last few days. I can sense it. You're ready for me to go. I'm ready for me to go too. Whether you're ready to go home is up to you.'

There was another silence, broken only by the weak cracks and pops from the fire.

'Thank you for being up here with me. I really do appreciate you, you know.' Toby walked over and gave her a hug, feeling her sparrow-like frame shrink a little as he did so.

'I worry about those nightmares of yours.' The words came out muffled against his hoody and he moved away from her a little.

'You shouldn't. I'm not.'

'Liar. Yes you are. Is it the one with the woman in it?'

Toby paused, ready to say no.

'Yes.'

'Don't you think it means something? Dreams can mean all sorts of things.'

'I don't believe in all that hocus-pocus crap, you know that.'

'I know but, is it the woman from the island, whatshername, is she the one in your dream?'

'Yes. Every night.' Toby thought he had said it to himself, then realised he'd said it out loud. 'Crap.'

'Well then. You need to tell her. Open up, Toby – you'll feel better for it.'

'But she's with someone, I saw the photos.'

'Still, doesn't hurt to tell someone you love them. Might make her day.' His mum smiled.

'I'm not. It's not...' *It's not love,* he thought to himself. *Definitely not.*

'You could use an excuse, say you need to talk to her because of your research. Ask her if her family had a visit whilst you were lost at sea.' His mum settled back in her chair as though everything was all settled.

'Hang on, what visit? You've not told me that.'

Toby had been researching the factors surrounding the four's disappearance and he'd quickly discovered that things didn't add up. In fact, the more he'd dug, the odder it had all become.

He also couldn't shake off the feeling his phone was being tapped; he'd noticed a few things creeping into the papers the last month or so, which could only have been heard from his chats on his phone. A lot of it was unnerving. But then, he did wonder if his mind was playing tricks on him – he was in the middle of nowhere, barely speaking to anyone. Maybe he was going nuts.

His mum drained her hot chocolate.

'The week you left for the island, I had a visit from a very nice lady. She'd contacted me and arranged a meeting and it all seemed above board, from the *Star Survivor* email address, you know.'

Toby nodded. *Skip to the end, Mum.*

'She came with a cameraman and they filmed us having a cup of tea and a chat about you, how proud I was that you were doing this programme, how good it would be for you. I assumed they'd use it on the show.'

'Okay.'

'Thing is. And I didn't really think about it until later. Much later actually. But when I watched the show – had to, didn't I, it felt like the only way I'd be close to you – no one had a film like that from any family, or friends for that matter.'

'Well, maybe it was for filler and they didn't need it. That's a usual thing for these sorts of programmes I think,' Toby suggested.

His mum shook her head slowly.

'I thought that and I forgot when you returned because I was so relieved to have you home. But now I come to think of it, she was asking some odd questions. She wanted to know how dependent on cigarettes and alcohol you were.'

'What did you say?'

'Well, I said you liked a ciggie and I couldn't see you giving them up any time soon. Same as the booze – but I assumed she was asking because you'd said you were doing a fitness thing there.'

'Okay.'

'She wanted to know what your pain threshold was like too.'

'Huh? That's weird.'

His mum looked at the fire.

'Sort of, but, again, I thought it was something to do with the tasks they'd be setting you.'

They both stared at the fire and Toby remembered the numerous nights sat on the sand, swatting away mosquitoes and setting the world to rights with the gang whilst staring into their enormous bonfire.

'But the whole point of *Star Survivor* is that it's all fake, Mum. It's not *I'm A Celebrity*. They wanted glamorous stars looking sensational, giving good gossip and occasionally looking as though they were surviving. I wouldn't need to do any tasks or eat gross things, or go without anything like cigarettes because it's all just for show.'

The room was still save for the sound of the wind rattling against the windows.

'Except you did have to do all those things. Didn't you?' his mum whispered, concern etched on her face.

Toby could feel his cogs whirring and he'd started to come to a conclusion that was so fantastical he couldn't say it out loud. Yet. But the evidence was there.

'Maybe you should speak to that producer woman again – Daisy isn't it?' his mum urged and Toby shook his head. He was reluctant to get Daisy into any trouble. These past few months she'd told him a lot about *Star Survivor*. In fact, she'd told him so much he'd begun to be worried for her, especially if Patrick Roberts found out she'd been leaking information to someone.

Especially as that someone was Toby.

Until now though, he'd only had Daisy's comments to go on and he had struggled to prove much. Edge Productions had been so careful. But what his mum had said might be the breakthrough he needed. The other families might have had similar weird conversations whilst they'd been away.

And if there were other conversations, wouldn't that mean more evidence?

And if he had more evidence, he could add that to his research. And more research meant more content for his book.

And then he'd have something people would be fighting to publish.

And then who would be the washed-up has-been?

Chapter Ten

Toby watched as Emily stepped out of a stretch black limo and saw her momentarily dazed by the flashing of cameras, the lights catching the sparkles on her dress. The amount of people yelling her name seemed overwhelming. Then she smiled. Less than a year ago that would have been him.

He looked away from the TV on the wall and pressed mute on Emily's big night, the flashes of light throwing odd shadows across his living-room floor.

Returning to the greenish glow of his laptop, Toby's heart flip-flopped as he reread the article he'd found buried deep in one of the entertainment columns dated two years before. He was sure it was a clue.

Distracted by something on the TV, he looked up again and saw Emily walking through a huge crowd. He turned it up a notch to hear the commentary.

'This is a huge night for the publishing industry and, frankly, anyone interested in books, records or a successful mum-boss.' Toby cringed for Emily; she would not want to be described as that.

'Her husband, Matt, accompanies Emily; she's wearing a dress from Needle and Thread, a brand favoured by down-to-earth celebrities. Hang on, I think we'll be able to... Ms...'

'It's Mrs,' Toby heard a muffled Matt correct the presenter.

'Mrs Chase—'

'Emily, please,' she corrected and raised her eyebrows at Matt who matched her expression. Toby wondered if there was a strain between them and smiled when he saw an aide come to the couple's side, freeing them of another interview.

Toby watched transfixed from his living room as fans held up posters of Emily – banners with *I slum it too* and Matt's phrase, *I tried*, repeated hundreds of times over. He shook his head at how enormous the love for Emily was now, and took a big sip of mint tea.

His phone rang with a video call.

'Are you watching it?'

'Hey Zo, yes of course. Wouldn't miss it, would I?'

'She looks amazing. Tired. But good,' came the response.

'Tired but good. I like that.' Toby looked around his room which was covered in meticulous notes stuck tidily to the walls, along with newspaper clippings from their disappearance and numerous other titbits he'd discovered which he thought were linked.

He was in his usual get-up of hoody and baggy tracksuit bottoms, but he was freshly showered. The flat was no longer a 'cesspit of masculinity' as his mother had described it on their return from Wales. Mainly because it was regularly cleaned by his scary Polish cleaner, Katrina, who had been angry when he'd been at the flat once, so he'd taken to going on two-hour-long walks when she arrived twice a week. He was tired, but feeling good too.

'Ooh, love her dress,' Zoe cooed down the line, her face in profile as she watched the same footage as Toby, from thousands of miles away.

'Yep. It's a dress.'

'Shut up, Toby. She was freaking out about what to wear – she called me from the middle of a store and basically stripped off, then tried on three dresses. That one is something she's seen the Princess of Wales in.'

'Right.' Toby's attention was wandering back to his computer screen.

'Is it almost midnight for you?' Zoe asked, snapping his concentration back to her and the TV. He looked at the clock on his wall.

'Yup. One minute to.'

'It's hilarious that all this is for a book. Look, the countdown is starting.'

Tonight at midnight marked the official publication date of Emily's hotly anticipated book. To celebrate it she was taking part in what would be the world's biggest reading and book signing.

She'd be a record-breaker.

Toby had thought he'd be jealous. Angry even at the way their lives had morphed into each other's. How her success should have been his. But he'd realised he wasn't. Instead, he just felt pride that one of his friends was doing as well as she was.

'I hope she'll be okay up there alone. It's a huge stage,' he heard Zoe comment as he thought the same. 'She's going to look tiny up there.'

Toby turned up the sound and listened. An ebbing soundtrack began. It sounded like a film score to an epic battle scene, not the unveiling of a book.

Searchlights began moving over the stage and out into the audience.

Lasers flickered across the dry ice, building in speed and intensity, working to the beat of the deep, throbbing bass.

'Bloody hell, they're going for it aren't they?'

'It's a bit much isn't it?' Toby heard Zoe's reply and he nodded absently.

'Wonder where she is.'

Toby heard the countdown hit five and looked to see an empty stage.

The crowd was yelling.

Four. Music was filling the stage like a headliner at Glastonbury.

Three, the lasers pulsed, speeding up.

Two. *And now... put your hands together for Emily Chase,'* called the male announcer.

One. Emily walked, a little shakily, Toby felt, to centre stage.

There was a moment of stillness.

Then the crowd roared.

'Fuuuuk, that's a serious audience. She looks

overwhelmed,' Zoe gabbled on in the background, but all Toby thought was thank fuck it wasn't him. There was attention, and then there was *attention*. Emily was getting all the heat and none of the fun.

'Hey, Zo. I think I've finally found something on Patrick Roberts,' Toby remembered, tearing his eyes from the TV and turning Emily down as she began to read aloud from an extract of her book.

'Yeah?'

'Yeah. I think, I think he has some money troubles.' Toby said it tentatively. Trying out the phrase. Hoping he sounded sure. He was sure but he'd need to sound a lot more so than he currently did.

'What kind of money troubles?' Zoe finally tore her gaze from her own screen and looked at Toby down the line.

'Well, it's just a tiny story from a few years ago – but there's something about a programme of his costing him a few million.'

'But he's a multimillionaire, that wouldn't affect him.'

'No, but the following year – about eighteen months ago, there's another article, this time in the *FT*, which mentions him as an investor in some companies.'

'That's because he's a businessman.'

'Yes, but I've looked them up – those businesses have gone bankrupt. So where does that leave his investment?'

'Hmmm. Oh, look, Matt's on stage with her now.'

Toby looked. The two were in a dramatic kiss, the position looked romantic but posed – it would be plastered across all the front pages by the morning.

Zoe's attention came back to him. 'You should be

careful, Toby, he's a powerful man. Don't start making accusations before you're totally one-thousand-per-cent sure you're right,' she left a beat, 'okay?'

'Okay.'

'Call me soon.' She hung up and Toby looked at his computer, trying to decide if he should force himself to bed. Glancing at the TV, he saw the muted jubilations of Emily's fans jumping up and down.

He watched as she smiled, waved, hung on to Matt for support, smiled some more. She looked happy. He watched as the cameras panned, catching his ex-agent, Angie, on the side in the wings. He watched as he realised he recognised who she was standing with and he watched the intimate way the man leaned into her.

The camera panned away to the crowd again, leaving Toby staring at the screen.

Patrick Roberts.

Chapter Eleven

Do you have the information? Toby practised the line in his head, then grimaced at how awkward and cheesy it sounded.

So, any info?

Nope, much worse. He wasn't trying to be some cool twenty-something. That's if cool twenty-somethings sounded like that. It had been a while since he'd spent time with any. Aside from Zoe, but she didn't count – she was a friend.

He wiggled a finger under his collar, his shirt felt tight around his throat. It had been so long since he'd made any kind of effort he'd forgotten how much he disliked wearing a shirt. And the new suit he'd bought, in a bid to reclaim a bit of normality after months of living in sweats in his flat, felt too sturdy. The cut felt wrong.

'Toby,' a blonde came around the shimmering wall

which set Toby apart from the rest of the diners. The luminescent curtain made up of thousands of fibre optics twinkled and acted as a discreet yet beautiful screen where they could enjoy the buzz of the restaurant without being seen.

The last time he'd seen Veneda was in what felt like another life. Another life where he'd spent a very fun night, not knowing she was the wife of Patrick Roberts. Not knowing that the next day the papers would be plastered with paparazzi shots of them in a very compromised position, taken of them as they'd been making out in a taxi on the way to his. The moment that cemented his place on *Star Survivor* in a bid to apologise to his boss for his indiscretion, if that's what you call screwing the boss's wife – even if you didn't know who she was at the time.

Toby still thought she was a stunner, with her tumbling wavy hair falling over her shoulders, her skin-tight dress that left nothing to the imagination and sensuous full lips. Lips that were smiling at him.

'Lovely to see you again,' she said as he stood to welcome her and they each kissed cheeks in a friendly but polite way.

'And you,' he smiled back, trying to ignore the feeling of awkwardness that came with seeing someone who the last time he'd shared a space with he'd been very intimate, 'thanks for meeting with me. It's good to see you again.'

'And you.'

She smiled at a waiter who had arrived silently at their table.

'A glass of champagne for me, and...' She nodded at Toby.

'I'm fine with this, thanks.' He nodded at his coffee and Veneda smiled in understanding.

'So, how are we going to do this then? I'll show you mine if you show me yours?'

Toby laughed, a little uncomfortably, and, feeling hot, shrugged his dinner jacket off. 'Well, I suppose we could start with what you know?'

'Or you could start with what you know?' she replied, her eyes narrowing at him, catlike.

'Okay,' Toby decided it was easier to lay his cards on the table, 'how about I ask you a question, and you can decide what you want to tell me?'

'Fire away.'

'Okay – I've heard on the grapevine that you're filing for divorce from Patrick, but can I ask about when you first got together?'

'Sure.' She sipped at her champagne.

'When you were married to Patrick, did he have any money problems?'

'Yes, and no.'

'Not a helpful response.' Toby smiled.

'Well…' She leaned in a little to impart the confidence Toby knew he needed as evidence, when their waiter materialised and lightly bowed as another, younger, waiter appeared bearing two small plates.

'Sir, madam, these are some amuse-bouche which have been prepared just for you. Enjoy.' The waiter placed the most delicate of white plates in front of each of them.

'Thanks,' Toby replied, wondering when the room had got so warm. He could feel sweat dripping down his back. 'You were saying.' He nodded at his dining companion, who had begun to nibble on her food. She reminded him of a rabbit and he thought about June and how she went from turning her nose up at the food they found on the island, to eating anything from fish to yams by the end of their survival.

June.

Toby tried not to let his mind wander. He needed to think straight. Instead, he sampled the miniscule platter of food that contained a soft cloud which he discovered was potato alongside a wisp of pea. The flavour was subtle but delicious and he savoured the tiny mouthful.

Their waiter reappeared to clear the plates and another refilled Veneda's champagne.

'I think you need to explain a little,' Toby tried again.

The blonde looked at him, her eyes inscrutable as she sized him up. Deciding, Toby thought, whether to trust him or not.

'He didn't have financial problems. I did.'

'What?'

'When we met, I had nothing. I was twenty-one, he was thirty-nine and he promised me everything. He was going to show me the world. And he did. It was magical.' She looked away and stared at the sparkling curtains. 'So, when we'd been married for five years, he made me an anniversary present of a building – an entire office building in the middle of London. Toby, I thought I was made.'

She shook her head.

'I honestly thought he was thinking of me. I thought. Well. I thought one day we might split up – people like Patrick don't stay with one woman for very long – but I thought he was setting me up for life. A property owner, with an income. It was a dream come true.'

'But?' Toby finished his coffee and nodded to the waiter that he wanted another.

'But it was a set-up. All of it. Now we're divorcing, it turns out the building was part of a company he'd set up, which has gone into liquidation and its assets are being stripped, so it isn't mine anymore.'

'What about the divorce? You must have had a prenup?'

'No prenup. I married at twenty-two: I was stupid and in love. In the last few months I've discovered I'm the owner of fifteen companies, all of which are either sham businesses for him to launder money through – not him directly of course – or they were companies which had folded. He isn't going to have to declare bankruptcy. I am. My lawyer has advised me the best thing is to declare I'm bankrupt, as I don't have any way to pay the huge debts the companies owe. It's in the millions.'

'Shit.'

'Quite.' She smiled and although he'd assumed she'd be bitter, she seemed almost whimsical. She absently moved a lock of hair behind her ear and looked away from Toby briefly, before returning his gaze.

'How is he getting away with it? Why don't you, y'know, put up a fight or something?'

'When you meet someone like that, you'll... I did anything he asked. He's very, very charming. Very persuasive,' she offered.

'How come none of it has made the papers?' Toby had become the world's number one expert on Patrick

Roberts and his dodgy dealings, but whilst there was a little coverage of the end of his first marriage, this one had gone under the radar.

'Let's just say, he's made it worth my while to stay quiet. He might have lost a ton of money, but there's still some floating around,' she explained quietly.

'Sir, madam, a starter of tuna carpaccio. Enjoy.' Their waiter had set their food on the table with a flourish and disappeared before Toby had registered his presence.

He tried to hide his queasiness at raw fish. He'd had his fill of it on the island; it brought back unpleasant memories of the times they'd eaten food which was undercooked or spoiled, only to spend hours throwing up or shitting themselves in the forest.

He waved their waiter over.

'Excuse me, but I thought we were having the "chef's choice"? Alain was going to create something exceptional for us?' he asked, knowing he sounded spoilt but it had been a year – more maybe – since he'd been out to a restaurant and as he could still afford the best, he had expected it.

'Monsieur, this is Chef Ducasse's very own menu, created just for you,' the waiter expanded his arms in Toby's direction. 'He was inspired by you and thought he could recreate island life. But you don't like it?'

Toby didn't want to make a scene. The reason he'd specified this area of the restaurant was to be discreet. He couldn't be caught with Patrick Roberts' wife again – even if she was soon to be divorced.

'Sure. No, it's fine. Thanks.'

'It's delicious,' Veneda said in hushed tones, as if

he were a petulant child trying to avoid his greens and though he was tempted to tell her what they'd endured on the island, Toby held it back. He knew he was still an oddity. Yes, he'd stepped away from the public eye – or been pushed, depending on who you heard it from – but people still wanted to know what life on the island had been like. How he'd got on with the three women who were making huge strides in their careers since.

He didn't want to tell her he still woke covered in sweat after dreaming he was back on the island and no one wanted to rescue him.

Or that he had to sleep on the floor because no bed seemed comfortable. Still. Even after six months. Or that his finger hovered over June's number twenty times a day but he always found a reason not to call.

Or that eating any fish, especially raw ones, would instantly cause his insides to recoil, as he tried to shake off the memories of the smell of gutting the catch the islanders ate daily.

Toby speared a shard of the tuna and placed it in his mouth.

'Mmm, good,' he lied.

'There, not so bad is it?' Veneda giggled and touched his hand gently. Toby knew it was an invitation. She had let him in and felt vulnerable; if he wanted, he knew he could ask her to join him in one of the stunning rooms at The Dorchester and have an enjoyable afternoon.

Instead, he took another mouthful of fish and swallowed it quickly with a gulp of sparkling water, the gas mixing violently with the tuna, and he willed it to stay down.

'There's more to it all as well. He's paid me for… other things…' Veneda began, 'maybe we could carry on the conversation elsewhere?' She raised an eyebrow at him and smiled. 'And you could tell me why you want to know about my terrible marriage and ugly divorce.'

'I don't think you'd believe me if I told you.' Toby raised his eyebrows back at her and she cocked her head to the side.

'Try me.'

'Sir, madam, this is our pièce de résistance.' The waiter bore down on them with a seafood platter. What looked like thousands of tiny shellfish eyes stared at Toby, frozen across a bed of jagged ice.

The smell hit him.

'I'm going to—'

He threw up all over the seafood. All over his new suit. All over Veneda.

And all over the beautiful, glittering LED curtain.

HAVE WE GOT SPEWS FOR YOU

DISGRACED AUTHOR Toby Masters really chucked things up this week.

The Mirror can exclusively reveal that Toby Masters and an unnamed blonde were dining at a posh restaurant at The Dorchester hotel when the star, who survived life on a desert island but didn't survive as an author, vomited all over his dining companion.

Instagrammer and Made in Chelsea *star LadyWhoLunches was in the restaurant at the time with best friend Robert French. She said:*

"It was super gross. One minute Bertie and I were enjoying a quiet lunch when we heard all this noise and we smelt the most grotesque smell. A minute or so later and the manager was telling us to leave the restaurant.

"The Dorch were lovely as they've said we can come back another time, but oh my god I felt sorry for that bloke – and his date. At first I didn't know who it was, but then I looked again and I realised it was that old guy who used to be a children's author. His date was so upset."

She added: "It's a shame cos that Toby guy looked quite a dish but who would hang about when you're covered in vom, eh? His suit, I think it was Hugo Boss, was totes covered in vomit and he looked very, very annoyed. The woman just walked out quickly before I could see who she was, and then he just, like, left the restaurant."

Toby Masters was unavailable for comment.

Chapter Twelve

'And the crew found a building with supplies in it. Where?' There was a long delay on the line but Toby needed to make sure he'd heard Zoe correctly.

'On the other side. It's ridiculous actually but if we'd walked off to the left, rather than straight ahead we'd have found a building with enough to keep us going, not in luxury, but we'd have had canned food, water, shelter of course and a first aid kit.' She laughed but it sounded distant and tinny.

'But instead we went to the opposite side.'

'Exactly. Apparently the atoll isn't inhabited but it used to be, which is why there was an airstrip for us to land on. The building is stocked for any rangers or scientists or whoever needs it, if they find themselves on the island.'

'Huh. Just think, when we were chewing on those disgusting clams, we could have tucked into what? Canned tuna?'

'Better… Soup. Noodles. All those sorts of things. The team that found it said they thought it was all in date.'

'I see.' It was 8pm for Zoe, but 6am for Toby and his mind was already whirring.

'What do you think it means?' As always, Zoe didn't muck about. Straight to the point.

'I think it's beginning to answer my big question, how did we end up on that island? And why didn't *Star Survivor* release any details about the pilot? Don't you think it's odd? Why call off the search and rescue so quickly? What do you think it's all mounting to?'

There may well have been a delay on the line but Zoe sounded hesitant and Toby knew why. What he was suggesting wasn't something that sat all that well.

'If I wasn't so sure it couldn't possibly be the case, I'd suggest we were set up,' Zoe suggested from across the other side of the world.

Toby nodded in agreement, the light from his bedside table throwing ink-blot shapes across the walls.

'So would I, Zo. There's too much going on here for it to be an accident. It feels a lot like a set-up.'

'I don't get it though. Why? Why us? Why then? Fuck,' she shrieked in frustration down the phone. 'But if it was a set-up, what the fuck were they doing? They were fucking with our lives.'

There was a pause and Toby wondered if the line had dropped. He'd have to use another phone if that were the case. He'd begun to switch around the numbers he used as he was sure he was being tapped. He'd seen people going through his bins too.

'We almost died, Toby.'

'That's because we didn't turn left.'

There was another silence.

'How can we prove it? How can I sue them? Fuck. How dare they?' Toby heard the anger in Zoe's voice that he'd experienced when he'd begun to investigate Patrick Roberts and Edge Productions.

'Because they did. Because they wanted publicity. Because it was a shit programme before we got involved and suddenly it far and away surpassed the US version. Because of greed?'

'Fuck. Fuck. Fuck.'

'I know. Look, Zoe, I have a lot of research. I have quite a bit of evidence. I've got quotes from other people including you, from a producer at the programme and some off-the-record chats with others. But are you sure you want to be part of this? For your quotes to be involved? We'll be pissing a lot of people off when this gets out. I don't have much to lose but they're very powerful, Zoe. Things are already getting weird for me. Are you okay with that?'

There was no pause; the answer was instant even across the time zone and thousands of miles.

'Fuck 'em, Tobes. Fuck the lot of them. If it's true, people should know.'

'Looks like there'll be some fun ahead then.' Toby laughed to cover the fear of what might happen when he went up against Patrick Roberts and he bid Zoe goodbye.

He paused for a moment and looked out towards the sea. Toby needed proof of what his hunch was telling him. It wasn't enough that he knew Roberts had a shady past, or that he'd discovered he'd set up his first wife. If what he thought was true, that Patrick Roberts had set up the celebs to go missing, banking on his programme gaining record ratings so his company would go back to the black again, he needed proof.

Toby smiled when he spotted some very brave beachgoers attempting to ignore the fact it was barely March. They were armed with a windbreaker and a picnic hamper and, by the looks of it, were in exceedingly high spirits. They were probably aiming for a breakfast on the beach. Typical Brighton.

'Good luck to you.' He grinned as he watched them from the warmth of his room, then returned his attention to adding in Zoe's findings to his notes.

Then there was the tricky question about why the four of them had been chosen to go missing. If he was correct, they'd have been pegged as the ones going missing from the very beginning. So why would Patrick choose them?

Toby looked up in shock. How had he forgotten? Patrick had only chosen Toby, Emily and June. Zoe had already told him she wasn't meant to be on the helicopter that day – she was collateral damage Roberts hadn't been planning on.

So what did he, Emily and June have in common? And how would Patrick know they'd say yes? Why were they expendable?

He needed to talk to Matt, find out if he'd had a visit like Toby's mum had when he'd gone to the island.

Toby's attention kept being taken by the view outside his window. The hardy beachgoers had made it to the pebbles of the beach – he preferred the pebbles any day to the sand from the island. Pebbles didn't make their way into arse cracks.

The couple were wobbling as they walked across the beach but soon chose a spot to make camp. They were clearly not from here, Toby realised, as he spotted them making the rookie error of opening the picnic box and leaving the lid off.

'Never do that unless you're about to eat, otherwise the inevitable is going to happen,' he commented as they were swooped on by gulls of all shapes and sizes trying to take off with the food. Toby noticed how the couple were unfazed. The guy had something and he was batting the birds away with it, whilst the woman closed the lid and they laughed hard. Toby watched as the man leant in, pulled his arm around her close and kissed her deeply.

He'd have to speak to June too, he realised. Even though he'd put it off for as long as he could. June's PA may hold the key as to why she'd been chosen.

Toby picked up his phone and found Emily's details. He pressed the call button and listened to the tone.

'Hi.'

'Hey Em, you okay?'

Her response was tired, toneless.

'I s'pose. You?'

'I am. I'm great, thanks.' Toby realised he was trying to compensate for her dull tones with false, bright ones of his own.

'Great.'

There was a silence. If it had been Zoe, Toby knew they'd have immediately begun chatting, but it was always harder with Emily.

'How's the second book going?' Toby prodded. The launch of her first had astonished Toby and ticked off numerous firsts for the publishing industry. She'd broken records left, right and centre and for a while he'd felt like she'd been on every page of every paper he'd picked up.

'It's not. Have you heard of writer's block?' she asked.

'Well, yes, of course – that's what the ghostwriter was for.' He laughed and hoped she'd join in with poking fun at him. She didn't rise to it though.

'Well, I have a house full of writer's blocks. What more do I have to say? I've only had six more months of being a parent, I've not learned anything else since the first book, other than I've not seen my children nearly enough. Maybe I should write a book on what it's like to be a parent and never see your kids.' She went quiet.

'Would that sell?' Toby asked, tentatively. It didn't sound quite as funny as her first one.

'No, of course it wouldn't sell,' she snapped and he was surprised by the outburst, she hadn't been like that towards him since the early days on the island. He decided it couldn't be because of him.

'Ah, I know what this is. It's the difficult second album. All artists suffer with it.'

'Yeah, but I'm no Adele. I think I might be more Mr Blobby – one number one hit, but nothing else to offer. I think I might be at a point where I've little else to say about being a mum.'

'I'm stunned, I thought everything was great – it looked good,' he uttered then caught himself. 'Sorry, I should know we shouldn't believe everything we see online and in the press.'

A very weak laugh came down the line.

'That's true. I hate to admit it though—' She broke off.

'What?'

Toby could hear her struggling to decide whether to confide in him or not.

'Come on, Em, what's going on?'

She sighed.

'I need the peace of our island. Everyone has a thought on what I say or do or wear and I thought I'd enjoy it. Honestly, I thought I'd be tough and have some witty retorts to come back with. I was ready for it.'

'Right.'

'But it's just so strange. I get papped going to the shops. I see my face on the front of magazines at the shop I've been photographed going to. It's so weird. I have thousands of messages from people and loads of them are lovely but some are just gross. Like, really fucked up. I think I don't want it anymore.'

There was a silence as he struggled with what to say but Emily broke it.

'Why did you call?'

'Oh – yes, sorry. I need to tell you something I've found out, but I'm not sure you're going to like it. Well, I know you won't. I think Matt might be able to help me too, is he around?'

'Yes, he is,' he could hear Emily's muffled shout to Matt to come to the phone. 'I've put you on speaker. Tobes, what's this about?'

Toby blew a long breath out.

'Okay. For a long time I've thought there was something really odd about our disappearance. The lack of searches for us. The immediacy to replace us on the programme, but keeping the programme on. Not long after I got home I started to get calls from a withheld number, and, long story short, they were from a producer on the show. She started telling me about the way our loss was handled at the production company.'

'Like what?' Toby heard Matt ask.

'Well. The day it was announced we were missing, adverts ran all over the place that the show was still going to be on, just without us.'

'So?'

'So, the print ads, the TV ads, the radio ads, they'd all been designed, shot or whatever, and they went up the very day we were announced as missing. How would they have been able to pull it all together so quickly—'

'Unless they already knew it was going to happen,' Emily finished for him. There was a silence as Matt and Emily took it in.

'But that's ridiculous. No, I don't believe it,' Matt said, breaking the quiet.

'I know, I didn't to begin with. It's so implausible. A TV company fakes our disappearance for ratings.'

'But it wasn't faked. We almost didn't survive,' Emily replied angrily. 'They were playing with our lives. We could have died.'

'Yes, and that's been one of many problems I've had with the theory as I've been trying to untangle what's true and what isn't,' Toby agreed, before rushing on to tell Emily what Zoe had told him, 'until Zoe called and told me there's a hut on the island full of supplies.'

'What?' Emily and Matt answered at the same time.

'There can't be. We'd have found it. We traipsed all over the place, Toby.' Emily's voice quivered with rage. Toby had felt the same when he'd begun to piece it all together so he allowed her anger to spill out.

'We did. But what the company hadn't accounted for were two things. One, in the middle of the storm we were set down in, we never saw the clearing that should have taken us to the hut. And two, the storms we survived blocked the paths we could have taken to the hut, so the further we walked into the island the more cut off from the supplies we became. Even though they thought they'd considered all possibilities, they forgot they couldn't control human beings and the choices they make.'

'But I don't get why they'd do it; it can't just be for ratings,' Matt said after a few seconds of crackling silence as they processed what Toby had told them.

'It was Patrick Roberts; he was pulling all the strings from the start. I've discovered he has serious money problems and the only way out was if his latest programme didn't flop. Instead, he invested in you, Emily.'

'Me?'

'Yes. And me. He made sure the ghostwriter story came out.'

'But…' Emily sounded confused.

'He has shares in Smith, Dean and Wooliss – your agency. It would only benefit him for you and I to sell more books – which happened even when my name was struck off their website. My books sold even more during the ghostwriter outing. It seems the old adage of there's no such thing as bad publicity is very true. Plus you became a record-breaker. Your book is second only to Harry Potter. Roberts is raking it in.'

'But what about June? He's not made anything from her?'

'Not directly. But it's his production company that makes her morning show and their ratings went up three hundred per cent when she disappeared. Even the outcry about the new look of the show made more people tune in. Plus, I think there might be more to it than that...' As Toby had been talking he'd had a thought which disappeared, a whisper about June he couldn't place.

'Which is?' Emily huffed a little.

'I can't... can't remember... can't put my finger on it... but I will. Matt, did you get any odd visits when Emily was on the island?'

There was quiet and Toby realised he needed a yes.

'Actually, now you come to mention it – I didn't get any visits, but we had that survey at the door, do you remember, Em? The week you were due to leave – the lady said she was from a skincare brand I think?'

'Did we?' Emily sounded confused.

'Yes – remember, I answered the door because one of the kids had just smeared peanut butter over the remote and you were dealing with that. She asked me about our household.'

'Er...'

Before Emily could distract him, Toby jumped in.

'What was she asking about? What brand?'

'Ha, well, now you come to mention it,' Matt laughed a little uncomfortably, 'I don't know if she did say where she was from. She had a lanyard around her neck and she looked like she was from a salon? I just… ah… fuck… but she asked about the whole family, not just Emily.'

'What did she ask?'

'She asked about whether we use sun creams, what SPF we use, whether any of us suffer in the heat and I thought how funny it was because I couldn't mention to her that the one person who never suffers is Emily who was going away to the sun.'

Toby heard the exasperation in Matt's voice.

'She didn't ask whether Emily could survive being on a desert island though. Or if she could cope with being near to death. How would I know that this was suspicious? I mean, it may not have been.'

Emily cleared her throat.

'I don't think that's all of it actually. I got an Instagram message from a fan, asking me about the kids and we had quite a long messaging chat. They asked about my life. My diet. My hopes and fears. But it was all presented in a way that was… I dunno… normal. Just like when I chat to anyone about my life. I was honest, but it wasn't out of the ordinary. Lots of people ask me about this sort of stuff.'

Toby had been taking notes.

'Tobes,' Matt's voice was authoritative, back in control, 'we need a plan. He can't get away with this – surely?'

Toby shrugged and realised they couldn't see him.

'I've written a book about everything how I see it. I've got anonymous reports from one of the producers at his company, I've spoken to his ex and his current wife – believe me they've got a lot to say,' he smiled ruefully, 'now all I need is to speak to Angie. I think she holds the key – but I don't know if she'll say something against him. It could harm her career.'

'He almost killed us. Surely she'll be able to see that's madness?' Emily sounded exasperated.

'Yes, but… I'm not sure she'll be on our side – she's likely made a lot of money out of us too.'

There was a pause, then Emily asked, 'Who's publishing your book?'

'Ah, well, of course no one will come near me now. So I'm considering printing it myself.'

'And then arming yourself with an incredible lawyer?' Matt sounded incredulous. 'I'm not sure that's a good plan. He'll come after you and you'll be in shreds.'

Toby looked at himself in the mirror. The grey around his temples had grown out over his ears a bit. He decided he quite liked the scruffier look.

'I'll figure out a way.'

There was silence.

'Maybe I can help,' Emily suggested.

Chapter Thirteen

Having tidied his flat, including clearing out the fridge and washing out the bin – tasks Toby would have usually left for his cleaner, but the last time he'd asked she'd shouted at him in Polish in such a way he was sure she'd cursed him – he realised there was nothing left he could distract himself with.

It had been over six months since Toby had last spoken with June. Five months since he'd begun having nightmares about her. Four months since he'd hidden all her social media posts from his timelines in a bid to rid himself of his memories of her. Three months since his mum had stopped asking whether he'd contacted her. Two months since he'd had lunch with Roberts' ex and all the papers had run opinion pieces on him.

One month since he'd promised Emily he'd call June straightaway to find out if she, or her assistant, had had any odd phone calls or any other evidence they could add to his argument.

With a shaking hand, he found her number and pressed call. Toby locked his attention on the waves, hoping the rhythm of the undulating greys and dark blues, mingled with the white froth of the breaks, would calm him.

The dial tone rang out as a long, low rumble and Toby realised June had to be somewhere abroad. He let it ring for a few goes, but she didn't pick up and it rang off. Shaking his head, Toby tried again, but almost instantly he felt irritated with her. Was she on holiday whilst he tried to find out how their lives were ruined?

His life.

Hers was fine.

Hers was so fine, she was abroad.

Toby heard the click and immediately felt like his stomach was going to fall through his arse.

'Hi, you've reached June. I'm somewhere in the world right now so please don't leave a message. Instead, call my PA if you have his number. If you don't, then I'm guessing I'm not interested in hearing from you! Bye!'

Toby realised he was grinning like a Cheshire cat at the bright and bubbly reply. It was so June – so full of optimism. He was instantly plunged into a memory of the two of them playing noughts and crosses in the sand, with stones and shells. They'd become highly competitive over the game and it had resulted in a tie – fifteen games each – so June had suggested they settle it like grown-ups. With an arm wrestle. Toby had known he'd win – he was twice the size of June – but he'd still agreed.

He realised he was smiling still but hadn't hung up and was now leaving a message entirely made up of dead air. He immediately hit the red button and ended the call.

'Fuck. Fuck, fuck, fuck. Fuck it.' Toby had begun pacing around the flat, like a caged animal, his hands clenched – the blood whooshing in his head. He hoped the message hadn't recorded. Just thirty seconds of nothing. He could have said anything but he'd just sat there, switched off. She'd think he was trying to scare her or manipulate her in some way – that was what The Bastard had done, he remembered her telling him.

'I need to call… shit, what's his name…' Toby paced, trying to remember June's PA's name whilst scrolling through his phone. He scrolled past hundreds of names; he couldn't remember who they belonged to and cringed at the descriptions he had given them: *blonde met at SoHo House, brunette with the tits.* Toby made a point of deleting those and worse, as he looked through his phone for a name which he'd recognise, whilst wondering at the same time whether he ever knew June's PA, least of all had his number.

'Who are these people?'

He read names of old school friends he'd not spoken to in a long time. Of famous pals who had stopped calling as soon as he received negative press. Of numerous names he had no recollection of ever adding to his phone but knowing they must have had at least a fleeting importance to him at that moment. Of takeaways. Taxis. Restaurants.

'So much for so little.' He realised, irritably, that everything he'd considered as important in his life, embodied by the numbers in his phone, were of no consequence if he couldn't be with June.

Giving up with ever finding the number, Toby decided to swallow his pride and messaged Emily.

What's June's PA's name? And number? Cheers.

He didn't have to wait long and saw she was typing.

I KNEW you wouldn't call her last month!!!! It's 07718338072. He's called Tom.

TOM. He knew she'd mentioned his name at some point, but in the mists of time he'd misplaced it.

Now he had the name and number, there really was no excuse to call of course. Toby picked up his phone and another message came through from Emily.

She might have told him she doesn't want to hear from you of course. If so, I'll call – ok?

Toby considered the message. He knew that despite their rocky start, he could count on Emily as a true friend.

But he had to be the one who spoke to June.

'Right. No more dicking about.' If he said it out loud, he was hopeful he'd become far more confident than he felt and quickly pressed call to Tom.

The phone rang twice and was picked up.

'Tom Yardley speaking, how can I help?'

'Ah... yes... hi... it's, ha, well...' Toby cleared his throat and focused on one of the intricate cornices that decorated his Regency flat. 'Hi Tom, we don't know each other, but I'm Toby Masters and—'

'Oh Toby, hello. I've heard a lot about you.' Tom's reaction seemed warm and, emboldened by this, Toby tried to push on.

'Right – well, all good I hope.' There was a silence and Toby rushed on, 'Anyway, it's just, well. I tried calling June and—'

'Ah, well she's travelling at the moment.'

'Travelling? Do you mean on holiday? Where?' Toby wanted to ask who with, but decided not to push it.

'She's filming a new series. It's called, *June in Every Country* – well, that's the working title. I think they're trying to make a pun,' Tom laughed a little, 'but it means she's filming all over the place right now. This week she's in Mexico, last week she was in Morocco and Dubai, and next week she's heading to Delhi.'

'Woah. June?'

'Yep,' Toby could hear the pride in Tom's voice, 'she was so invigorated by the experience you all had that she couldn't settle with being at home and living the life she had before. She pitched the idea to Channel 4 and they loved it – certain demographic and all that.'

'Is she alone?' Toby heard himself ask.

'No, she's got the crew there of course. But it's a small team – and the idea is they basically leave June in the middle of somewhere and she has to survive for a couple of days. Of course, she's been briefed on places to visit, but she's loving it.'

'Wow.' Toby broke off as he realised that June had moved on. He'd spent the past six months thinking about and longing for her, hiding away from the world and investigating Patrick Roberts. Meanwhile, June had upped sticks and gone away.

'She always was the bravest out of us,' he admitted, remembering how much June had grown whilst they were on the island. How her timidity had fallen away as she'd learnt how to survive.

'How can I help?' Tom prompted, and Toby shook his head, clearing the feelings of nostalgia.

'Right. Well, I really need to get in touch with June, and her number goes straight to answerphone? I need to ask a couple of questions.'

'No, sorry Toby, but she made it clear she wasn't going to take calls from you,' Tom said honestly.

'Don't spare my feelings.' Toby forced a laugh.

'Sorry, but she was quite specific.'

'Shit.' Toby sat on his sofa, wondering whether he could finish the book without June. He needed her story as much as the others. And he needed her.

'Was there anything I could help with?' Tom, the ever-helpful PA, asked. Toby was just about to say no, when he realised he could ask the questions of Tom.

'Actually, there is. Can you remember, either before June left for *Star Survivor* or when she went missing, whether you had any odd communications from anyone? A visit? A phone call?'

Tom was silent.

'Not that I can recall, no, why?'

Toby outlined his theories on their disappearance and how his mother and Matt had recalled odd encounters which could lead to evidence that their accident was actually a set-up. He explained how Patrick Roberts could stand to make money out of himself and Emily, and to an extent June because of his link to her programme. But he was drawing a real blank about why she in particular had been chosen.

Tom took in everything with audible gasps of surprise.

'And there was me thinking you were calling to ask her out,' he replied when Toby had finished speaking.

Toby smiled to himself.

'Well, I had hoped to do that too.'

There was another silence.

'Of course, if you were to say it was an emergency and you absolutely *had* to speak with her...'

Toby allowed himself to smile again.

'Thanks Tom.'

'And Toby?'

'Yep.'

'She's been really good lately. Really good. Her ex was trying to get back with her and she almost wobbled, but stood firm. Don't, well...'

'Don't fuck it up?'

'Yes, exactly.'

'I promise, if you put in a good word for me, I won't fuck it up. Again.'

'Huh, funny – did you say the guy is called Patrick Roberts?' Tom added, just before Toby was about to hang up.

'Yes, why?'

'I just... feel like I recognise the name... I can't think why though.' Tom sounded hesitant and Toby shrugged.

'It's probably just because he's fairly well-known.'

'Yes, probably.'

Toby hung up and grinned when he heard his phone ping, with what he expected was to be a message from Tom confirming his call with June.

Instead, it was from an unknown number.

Go back to children's books, that's where fantasies belong.

Chapter Fourteen

'Hi.'

'Hi, you look – well.' Toby's urge to tell June how hot she looked conflicted with wanting to say how serene and beautiful she appeared, and he didn't know if women were keen on being described as serene. But she was. Not just in how she was dressed, a simple black dress which skimmed her tiny figure, showing off lean and toned arms, but also the glow emanating from her entirely unmade-up face.

'You look well, too.' She smiled and popped a kiss on his cheek. 'Nice to see you lost the *Cast Away* beard. Not your finest hour, darling.'

She turned to the waiter. 'Can I have some water with a slice of lemon please, and…' She looked at Toby who realised he'd been gawping at her, his eyes wide with the reality of the woman in front of him.

'Er, same. Thanks.' He smiled at the male twenty-something waiter in jeans and a tight-cut T-shirt which suggested a very good six-pack underneath. 'I used to look like that, you know,' he mentioned to June, causing a tiny ripple of a smile to flit across her face.

'I know. We used to do the segment "six-pack or multipack" on *Wake Up*, where we'd rate male celebrities on how fit they were. Or are.' She winked at Toby.

'I'm pretty certain I should be horrified at that. Claim sexism or something?' he replied, but grinned. 'Did I do all right?'

June laughed. 'Of course. Body like yours is easy to rate,' she smiled again at him, 'but we're not here to talk about your abs. Or are we? Tom was fairly cryptic on the phone.' She nodded thanks as the waiter placed a tall, thin glass of water filled with ice and lemon, in front of her.

'This place is beautiful by the way,' she added, looking around at the courtyard they were sitting in, which was filled with roses of all colours that climbed erratically up walls, grew in tiny shoots from large reclaimed wood pots, and sat in tiny bunches on the tables. Dotted between the roses were pinpricks of soft warm lights, twinkling and hinting at their presence. To complete the effect, light flickered against the walls courtesy of the church candles placed on the tables or sat in hurricane lamps nearby.

'Yeah, I can't take the credit for it. Tom organised us.' He smiled at June, knowing she wouldn't be upset that her PA had helped mastermind their first meeting in over half a year. It had been his idea to meet somewhere rather than discuss anything over the phone, and a secluded pop-up that was only in existence for a couple of days seemed perfect.

'Okay. So I'm intrigued. We're in a stunning place, you won't talk to me over the phone and you've not spoken to me in months. Why now?' June was straight to the point.

'Yep. I know. I don't know which bit to start with,' he admitted, and shrugged a little to emphasise this.

'The most important bit I think,' June replied evenly, smiling at the waiter as he placed a delicate bowl of velvety green soup in front of each of them, the hints of wild garlic causing Toby to salivate.

'There's, ah, no menu here by the way. They cook what they've foraged or bought on the market that day,' Toby explained, worried June might think him presumptuous.

She smiled broadly. 'You're talking to a woman who ate dried sheep's testicles last week as she was told it was a delicacy. There's nothing I won't try now; I'm happy for someone to tell me what's best to eat.' To emphasise this she dipped the smooth copper-coloured spoon in the soup and savoured the mouthful.

'That is gorgeous. Before you tell me the big important news, enjoy this,' she ordered and Toby did as he was told. It was the way things had worked on the island – she'd tell him to do something and he'd do it.

'That's exquisite,' he managed, after appreciating the few spoons of the earthy, rich soup that had been served to them.

June patted her mouth with a thick cream napkin and sipped her water.

'Now. Tell me what we're doing here.'

Toby was about to launch into everything he'd

discovered, the severity of the cover-up of their disappearances and his theory about Patrick Roberts. He looked up to tell her and opened his mouth.

'I missed you.'

The words came out before he'd had a chance to catch himself.

'Sorry. Sorry, I wasn't going to blurt it out... like that... but... and, well, that wasn't why I wanted to see you.'

June looked hurt.

'Wasn't it?'

He shook his head. This had all gone very wrong, he didn't want to lose June again.

'I did miss you. I do. You're pretty much all I think about, when I'm not trying to work out why a company would send us off to a remote island, not caring if we survived or not.'

She was silent and he reached his hands over to hers.

'June, I'm so sorry I didn't see it before, didn't recognise that you... and I...' He scrambled for the words, hoping she'd help him but she continued to just stare at him. 'After we got back, I had such a hard time and, well, I thought you'd be better off without me.'

'That wasn't your decision to make.' Her words were quiet, but calm.

'No. I realise that,' he paused and scratched his stubble a little, 'but when we were on the island, after we kissed by the fire that night, I thought you'd mention it, that something might happen between us. And when we were rescued, I just assumed we'd get together. But days passed and I convinced myself we wouldn't work.' He breathed out and smiled at the waiter who replenished his water.

'I didn't mention it because I didn't know if we'd live. I wanted to know we could build a life together – not die together, Toby.' June's eyes were sad and he remembered the day he'd had to wave goodbye to her as she'd swum away. He'd had no idea if she'd make it, or if the rest of them would.

He'd had no idea it would be the last time they'd see each other either. Would it have been different? If he'd known? Would he have insisted he took her place? He shook his head. No, if the last few months were anything to go by, he needed to learn from his mistakes. Not dwell on them.

'If you're worried about the age difference,' she began, but Toby had got up from his seat and stepped the short distance to June's side, pulling her gently out of her chair.

'I'm not,' he replied gently, holding her face in his hands, and leant in to kiss her.

STAR ROMANCERS

DISGRACED former author Toby Masters has been spotted canoodling with fellow island survivor June Sharp.

The couple were spotted in a pop-up restaurant near Covent Garden yesterday and other diners were quick to snap the pair as they cosied up.

TV presenter June, who's fifteen years older than Masters, has been filming around the world for her latest TV show but clearly had time to fit in a few mouthfuls of her latest squeeze.

Diners watched on as the couple, pictured, engaged in a "swoon-inducing snog" as one Instagrammer described it.

Halle, who was dining at the time, posted under her Instagram handle MummaEats, "Just watching the most romantic PDA – bit worried he'll eat her entirely before the meal is over though!!!!!!!!!!"

There has been long-held reports of the two getting together on the island they were stranded on last year, but nothing has been seen of them in public until now.

It had been rumoured June had reunited with her ex-husband, with photos emerging of the two just a month ago, however this coupling up with Masters would suggest her marriage is well and truly over, something which concerns her friends.

A source close to June said:

"June has changed a lot since her return from the

island and is playing a huge game of risk with a lot of decisions she's making right now. We're worried she's going to get her heart broken by this fling with a man so much younger than her."

GOT a story? RING The Sun on 020 7946 0981.

Chapter Fifteen

'Aww, I think it's just so lovely you guys have got together.' Emily's face beamed out of June's phone as her and Toby bowed their heads into the frame.

'Are you surprised?' June asked, her body pressed firmly against Toby's, taut under the loose navy silk jumpsuit she'd changed into minutes before from a selection of clothes Tom had sent round to Toby's flat. Toby smiled at the memories of the last three days. They'd barely left the bedroom, alternating between grabbing at each other like teenagers with out-of-control hormones, to talking about everything, napping a little, eating delivered food and then repeating it all again.

'So what's the plan, Toby? You've got the girl, now you destroy Patrick Roberts?'

He laughed. 'Not sure I'll be able to destroy him, but I'd like the world to know what a shit he is. He spouts on about being authentic, but nothing about him is.'

'That goes for the rest of us then.' Emily laughed, a little crazily.

'You okay?' June asked, full of concern. Toby, meanwhile, had realised he could see June's nipple grazing up against the jumpsuit material and the more he could see it, the more he couldn't control his erection.

'Sure. It's just that it's been a gruelling month of book promotions including signings, talks at numerous locations including a playgroup and a vineyard, podcast and TV appearances, book-club chats, online blog tours and radio broadcasts. I'm a bit fed up of it all – hang on.' She looked away from the camera but they could still hear her speaking, 'Okay, I'll be right there.' Emily looked back to the screen.

'Sorry, they want me in the studio. I'm on Radio 2 in a mo, why don't you pop it on – it'll be the only way to dampen that one's lust.' She laughed and nodded at Toby, who hadn't been listening. He'd been too busy snaking his arm around June and placing his hand inside a gap he'd found in her jumpsuit. Her bare skin was cool and soft to the touch and he could rub his thumb over the hipbone which jutted out a little. His cock was getting harder and it was all he could do to smile at Emily goodbye as June hung up.

She stood up and he allowed his hand to fall away as she stepped a little from him.

'Alexa, Radio 2,' she said clearly, holding his gaze.

As he watched on, leaning back a little on his bed, she slowly undid the buttons on the front of the jumpsuit. When three had popped open, the capped sleeves on both sides fell away from her shoulders, exposing the tops of her breasts.

Toby made to move.

'No touching. Wait,' she told him and, turned on, he did as he was told. In the background, the radio was playing the song that was still on everywhere from the winner of *Star Survivor*, Cyan.

Toby looked on as June painstakingly undid the last three buttons, exposing more flesh as she did. Her breasts revealed themselves, the dark pink nipples hard with arousal.

'Last one.' She smiled, and undid the final button.

'Welcome back, that was Cyan and You Loved Me,*'* Mike, the radio presenter said in the background, *'and today we have a special guest in the studio,'* he continued.

Toby looked on as the jumpsuit fell to the floor, exposing June's mound with its lightly covered bush.

'Fuck, bugger, shit, ouch. No.'

Both looked at the radio.

'Apologies, listeners, if you caught any of that, we have Emily Chase, or as most of you will know her, "SIMI" with us in the studio. The blogger who survived being deserted on an island and has since, on her return, seen the most phenomenal rise to fame. But still, I take it, still trying to balance everything.' He laughed in what Toby could only assume was a phoney fashion.

Emily's voice came over the speaker.

'I am so sorry for my outburst there. I took a sip of coffee and basically everything went wrong. Live radio, eh?' She laughed and the DJ joined in.

'Live indeed. Sounds to me like you've got your hands full. We'll have another song, then we'll find out how things are going for you these days.'

Toby moved to the end of the bed and pulled June

towards him, her legs gave little resistance and she stepped closer. He began to kiss her thigh, lightly, his hands cupping the curve of her ass.

The radio was playing *Seven Nation Army* by The White Stripes whilst Toby continued to feather the tops of June's thighs with light kisses, aware his cock was straining in his boxers, begging to be released.

As the song faded out, the presenter started again.

'So, Emily. Your book is all about parenting and offers numerous tips on, let's see, what does it say on the back, "the perils and pitfalls of parenting from someone still living it". Sounds good. Must admit, I've not read it as I don't have any children, but I know lots of people are swearing by your advice. How does that feel, to be a voice for your generation?'

June had stopped caressing Toby's hair and he could tell she was half listening as they heard Emily explain she was thrilled so many people felt empathy and understanding to her experiences and if she could make it so that one parent didn't feel alone, she knew she'd achieved her goal.

Toby ignored his island friend and began licking June's thighs, working his way nearer and nearer to her mound when he heard a ping.

'You don't usually make that sound.' He looked up at her and grinned as she laughed.

'My phone, I better check it…' She moved away a little and read it. 'It's Emily, she must be texting whilst in the studio.'

'What's she saying?' Toby realised he was unlikely to get the ending he'd been hoping for.

'"Why is this man interviewing me if he hasn't read even a bit of the book? What was the point in adding to my week if he doesn't care whether I'm a parenting writer or a fucking nature lover?".'

'Ah, she doesn't sound happy.'

'Neither do you, let's help you out with that.' June threw her phone aside and looked suggestively at Toby's crotch as he laughed. She straddled him as in the background they could hear the DJ.

'You're, ah, very free with your words,' the DJ laughed, *'as we all heard. I just wondered if you worry your kids will pick them up? Surely swearing and drinking gin at 3pm isn't the best influence on your children?'*

'Christ, what's his problem?' Toby murmured as June went to pull his boxers down.

'Shock jock crap, I should think; now, let's just take care of this.' She smiled and went down on him, taking him fully.

He took a deep breath in and felt his brain go blank. Somewhere in the distance he could hear Emily stammering on the radio.

'I...' she managed.

'Don't you worry, you'll be responsible for a generation of parents, mainly women, who will think it's okay to be lazy and reckless, swearing and drinking whenever, because people like you posted it on social media?' The DJ laughed again.

'Fuck, June... fuck, you're too good at this... fuck...' Toby could feel his entire body release itself.

'I'm just asking, I think it's a really interesting debate to discuss. Nature-nurture and all that,' the DJ suggested

in the background, not giving Emily a chance to respond, *'because a lot of what you and those other so-called influencers appear to celebrate is ineptitude or terrible parenting. That's the gist of your book, isn't it?'*

'Ah fuck, June, fuck-fuck-fuck.' He shuddered as he came, relishing the clarity his un-fogged brain brought.

'Mike,' Toby could hear the smile in Emily's voice, so sweet, so calm, *'I think it's great to have discussions around this. Of course,'* she allowed the words to drip like honey, *'it's often easier to speak on a subject you're not familiar with.'* She forced out a light tinkle of laughter.

'Here it comes,' Toby muttered.

'I thought you already had.' June lay next to him, his dressing gown wrapped around her frame.

'Funny lady,' he shook his head. 'No, Emily's about to lose her shit, I recognise the tone.' June lay on his chest as they listened to their friend.

Emily continued.

'As you're not a parent, I doubt you've ever had one of those unbearable moments in the day when two children are screaming at you, you've run out of nappies, you've had zero sleep for days and you go to the fridge and realise the milk is gone so you can't have a tea.' She paused, Toby knew, to allow the words to paint a picture, but continued before the DJ could reply.

'And you can't pop out to the shops, because popping out, Mike, is impossible with one, two or a thousand children, so what do you do? You dry the tears as best you can – theirs and yours – and you put the children in their cots and hope, no, pray they finally bloody go to sleep, so that you can have a moment, one single, blissful,

soul-enriching moment, when there's silence and you can just be.'

'I think you're right. What I'd pay to see that DJ's face right now.' June grinned.

'And in that moment, Mike, you see, you reach for your phone. Your only access to the world outside the four walls which have shrunken in on you so bloody much that you're convinced the house is disappearing, and you go on social media because you want to know that despite appearances, despite not seeing your other half for days, or despite not getting to playgroup in weeks, you are not alone.'

The two of them lay on the bed and heard the deep breath Emily took. They could sense the spiky frustrations coursing through their friend, feeding her and giving her the energy she needed.

'You scroll, you click and you find other people like you, having the same awful day or week or month or year, and you say "Yes, that's me, I'm having the same time as you. Thank god it's not just me. Thank god I'm not doing this all wrong". And who cares, Mike, if the way for some is a cheeky glass of wine with lunch, or gin o'clock starting at 3pm? Who really cares as long as their children are safe, fed relatively well and you've got through another day?' They heard her take another deep breath. *'Because, Mike, that's what parenting is. It's getting through a day, then a week, then a month and then you realise that the thing that was upsetting you so much has faded – it's been replaced by something else. You know things will change. But until they do, you look for people, like me, to tell you it's okay to get things wrong.'*

Emily's breath was caught on the microphone, a deep inhalation.

'Tenner says she walks out of the interview.' Toby turned to June and she smiled.

'No, she'll stay put.'

'And I got this wrong today, Mike. I should be at home making a costume for my daughter's school play but today I gave up my time, to talk to you. To someone who couldn't be arsed to even read the back of my book before speaking to me, let alone the crib notes for it.'

Toby's eyes widened as he heard Emily shout, *'Bye Mike,'* and a whine of silence as she was no longer on the airwaves.

'She fucking did it – ten pounds to me I think.' He laughed.

'Wow.' June looked shocked. 'I can't believe she called him out like that.' Toby was looking thoughtful and shook his head, his mind still post-blow clear.

'No. She's done what I should have. She's used her voice and spoken up. That interview will be replayed a thousand times over and the message is loud and clear. Don't fuck with her.'

SLUMMING IT/HIDING IT?

BLOGGER and island survivor Emily Chase has gone AWOL since an out-of-character outburst on BBC Radio 2 three days ago.

Nothing has been added to her social media channels since she last posted on Friday with the caption *'listen to me in five minutes talking rubbish on the radio!!!'* with a photo of her at the studios.

Chase was due to be promoting the paperback version of her multimillion bestseller on the drive-time show, but the interview was cut short after a lengthy outburst by the blogger to DJ Mike Rendell who was verbally abused by the star before she left the studio abruptly.

Mike was unavailable for comment, however online he wrote:

'Sometimes people can't take criticism. If you're in the public eye, you need to be prepared that not everyone will love you. However, of course she's welcome back to the show any time.'

Chase's outburst came when she was being pushed on her role and responsibility to her millions of followers, something which angered the blogger.

Her publicist said: *'Emily is obviously very sorry for any hurt she may have caused. She has been working incredibly hard lately and we believe she needs a few days' rest before any further promotions.'*

Comments on the star's Instagram page have varied, with many supporting the blogger for her response.

Triciasmum said:

'Poor SIMI, she's been working so hard and all she wants is to see her lovely girls. That DJ should have done his research.'

Some others were less impressed with the blogger's response.

Mumof3boyz said:

'You should be ashamed of yourself, you've become popular because we all want to support you. If you can't be nice then you shouldn't be supported #BOYCOTTSIMI.'

Emily was unavailable for comment.

Chapter Sixteen

'Tom, you okay? She's not with me, she's filming.' Toby tried to calm his breathing a little as June's PA had called him mid-run.

'No, it's okay. It was you I was after,' Tom explained. 'I thought you should know something though. Well, two things.'

Toby jogged a little on the spot to stop his heart rate coming down.

'Okay?'

'We spoke, what, about a month ago about your theory?' Tom checked, with his head on his side, enquiringly. The image on Toby's phone was grainy.

'Yep, must be, because I've been with June for about three weeks.' Toby laughed, and gave up on running, choosing to lean against a turquoise street light on Brighton seafront. Today was the first one he'd not spent with June since the two had met for dinner in the rose garden and he couldn't believe how odd it felt not to have her around.

'You two are so sweet.' Tom smiled and Toby beamed back, noting how happy he looked in the small picture on the bottom right of the screen. A gull screeched overhead and he looked towards the pier, its structure silhouetted against the bright morning. The traffic was just starting to get busy; soon the area would be choked with day-trippers and tourists, workers and students all racing to their part of the city.

'Okay. Well I knew I recognised Patrick Roberts' name, not just from the newspapers, and, whilst I was going through some filing for June yesterday, I came across a letter which must have got mixed up with it. It's dated from two years ago and to her ex – but, Toby, they were in business together and by the sounds of it, her ex had bailed out Roberts in some way. In the letter he – Roberts – says "*if I can ever repay the favour, let me know*". What if the favour was to send June to that island to… get rid of her?' Tom said it in a way which was light enough that if Toby scoffed, the PA would be able to say he was kidding, to save face. But Toby looked at the phone and didn't scoff.

'What?'

'"Repay the favour".'

'You could be right.'

Tom sighed. 'I didn't want you to agree with me.'

'I didn't want to, if that helps.' Toby kicked a stone across the pavement and tried to quell his fears.

'Do you think they sent June to that island on purpose? To punish her?'

The way Tom asked it, the fear in his voice, brought Toby back to the present.

'I don't know. But it seems plausible.'

There was a silence at the other end of the call and Toby looked out at the sea, drawing strength from the crashing of nature around him. He watched on as the sea threw its surf on the pebbles, then slowly sucked it back again. Back and forth. Push and pull. Never ceasing, unrelenting. Powerful.

Just like Roberts. He'd been playing them all – treating them as puppets.

'Send me a copy of the letter, and anything else you see.'

'What are you going to do?'

Toby grimaced; he was relieved the conversation wasn't in person or he wouldn't have been able to meet Tom's eye.

'It's probably best you don't know, but I hope to set the record straight.'

'Toby – don't let anything happen to June, not again. She means a lot to me.' The PA smiled sadly and Toby was reminded again of what their losses had meant to their relatives and friends. The trauma. But it was Patrick Roberts' fault. 'Oh, and Toby. Whilst we're on the topic of, erm, odd things happening...' Tom squirmed and Toby looked on, confused.

'Go on?'

'Er, I'll just have to get this over with. But, okay... a couple of days ago I got asked out on a date by this guy and he was incredibly beautiful, like stunning. Too good for me to be honest.'

'Right? Good for you, but what's that got to do with me?'

'It's... well. I'm not proud of myself but with June away at yours at the moment, I've been staying in her house to keep things secure – she knows by the way, I'm in the guest room – but the guy invited himself back to mine. Hers. And I never do that. Not whilst I'm at her house; it's her place and she should trust me. But he was so good-looking, and funny and into me, I brought him back. And...' Tom broke off, clearly uncomfortable with where the conversation was heading.

'What?'

'After we'd... you know... I must have fallen asleep... and when I woke up Hot Guy had disappeared. And when I went to the kitchen for some water, well... everything felt weird. Everywhere.'

'Weird, how?'

'Weird like it all seemed like it had been moved. Everything seemed slightly out of place – like it had all been set down slightly off-centre, and when I checked the clock I realised I'd been asleep for over twelve hours. I think, I think he slipped something into my drink. And I think someone went through the house.'

Toby looked at the phone in horror.

'Was anything gone? Did you tell June? Is anyone on the CCTV?'

Tom shook his head and looked full of remorse, answering the questions in the order Toby asked them.

'Not that I could see. No... I don't want to freak her out and, no, it's not been working properly for ages – it's due to be fixed next week.'

'Shit, Tom. Shit. Fuck. And you've waited two days to tell me. To tell us? I'm going to have to tell her, you know.' Toby's voice was hard. Frustration tumbled out of him like the pebbles being thrown around by the shoreline.

Tom raked his hair with his free hand and sighed.

'I know. I'm sorry but I was just so embarrassed. She trusts me and I... I just don't know how I would forgive myself if anything were to happen to her,' he allowed a pause whilst he thought about the possibilities, 'again.'

Toby shook his head, watching a man idly walking at the front of the pier. He looked lost. He knew how the man felt.

'She trusted you, Tom. Hopefully she'll see it as an incredibly stupid mistake, but who knows who that guy was and what he was after. He could have been trying to get some sort of scoop for one of the red tops. Or maybe her ex is looking for a way to get back with her.'

'She told you about the letters then?' Tom asked, then put his hand to his mouth at the look of surprise which skittered across Toby's features.

'What letters?'

'Er, probably best you speak to her.' Tom shifted uncomfortably.

'What. Letters?' Toby could feel the old white rage, the one he'd associated with drinking. June hadn't mentioned anything about letters from her ex.

'Oh, it was a load of nonsense. He sent a few letters when she came back from the island, asking her for forgiveness, saying that he loved her, he missed her. Usual nonsense from that dreadful man,' Tom explained and

Toby understood he was trying to undo any damage he may have caused by diminishing it.

'Does she still have them?'

'I don't think you need to read them,' Tom replied, looking pained, his image pixelating a little.

Toby took a deep breath in. He was not going to manage this like the old Toby. He was going to think sensibly.

'I don't care about them. But if she did keep them, they could be used as evidence potentially, of how he was involved in June's disappearance. If it was as a favour to him and he discovered she almost died, when he was actually hoping to just scare her back into his arms, well, he'd ask for forgiveness wouldn't he?'

'I can have a look. Should I ask her where they are?' Tom cocked his head to one side and Toby nodded.

'There won't be any secrets between us – there's been enough of that elsewhere. I'll talk to her tonight and tell her I know and don't care – really, I don't – but if she has kept them, they could be vital to us undoing what her ex has done.'

Chapter Seventeen

'You'd love the beaches we have near to mine, you know.' June smiled up at Toby from her position on the red tartan blanket they'd brought down to the shore to enjoy the sunset on. She stuck a wooden fork into the polystyrene tray that held a collection of golden-hued chips.

'This smell is heavenly,' she inhaled the food and grinned, 'just the merest waft of vinegar and my mouth is watering. I'm sure being by the sea makes these taste even better.'

Toby watched as she tucked into a couple of chips.

'I can't believe how much vinegar you've put on those. They're dripping.' He laughed, and enjoyed his own, slightly drier versions.

'Only way to enjoy them,' she said through a muffled mouthful.

'Any luck remembering where you put the letters then?' he pushed, lightly. When June had arrived back from filming she'd been tired and crabby, so when he'd brought up the topic of her ex, all she'd done was say she didn't want to discuss The Bastard, and had taken herself off for a long bath.

It was only the lure of chip-shop chips on the beach that had tempted her out of the bathroom, and Toby had done his best to keep the conversation away from her ex until she'd eaten something. If he'd learnt anything from surviving the island, it was that if you were hungry more often than not it meant you'd be grumpy. Even if someone told you you'd won the lottery.

June licked her fingers, savouring the salty tang, and bundled up her rubbish. She took a swig of water and replaced the bottle on the blanket.

'I don't know. A lot has happened in the past six months.' She looked to the quietly lapping water with the pink light reflecting off it. 'I remember seeing one and being shaken up about it.' She turned to Toby to get his attention. 'He asked to meet. I think he said he missed me and I, I was tempted,' she admitted, reddening a little.

'It's okay – that's normal, he's been a large part of your life,' he said quietly, hoping she'd continue.

She shook her head.

'No, it wasn't like that. I was tempted to meet to tell him it was over and that he needed to stop trying to get in touch. When you and I... you know... kissed, on the island, it was a turning point for me.'

Toby smiled in a lascivious fashion. 'Well, thank you.'

'Hey, shut up you,' she leant into him and pecked him

on the cheek, 'I don't mean it like that. Yes, it was lovely to have a kiss – but for me it was the actual moment I realised I was able to move on from... him... even if it meant I had to survive on an island to do so.'

'But?' he prompted.

'But I didn't tell him. I was going to and then I came to my senses. He had always manipulated me and he was trying to do it again, but with the letters and trying to meet. This time I was in control.'

'What did you do?'

June sipped her water thoughtfully.

'I wrote him one back. I told him if I hadn't recently survived living on a deserted island, if I was the old June, I might have been weaker and invited him back into my life. But I'd come to the brink of death and I'd learnt how to live. I told him I'd made friends for life who had taught me far more than he'd ever done, and I told him I was happy,' she smiled. 'I didn't hear from him again.'

'And the letters?'

'It's you, June.' The shout from across the beach distracted the two. A woman of June's age came walking carefully across the pebbles to them; she had a red-and-white-spotted bandana tied around her hair, huge sixties-style glasses and a floaty white dress. She was accompanied by a man of a similar age, greying to almost white, with a deep tan, a Hawaiian-style shirt and light-coloured shorts.

'Hi, yes I'm June.' The presenter smiled.

'I said so. I told you, didn't I, Phil?' The woman turned to the man June assumed was her husband.

'We've watched all your programmes. Are you doing another one? You're such an inspiration – we've booked to go on a safari. You've inspired us to really go for it when it comes to our holidays,' the woman said enthusiastically. 'We used to go to the same place, didn't we?'

Her husband smiled and nodded in agreement.

'Yes—'

'Anyway,' the woman interrupted him and smiled knowingly at June, 'we were bored of the same thing all the time and I've been watching you. Well, you survived that awful island and now you're popping up all over the world and I thought, well, if she can do it, then so can I. Well, we – I had to bring him along didn't I?'

June laughed. 'Yes, only fair.'

'Anyway, I wanted to say thank you for inspiring us. And well done you for just getting out there – very brave. Oh, and I'm going to say – I said I would if I ever ran into you – well done for getting rid of that... well, that man, you're well shot of him. You should have some fun.'

'Thank you.'

'No, thank you. Come on, Phil, let's leave them to it.' She nodded in Toby's direction.

June watched the couple walk off hand in hand and smiled broadly. As they walked away, they could hear the woman's voice carrying on the wind.

'I'm sure I recognise that chap too. I'll ask one of the girls – they'll know.'

'You've inspired someone,' Toby grinned, 'and I might be someone. It's a good day for the both of us.'

June laughed, colouring a little, and shuffled on the blanket – the pebbles were starting to dig into her backside a little.

'I get a bit of that now. I never did when I was on *Wake Up*.'

'You're being you – that's why,' Toby said. 'People like that.'

'Huh, and to think I'd never have any of it if it weren't for surviving on the island and being removed from *Wake Up*. My ex has done me a favour.' She grimaced.

'Sort of. Apart from almost getting you killed. It's more like you've taken advantage of what could have been a shit outcome.'

'Point taken.'

They both looked out to the sea. The sun had disappeared behind the horizon and a chill had settled over the beach.

'They're in a Jo Malone box in my wardrobe. Right at the back, under a pile of shoes,' she paused and blew out a deep breath. 'I don't know why I kept them.'

Toby put his arm around her and pulled her into him.

'Because it's what we do. But now we're going to move on together – sound good?' He cupped her chin with his free hand and kissed her gently on the lips. She tasted of salt and vinegar.

'Let's go back to the flat for dessert,' he suggested quietly into her ear, enjoying the gentle shiver of anticipation from her.

'Sounds good.'

As they packed up, he sent a text to Tom, knowing they had the evidence he needed to help hang Patrick Roberts out to dry.

Just as long as someone else hadn't already found them.

DON'T BE SHELLFISH

INSTAGRAM influencer and Times Bestseller, Emily Chase, has broken her self-imposed media blackout with a cryptic post that has left her followers baffled.

The post appears to relate to the countdown of a launch, but no one is sure what the star writer and island survivor is counting towards.

A picture of five shells is accompanied with the phrase "five days".

The mother of two, who had an on-air disagreement with Radio 2 presenter DJ Mike Rendell, has not used any of her social media channels for three weeks and has cancelled all appearances, since the out-of-character outburst.

Her agent, who was approached about the post, has replied with "no comment", leading some of her fans to come up with their own conclusions.

One posted underneath, "Are we soon to hear the pitter-patter of more SIMI feet?" whilst another asked, "Ooooh, are we getting book two earlier than expected?"

Meanwhile, one of Emily's fellow islanders, Zoe, has been photographed out and about in London, visiting various stores with her entourage, with fans hopeful a new British film is on the horizon. The star has said she's in England for "personal reasons".

If you have any information, contact The Mirror *news desk on 02284 724702.*

Chapter Eighteen

'This is happening fast,' June said, looking around the lounge where cardboard boxes were stacked and others of varied sizes sat, open and empty, surrounded by packing materials and potential contents. Walls were left bare, save for random picture hooks and sun-bleached marks.

Emily looked up from the chow mein she was inhaling quickly, barely giving it time to touch the sides, and nodded, waving her chopsticks in the air to emphasise her point.

'I know. It's been a bit of a whirlwind, but the time was right – wasn't it?' she said to Matt who was sat to her side on the floor, eating equally as quickly as his wife, a baseball cap pulled on backwards and his oversized jogging bottoms covered in dust and debris.

He smiled. 'Yep. We were talking about what the future should look like for us, and I've been working a little on a project this past year or so which gave me an idea and when I put it to Em, she was thrilled. And, let's be honest, when your stuff goes out there,' he indicated Toby with a slight incline of his head, 'we're going to want to be as far away as possible from it all. It makes sense to disappear and keep our heads down for a bit.'

'Well,' Zoe interrupted, taking a sip of cola and wincing at the sugar, 'I think it's a brilliant idea and I couldn't think of a better one for you both.' She grinned and raised her can to mark a cheers.

June's laugh caused the large earrings she was wearing to move vigorously around, reflecting the log fire and throwing sparkles around the space nearest to her.

'You would think it was a good idea – Matt's got you as an investor.' She smiled at Zoe's wide grin, a grin which stretched further on the actor's face as Annie leant in and hugged her girlfriend with happiness.

Toby watched the interactions between his friends and felt a moment of the terror which had been seizing him the past few weeks dissipate briefly as he enjoyed their pleasure. He'd been thankful when Matt had told him a week ago that he and Emily had decided to take on a run-down château in the South of France, with the aim to turn it into a B & B, but that they needed to move quickly to secure the girls their school places. It had been a joint dream for them for years and meant Matt had a chance at working on something architecturally difficult, which he could call his own.

It had made sense, too, for Zoe to invest, as she'd been looking for a suitable location for her next film, especially with the Oscar buzz around the one based on their disappearance.

'What time's your flight tomorrow?' Toby asked of Zoe, aware she was returning to the USA now the paperwork was official between the Chases and her.

'We're out of here at 5am, but we're going to make a stop or two before we get back.' She grinned at Annie who nodded.

'That's right. We decided we could do with a little break – and laying low wouldn't be bad for us either, but,' she looked at Matt and Emily, 'we won't be doing anything as tiring as you two. Our plan is to lie on a beach somewhere and just soak up the sun.'

'Watch out, you'll have to make sure she doesn't try spearing any fish for your dinner,' ribbed Emily, blowing a kiss to Zoe.

'Oi. Now, if it hadn't been for my fishing we'd have never made it.'

Emily nodded gravely.

'Very true. And I wouldn't have learnt about a Hollywood wax either. The whole experience was really very worthwhile.' She laughed hard and Matt blushed a little, his eyebrows raised.

'Did you discuss that?' He looked between Zoe and Emily who both giggled furiously.

'Oh god, we discussed *everything*,' Zoe intimated, pointedly looking at Matt and raising both her eyebrows in reply.

'And what about you two? You're hardly going to want to be in the UK when it all breaks, are you?' Matt turned his attention to June and Toby, sat together companionably as if they'd been together for years, not a couple of months.

'I've got a new series to shoot, but only Tom knows where I'll be travelling over the next few months so I'm taking my very own, personal video recordist and sound-man,' June answered and smiled at Toby who swallowed his mouthful.

'I've got a vested interest in the star.' He grinned.

'Won't the director or whoever want to be more involved?' Annie pressed. June shook her head and placed her food on the floor for a moment.

'Actually, as it was my idea for the show in the first place, I've decided to set up my own production company, so I'm going to make it and get it out there myself. I've had enough with other people deciding what's best for me.'

'That's amazing, June.' Toby watched as Zoe leant over a packing box acting as a makeshift table and hugged his girlfriend. 'You know, if the rumours are correct, I'm likely to be an Oscar-nominated director, so if you needed someone to look over anything…' She left the offer in the air and June whooped.

'Oh thank goodness you offered – I had no idea what I'd do if you didn't say anything. Cheers to that.'

The six clashed together cans of beer and soft drinks and Toby made sure he savoured this last supper. They had no idea when they'd all be back together again, and he hoped he wasn't gambling with anyone's life or career – other than Patrick Roberts' of course. He just hoped he was doing the right thing. The easiest option would have been saying nothing, but he couldn't do that.

Not anymore.

'Well, we need to carry on.' Emily smiled, a little apologetically, starting to collect up the rubbish around them. 'The kids are at Mum's and the first van is with us at 9am tomorrow to take all the big stuff. If we want to be out of here in two days, we're going to have to get our arses in gear.'

The others nodded and began gathering their bags and coats.

'Right. Well. Good luck all.' Zoe kissed everyone, pulled a baseball cap deep past her eyes to help disguise her a little from any passers-by and made her way out with Annie, entreating them all to come and visit them in LA as soon as possible. Her security had remained in her car, alert but distanced from the star, as she'd requested.

'We better go too,' June smiled at Emily and Matt. 'I'll just use your loo, then we'll be on our way, okay?' She checked with Toby who nodded.

Once she'd left, he turned to Emily.

'Are you totally sure about this? Once we do it, there's no going back.' He gripped her wrist a little and she looked at him intensely.

'Toby, I've never felt so strongly about anything in my life. Apart from marrying him, having the kids – and buying a fucking castle in France sight unseen.' She grinned at Matt who nodded.

'It's okay, mate, we trust you to do what needs to be done.'

'Thanks.'

'Right, I'm ready,' June popped her head round the door. 'Bye both.'

Toby shook Matt's hand and kissed Emily on the cheek. As faintly as anything, he heard her whisper, 'Don't fuck it up. Good luck.'

Chapter Nineteen

Toby's phone alarm buzzed next to his bed, but it wasn't necessary. He'd been awake for most of the night, waiting for today. He turned it off quickly, in case June woke, but she barely stirred.

The last two days had been a blur since leaving Matt and Emily's. They'd decided to pack just the bare essentials, knowing they could buy what they needed as they travelled the world. June had left Tom in charge of her house – under strict instructions not to bring anyone back there again – and Toby had asked his mum to look in on his flat from time to time. He'd warned her she might need to lay low for a little while too, but she'd laughed and told him she wasn't afraid of anyone.

Still, she'd agreed to him having CCTV installed inside her house in Saltdean as well as trained on the back and front of her three-bed semi, which gave him a small crumb of comfort.

The two had left London's grey and stormy skies and had travelled to Patagonia, where Tom had booked them under the names Mr and Mrs Smith, to preserve their anonymity, into the Antumalal hotel in Pucón, right on the edge of the Villarrica Lake, beneath a volcano.

Toby and June had settled quickly into the chalet they'd been upgraded to by the beaming assistant who assumed they were on honeymoon. They'd been enveloped by the chalet's warm honeyed wood walls, accompanied by soft fake fur furnishings and a cosy open fire in the living room, where the night before the two had watched the view over the lake which opened out to the range of mountains.

Moving quietly around the chalet, Toby made himself a thick, strong espresso and took it onto the terrace. The day was beginning to warm up and he smiled at the beauty of the place. He checked his watch, 6.30am. Perfect. In London it would be 10.30am, and his first Instagram post was due to go out at 11am GMT.

It had been Emily's idea to use her social media platforms to expose the truth about Patrick Roberts.

'I've got over 20 million followers, Tobes,' she'd told him a month before, 'and I reckon if we give you access, it'll take a day before anyone will be able to get the account closed down, which will give *you* more than enough time to post up as much as you can against him. By the time it gets shut down, there'll be thousands of shares and screenshots out there, and no one will be able to stop all of them.'

Toby looked at the lake and enjoyed the way the light caught on the water. He and June would be doing some filming out there soon, but not today. Today he was going to watch what happened when he exposed a media mogul to the media madness.

When he'd explained the plan to June, she'd been sceptical. She'd wanted Toby to push for a book, a publishing deal. But he knew he'd never be able to get the book published. If he'd been lucky enough to get a chat with an agent, despite the bad press about his previous writing career, when they discovered who his book was on and what he'd be saying, he knew it would end up never seeing the light of day.

He'd reminded June of the odd texts he'd received the last few months as his digging had got ever closer to the truth, how sure he was of being followed daily and the break-in of her home. She'd winced at the intrusion of their privacy and agreed, admitting Emily had confided that she'd been convinced her phone had been tapped.

What had puzzled Toby, though, had been the lack of cover-blowing from Roberts' side if they'd known what he was up to. He'd wondered why they hadn't come out into the open and forced him to talk.

It was June who'd cracked it, of course. Toby had been lamenting how she never received favourable reviews from the red tops, when everyone else seemed to love her new programme.

'Well, they're owned by Roberts aren't they? I wouldn't be surprised if we were to take a look over the last year or so that ninety-nine per cent of the negative reviews, or scoops of us that told total lies or maybe even the coverage when we'd gone missing that suggested we were dead, were all the red tops. And all owned by Roberts. It'll be all his media outlets controlling what's being said about us. And for the last few months, it's been a pretty consistent shit-smearing campaign about you, Emily and me. They wouldn't touch Zoe – she's the nation's darling.'

Shaking his head, Toby swallowed the last mouthful of bitter coffee. He'd been so slow. She was right, of course. A quick internet search and they'd established very quickly that the majority of negative or speculative press about them had been from Roberts' companies.

It was a phone call from Roberts' soon-to-be ex-wife, Veneda, who'd led Toby into the *Star Survivor* mess in the first place with the very publicised fumble in the taxi that meant everything fell into place, giving him the answers to his one outstanding question. After which Toby had spent some time on the government's website looking up the numerous companies Roberts had been associated with over the last twenty or so years.

Checking his watch, Toby felt his stomach flip-flop. Ten minutes to go.

'Morning,' June wandered out onto the terrace with a white waffle dressing gown pulled tightly around her slight frame, 'you weren't going to let me sleep through this were you?' She indicated the set-up Toby had outside. His precious laptop with the evidence secured safely – there were numerous other copies too, of course. Some were on their way to Barbados, others to the South of France, some in a little house in East Sussex and others emailed to a PA who'd do anything for them.

Next to his computer, three phones. One bought solely for monitoring the social media posts as they went up that day. The second, a burner which he'd be using to call Patrick Roberts on, and a third, the only one he'd be keeping after today, which had just four numbers programmed in.

'Are you ready?'

'As I'll ever be.' He breathed in deeply and smiled at June who handed him the phone he'd be calling Roberts with.

'Go for it.'

He picked up the phone, aware of how calm he felt. Looking up, he could see June leaning over their balcony, soaking up the sun's rays and enjoying the spectacular view.

The phone took a while to connect but eventually Toby heard the click of it being answered.

'Hello?'

'Good morning, Mr Roberts.'

'Who is this?'

'I'm a friend.'

'Who is this? Who gave you this number?'

'Your wife. Or your ex-wife, Mr Roberts.'

'What does that bitch want?'

'She wants nothing.'

'Who is this?'

Toby smiled as he could hear Roberts sounding particularly ruffled. He clicked his laptop and smiled.

'I see you're working hard today then? Who's the brunette? Anyone we'd know?'

'What the fuck? Who is this?'

Toby watched on his screen as Roberts pushed away the woman who'd been kneeling by his desk and zipped his trousers, looking around his office. His sanctuary. Unsure how his privacy was being intruded upon.

'She's cute. Bit young – mind you, bet she's wife material isn't she, Mr Roberts? Bet she'd be a good director of your next company. Or is she a director already? Maybe she's the one who's £200million in debt?'

Toby chuckled as he saw Roberts standing away from his desk and begin pacing around. He was looking into plant pots and scanning the windows.

'Oh no, Mr Roberts, we didn't need any of your devices. None of the ones you used on the island, to watch us. To decide if we should live or die depending on how your viewing figures were looking.'

'Masters.' Toby watched as the penny dropped. It hadn't been too tricky to be hooked up to the security system in Roberts' offices. Turns out, if you're a dick to people enough times, they're readily agreeable to helping undo you. And a small wad of cash from a pretty face can help.

'Because it was all about the figures, wasn't it, Roberts? It was about the revenue, the streaming, the advertising, the coverage. If that worked in your favour then maybe, just maybe, the shitty programme you sunk everything into, because it was so successful in the States, might not flop, as you discovered it was going to do, when it aired in the UK with its low-rate celebs and a disengaged audience who'd moved on from reality TV shows.'

'Fuck off, Masters, I've got people.' Toby watched as he saw Roberts furiously typing on his computer, and calling someone on another phone.

'I can see you, Roberts. More than that though. I know you. I know everything you've done. I know how you managed it so that myself, June and Emily were on that

334

helicopter that was lost. Zoe was never meant to be on there, was she? But when you found out she was, well, it was a gift. Meant to be, eh? And so you waited. And watched.'

He could only hear breathing.

'And whilst you watched, so did the rest of the world. Your programme was huge. So big, in fact, that you decided we needn't be found. You encouraged the reports of our deaths. Enticed my ghostwriter to tell all. Cajoled ex-lovers to sell stories. Encouraged the mourning. Populated and furthered the hashtags across your media sites. Sex sells. But dead celebrities sell more, don't they?'

'You have no proof.'

'Oh, is that the time?' Toby jeered a little, 'Probably a good idea to check your social media. Oh, look at that – you don't need me to tell you.' He watched as Roberts' desk phone and other mobiles began ringing and pinging with notifications.

'One every hour. Good luck.' Toby smiled and pressed end on the call, breathing out shakily.

'You were amazing, Toby,' June squealed and sat on his lap, kissing him deeply. Toby's phone began dinging with notifications, but he knew what it would be about and returned the kiss. There was a knock on the door and a member of staff came in, carrying a tray laden with fresh fruit, delicate pastries, freshly squeezed orange juice and an aromatic jug of coffee.

'Aww, Mr and Mrs Smith, you look so happy,' she said, smiling at the two of them. Toby grinned back.

'Love's young dream and all that,' Toby replied as the room-service waitress bowed her head a little, smiled and walked out of the chalet.

'Young?' June cocked her head to the side.

'Nah, you're far too long in the tooth. Love's old dream?' Toby replied, narrowly missing the cushion June lobbed at him from beside them.

'I am not old,' she said, grinning at him. Her face tanned and smooth, eyes glittering as blue as the lake behind them.

'Okay, but love you'll take, right?' Toby stopped mucking about and looked at her seriously. He pulled her in close so they were almost nose to nose. Eyes looking deeply into each other's.

'I love you, June Sharp.'

It was the first time the L word had been mentioned, though they'd both known it since they'd met.

There was a silence in the air and shafts of sunlight spliced through the canopy of trees onto their terrace, causing glints of light to flutter around them.

June took a deep breath and smiled.

'I love you too, Toby Masters.'

Chapter Twenty

The Times Online

JUST MY OPINION

Fiona James

*T*HE art of celebrity should not only be to get noticed, but to harness it so you can do something with it – a thought which one particular celebrity has taken completely to heart this week.

Toby Masters, the disgraced children's author and island survivor, managed to break Instagram yesterday when he took over his fellow islander's profile, mummy blogger Emily Chase, and released what he described as 'evidence' against media tycoon Patrick Roberts to her 20 million followers.

Masters posted his evidence on an hourly basis from 11am yesterday on the Instagram takeover, starting with an image of a document and the caption, 'Let's play the game Join the Dots and see if you can work out what we already know'.

The image was shared as a post and on stories, enabling fans to see the information and screenshot to other social media sites or 'regram' – which they did in their thousands – the claims being made.

All previous posts from Emily Chase had been removed, except for her cryptic clues pointing to the takeover with a three-day countdown and, at 10.59am, a ten-second story which she uploaded saying,

'The truth needs to set us free. To do that, we've found the key and I'm letting my friend, Toby, turn it.'

It soon became apparent that his intention was to post something with huge libel implications on the hour. Whilst we, at The Times, *cannot print the claims being made due to their libellous and potentially defamatory nature, we can report the facts.*

Fact one: Patrick Roberts doesn't own our group of papers.

Fact two: Patrick Roberts has been removed from the boards of all the media groups he is associated with, as of 5pm yesterday.

Fact three: The super-injunction preventing any discussion of the divorce case between Roberts and his now ex-wife, Veneda, has been overturned due to latest claims, and has resulted in her being paid over one hundred million pounds. However, solicitors on Roberts' side are claiming he is bankrupt and therefore cannot pay.

Fact four: Veneda Ashby, Roberts' latest ex-wife, has given an exclusive interview in our paper today, in a tell-all about their secret divorce, and claims Roberts involved her in a plot to trap Toby Masters, which included being caught in a compromising pose with him.

Fact five: Whilst some of the captions Toby Masters posted are potentially damaging to Roberts' reputation, we can report what the photos were of:

11am – a hut appearing to be on an island, stocked with food and long-life drinks.

Midday – a cheque written to Roberts' ex-wife, signed by Roberts, with a note saying, 'I'm sorry it came to this, but at least you made the front page. P.S. He'll be fine.'

1pm – an image of an emaciated June Sharp, taken by the scientists who found her.

2pm – an image showing more than ten listening devices.

3pm – images appearing to have been taken from security cameras of three balaclava'd figures going through the bins next to a lavish house which is known to be the UK home of Zoe Stenson.

4pm – story after story demonstrating the upward rising of Star Survivor *programme statistics.*

5pm – a non-disclosure agreement between Toby's ghostwriter and the literary agent Angie Smith, with a sentence circled in neon yellow which reads 'all elements relating to the provisions made within this contract are non-binding in the event, or suspicion of, Toby Masters' death'.

Fact six: Emily Chase's account was suspended at approximately 5.07pm, with the entire site crashing for well over an hour not long after, with a spokesperson for Instagram saying, 'The platform has crashed due to an unprecedented volume of site traffic. Our experts are working tirelessly to reinstate it.'

When asked about the suspension of Chase's account, The Times *was told* 'no comment'.

Fact seven: Whilst all efforts have been made to contact Toby Masters, Emily Chase, June Sharp and Zoe Stenson, none of the four have been available for comment.

Fact eight: Toby Masters has been offered a six-figure sum for the rights to the tell-all account around the circumstances of his island survival.

Fact nine: Star Survivor UK *is due to begin airing its second series next month.*

Acknowledgements

First and foremost, a huge thank you to you, the reader. With so much competition out there, it means a lot to have someone choose my novel to read. I hope you enjoyed it and, if you did, feel free to leave a review. Do share photos of where you are with *Star Survivor* too – my dream is that this novel gets to be on a sandy white beach – tag me on Instagram!

Thank you to my wonderful agent, Annette Crossland, at *A For Authors*. Ever since the day I signed with her agency, she's been an unfailing supporter of my work and always there with a well-timed gif when needed. Not sure we're *quite* at Lear jet stage yet, but let's keep our fingers crossed.

Thank you to Danielle Price - if ever an author needs a cheerleader, speak to her! She is surrounded by books, obsessed with publishing and is super knowledgeable. As a friend and passionate supporter of my novels, I truly can't thank her enough for her help.

Thanks also to Ian Skewis – editor extraordinaire. You made editing a joy. I'm thrilled working on my novel meant you had to search up the correct spelling of Shewee.

Chloe May and all of the team at The Book Guild. What can I say? You've made my dreams come true, and I'm thrilled you breathed life into Zoe, Emily, Toby and June.

Thank you to two amazing women I met on a Curtis Brown course – Costanza Casati, an incredible novelist who is immensely talented and has been an invaluable source of advice. Thanks also to Emily Cronin who I met on the same course. Not only did Emily beta read my novel, as a fashion editor for her day job, she made sure the characters were dressed incredibly well. If it had been down to me, they'd have been wearing Designers by Debenhams.

There's a team of wonder women including Michelle, Becky, Sarah, Mel and Kaye, all part of a tightknit networking group which (due to lockdown) swiftly became a friendship/swapping silly stories/supportive as hell group instead. Thank you for keeping me uplifted through the numerous rejections, and celebrating every tiny victory with a variety of dodgy gifs.

Thank you to my wonderful friend, author Daisy White. Thank you for being a steady ship whenever I got the jitters about anything during the publishing process, and forever pushing me to keep going. Even when I hit ten rejections, I remember you saying 'tell me when you get to

50'. Thankfully it didn't take as many. Looking forward to more gins in the garden.

Thank you to my darling sister, Fiona. It's her experiences on a real island in the South Pacific for a TV programme, that I drew on for the first part of the novel. Thank you for sharing all the wonderful memories you had and putting up with me asking some very odd questions. I hope you appreciate the crabs making an appearance...

Thank you to my supportive Pops, the man who introduced me to newspapers and journalism, thereby ensuring I had my career path set out at five year's old. The articles written for this book are founded in my journalist training. I hope you enjoy your walk-on part.

Thank you to my first beta reader, my wonderful Mum, Elayne, who tells me everything I write is great, but who particularly enjoyed the very first incarnation of *Star Survivor* and spurred me on to take it further. Thank you for the constant cheerleading and support.

Thank you to my two brilliantly wise children, Dylan and Bethan. When I first drafted this, we were in the throws of lockdown and they helped me in various ways with the plotting of the book. They forever endured their mother asking them their opinion on how the celebs could survive and came up with ingenious solutions. I love you both dearly and would swim from one island to another for you.

Lastly, thanks to two very influential men in my life. One I know well, the other not at all:

The first is Simon Cowell. Thanks for coming to me in a gin and reality TV infused dream and sitting with me on a beach, telling me the full plot to *Star Survivor* over numerous cocktails. Now, if the real Simon could just option the TV rights for this book *that* would make the whole thing come full circle.

Finally, thanks to my husband, Owen. Thank you for having the belief in me for both of us, for supporting me, for the cups of coffee and glasses of wine, for the hugs when things went wrong and the glasses of champagne when they were good, love you.